LEAVING BASILE

by

Mechelle Randall

Mechelle Randall

CHAPTER ONE
Basile, Louisiana - 1954

BOOM! Papa's shotgun blast echoed through the yard behind the old wooden house. The instant he pulled the trigger, bright, red blood spurted out of the left temple of the large hog's head. The hog stumbled once or twice, then fell, and was completely motionless by the time Papa walked over to the carcass that lay on its side like a beached whale. Papa lifted its massive head by the snout and sliced its throat as quickly and effortlessly as if painting a quick stroke on a canvas. He placed a bucket underneath the wound to collect the thick, dark blood that flowed into the bucket as easily as water flowed from the pump that stood a few yards away.

Ann slouched comfortably in the rocking chair on the back porch, watching the slaughter, thinking about how tired she was of eating pork. She and Papa hadn't had time to go fishing lately and they only had beef on special occasions like Christmas, or a wedding. Ann closed her hazel eyes and relaxed under the early morning sun. She stretched out the long legs of her five-foot-seven inch frame as she leaned back in the rocking chair. She locked her thin fingers together and stretched her brown arms out over her head. The warmth of the humid, southern spring air produced tiny droplets of sweat that covered the light brown freckles on Ann's straight nose. She had grown up in this type of weather and loved it. But what Ann dreamed about, on these warm, spring mornings, was what she would do when she was able to leave Basile, and live a life no one in Basile ever had.

"*Amener ce'a la maison,*" Papa shouted at Ann. He mumbled something under his breath and scratched his gray hair. Ann laughed at the way he always mumbled after he asked her to do something, and pulled herself upright indolently. She strolled over, lifted the heavy bucket of blood and carried it in through the back door into the kitchen. Ann slowly ladled the fresh blood into the mixture of onions and rice that was already cooking on the black, wood-burning stove. Later, Papa would cook the organ meat from the hog, chop it up and add it to the rice mixture. Then, he would stuff the mixture into the hog's intestines to make delicious *boudin* sausages. Ann didn't like to cook very much, so Papa did most of it. She stirred the mixture slowly as she read the Sears catalog pages that covered their kitchen walls and most other kitchen walls in Basile, and thought of some particular women in town she knew who could benefit from the girdle she was reading about. She covered the simmering pot, returned to her spot in the rocking chair, and resumed her reclined position.

Pretty soon Papa would yell to Ann to go get salt from the general store in town for curing. Ann's mouth watered when she thought of eating *tasso,* the dried, pork jerky treats they made by letting the salt cured pork dry on the roof, then returning later to find the pieces shriveled and tough. She could put a piece in her mouth and chew on it practically all day.

Ann lifted her head a little to see how far Papa had gotten with his slaughter. Ann had watched the hog walk around inside his own private coop for the last six months, enjoying the special attention he was being given. He had eaten fresh corn and grain happily, the whole time oblivious to Papa's motives for serving him a king's supper. Papa had been planning meals of fresh pork chops, pork roast and tasty pork treats which he had grown up on himself. He had already sliced the sow opened from neck to nipples, gutted it, and was dragging it to a tree to hang up to dry when Ann looked up.

"Ann," She knew it was coming. "*Vous plait de sel.*"

Ann saw his slim, overalled physique in the distance, the bloody knife still in his hand and the hollowed pig in the background hanging from the tree like a festive piñata. He wiped some sweat from his wrinkled forehead with his forearm, "*Et presser!*" He waved Ann toward the general store with his knife, splattering some blood onto the ground in front of him as he mumbled to himself again and walked toward Ann. She rocked forward into a standing position sending her waist-long, dark brown braid into a spin, and tugged at her cutoff overalls.

Papa approached Ann and rested his gray-haired arm around her thin neck as they walked around the side of the small wooden house. She was a good girl, Papa thought. She looked so much like her mama. He yanked gently at her thick, heavy braid. It hung down her back like the rope that rang the church bell. Her mother's hair had been just as long and thick, except she used to twist hers around at the nape of her neck, and spiral it into a large bun. Papa had never thought he could raise a child alone, a girl at that, but he wouldn't have raised a son any differently. Ann hunted and fished right along side him as good as any son could have, maybe better, he thought. But now she was almost grown up, and had become a beautiful young lady, so tall and slender, like her mother. She would have been proud of her little girl.

Papa got Ann lots of things other kids in town didn't have. But he knew she looked forward, more than anything, to the books he brought her. Ann studied and studied in the hopes of someday going off to college. After elementary school, most kids in Basile couldn't even go on to high school. They had to work to help support their families, either by working in the field or on the farm, or by caring for younger children, cooking and other domestic duties. But Ann had wanted to go to high school more than anything and Papa was able to afford this luxury since she was an only child. She loved to read. He watched her read everything she could get her hands on. She had breezed through the simple text books at school, then started at home on some old books the George's, the white family Papa used to work for, had given Papa for her. Ann went through them by the dozens. She studied day and night, and even tutored some of the other children after school. Although Ann grew up speaking mostly French, she had perfected her English grammar, vocabulary and diction until no one could guess she was from a small town in the South.

Although Papa knew of Ann's dream to go off to college, he could never allow her to leave Basile unmarried. But he did understand why she was aching to leave. He saw how excited she became when she read about life in places outside of Basile. About new and different things. Things she would never see in Basile. But the Fruge's had been a very proper, upstanding family in Basile, and it wouldn't be right for her to leave single. After Ann graduated from high school next year, she could marry and would then be able to leave and fulfill all her dreams.

Papa leaned on Ann as he climbed the three steps onto their front porch. He paused on the porch as he remembered what he had walked over to tell Ann.

"Ann, next Spring we gon start buildin a new chuch in town."

"A new church!" Ann was delighted. She liked going to

Leaving Basile

church. It was a place where all the townspeople got together and she was able to see all her friends. Going to church was a social event. Often they had food and music after church. Ann had made her First Communion and Confirmation at St. Augustine's, but it was very old and a new church was needed. Ann couldn't wait until it was built. She knew if Papa was working on it, it would be grand.

"Na go on an get dat salt, Ann." Papa went into the house and Ann walked out of the yard and turned onto the dirt road toward the general store to fetch salt.

The sun had moved closer, it seemed, and the morning warmth had become a moist heat overhead. She wiped a small amount of perspiration from her hairline, spreading soft, wet, curls around her slim face. She squinted and visored her hand over her eyes, then let her long arms hang at her side like shirt sleeves on a hanger. Her legs stepped forward loosely like a pair of empty trousers. Ann let her narrow body bounce up the road, as she hummed a tune Papa had taught her as a child, and bobbed to its catchy rhythm. She could picture Papa singing the words to her in French. His scratchy voice never carried the tune very well, but she loved the way he always waved his hands in front of her, conducting her to sing along.

Ann knew Papa spoiled her terribly. Mama had died ten years ago when Ann was seven, and Papa had raised Ann alone since then. She remembered one Christmas some years back when Papa had given her the best present she had ever received. It had been wrapped in tissue paper and placed in a small box and on Christmas day Ann had unwrapped the biggest, roundest orange she had ever seen! Well, it was the *only* orange she had ever seen. And right next to that, was a dark, red, shiny apple! Apples and oranges were not available in Basile, but Mr. George had given them to him that Christmas. Ann didn't eat them right away. Oh, no. She pushed the orange back and forth on the table between her hands and smelled its citrusy aroma through the thick skin. She tossed it up in the air and caught it and rolled it around in the palms of her hands until they absorbed its sweet scent. Then, she covered her face with her hands and inhaled deeply through her nose and sighed out pleasurably through her mouth. She held the cold apple up against her face and licked its tight skin, then puffed some breath on it and shined it on her dress until she could see her smiling face in it, but she didn't eat them until Papa warned her that they'd go bad if she didn't. Then, she lay on her back in the grass, and with each bite fresh juice ran down the sides of her face and she licked up as much of it as she could before it hit the backs of her ears. She tried to chew each bite a thousand times until there was nothing left. Her mouth watered thinking of that Christmas. Yes, that was the best present Ann had ever received.

Papa and Ann often went fishing and hunting together, and she could kill and slaughter a hog as well as he could. Ann loved to fish, but that took a lot of time and they had other things to do besides sit by the river half the day and wait for a giant garfish to tug at their lines. Papa's trade was carpentry. He built outhouses, furniture, pull carts for horses and chimneys. He could make as much as three dollars for building one chimney! When he wasn't building, he picked cotton. That was pretty much what everyone in Basile did. During the summer, when Ann wasn't in school, she'd hop onto the back of the truck that picked folks up in town at five in the morning to drive them out to the fields, and pick cotton with Papa.

When she was younger, she remembered, Papa would comb her long, wavy hair down flat, braid it into two plaits and twist them onto the top of her head. Then, he would tie a scarf on it and place a small straw hat on top of the scarf. This would keep her hair from getting dusty, he used to say, but it only made her hot and by midday she had pulled it off and stuffed it into her cotton bag.

Ann hated the early mornings in the fields. The dew on the cotton plants brushed against her overalls as she traveled between each one until her clothes were drenched. It was cool in the mornings and she always shivered miserably as her wet hands stuffed the soggy cotton into her bag. It was on those wet mornings that slimy, chartreuse lizards clung their prickly little claws onto the cotton plants. Whenever Ann happened to startle one, it would fling its clammy little body off the plant and usually land on top of her hat or suction itself onto the leg of her overalls. Once, one had leaped onto her collar, then slid its way down the inside of her shirt. She had dropped her cotton bag, shrieked out loud, and did a dance out in the fields no one could have imitated until the little monster dropped out of her pants leg and scurried off.

The only thing Ann disliked more than lizards were snakes. They slithered between the stalks, through the dirt, and around

Leaving Basile

Ann's unsuspecting ankles. Whenever she spotted one, it just kept moving in its serpentine fashion as if she were another cotton plant. Ann knew to remain perfectly still if she felt one, until it passed. Years ago, David Mouton's uncle had gotten bit and his foot swelled to twice its normal size. He had nearly died, she remembered.

Ann and Papa got along fine with the money he made from his cotton and with his carpentry, so Ann saved the money she made picking cotton in an old mason jar under her bed. She and Papa didn't really have much use for spending money. There were only a few things they actually bought. They had chickens and hogs in their yard. Potatoes, corn, sweet potatoes, greens and all kinds of peas and beans grew abundantly in their garden. They cut sugar cane from the fields, mashed the juice out and cooked it to make a sweet syrup that they used to make cake, candy and biscuits. They got plenty of eggs from the chickens and milk from their cow. They did, however, buy flour, salt and kerosene from the general store in town.

They didn't have to spend money on clothes either. Mrs. Thibideaux, the town's seamstress, had been Mama's best friend. Mrs. Thibideaux was a short woman with wide hips, clear olive skin and a mustache. She made all of Ann's clothes, everything from overalls to pretty, fancy dresses for church since the day Mama had passed, and wouldn't take a cent for them. She even made Ann's underwear. Ann always had to boil them for hours, though, before she wore them, to soften up the tough, scratchy material. The underwear she had on definitely had not been boiled long enough. She rearranged them through her denim overalls and continued on to the general store.

CHAPTER TWO

"Ann!" She heard a shout from nearby. "Ann Fruge´!" She turned, looked, and saw no one, but she knew Edward Broussard's voice when she heard it. He leaped out from behind a bush and nearly made her drop the canvas purse Mrs. Thibideaux had made for her. Ann gasped as she turned toward his abrupt appearance, then slowly relaxed her shoulders and rested her hands on her narrow hips.

"Edward Broussard! Why, you almost scared me to death. I could . . ."

"You could what?" He smiled into her hazel eyes. She shook a thin fist at him and they continued their leisurely stroll toward the general store. Ann and Edward had known each other since they were born. They lived down the road from each other and the midwife had paid visits to both their mothers a few months apart.

"What you gon buy?" Edward knew it could only be one of a few things.

"Salt." She swung her purse back and forth as she walked, kicking up a small dust cloud behind her with her bare feet.

"I'm gon buy one a dem magazines dey got." Edward pulled his accordion up on his shoulder by its strap. It had been given to him when he was ten and he had been playing it ever since. He played it at the *zydeco* dances and other social functions, and had learned quite a collection of songs over the years. When Edward wasn't playing his accordion, he was reading his movie magazines, gloating over pictures of fancy movie premieres and glamorous stars. Ann was always interested to hear the stories Edward told her about the star's lives in Hollywood. Ann and Edward had no televisions and had never seen a movie, so this was all Ann knew of movie stars. She especially enjoyed the stories about life in California. Everything about it sound so wonderful. Edward knew this. He would keep Ann captivated for hours at a time with his tales of warm weather in the winter and concrete swimming pools. Ann pictured herself lying near one in a real swimsuit. Not one Mrs.

Leaving Basile

Thibideaux had made. One bought from a store. He liked the way her eyes lit up every time he told his stories and how she sat close to him so she wouldn't miss a word. Ann could have read the magazines herself, but Edward had a delightful way of telling stories and she enjoyed his dramatic descriptions. He always spiced up the articles and knew Ann wouldn't mind his exaggerating a bit to make the stories even more interesting. She and Edward stared at their dusty feet as they walked, kicking pecans that had fallen from the trees lining the road.

"Did you know," Edward asked, "dat dere's a high school in Hollywood call Hollywood High, and all de kids dere is movie star's kids?"

"I wish I could go to school in California." Ann thought out loud.

"Well, we almos outta high school."

"Not high school. College." No one Ann had ever known had gone to college. Most people from her town were content with their high school education. Some were content with less.

"You know yo daddy ain't gon let you go to no college. Never knew why you want to do dat so bad no how."

"Because all the girls in Basile are content with being housewives and mothers."

"Wha's wrong wit dat?" Edward asked. He didn't understand why Ann thought of this as such a horrible fate. This type of thinking was very unusual for a woman, especially a Creole woman from a town like Basile, but Edward had always thought Ann was unusual. The way she would much rather build stuff with her Papa then cook or do things other girls liked to do. She spoke differently too. Like the people they heard on the radio shows. Ann was the only girl Edward knew who had her own thoughts and ideas about everything, who was independent in everything she did. He guessed that was why he liked her so much. But Edward always felt he liked Ann more than she liked him. If she set her mind out to do something, he had a feeling she'd find a way to do it. She was very determined, and the one thing Ann wanted to do was to leave Basile.

Although Ann and Edward were the same age she had always felt older than him. She had been five foot seven since she was fourteen so she towered over him for many years before he grew to his present height of five foot ten. He was sort of cute, Ann thought, but in a simple, homely sort of way. His woolly hair was a sandy mixture of brown and orange and his skin was just as ruddy as the orange in his hair. When he wasn't pushing his hands as deep down into his overall pockets as they would go, he was wringing them together like he was trying to lather them up with soap. He always laughed a sort of hissing laugh through his teeth where his lip covered his top row of teeth completely and only the bottom ones showed.

"Nothing's wrong with that, Edward. It's just that there's so much going on out there. So much available to us. Basile isn't the only place in the world. Besides, if I stay here, all I can do is work in the fields or build things with Papa. I've already done that. I'm almost eighteen and I'm ready to move on to something else. Did you know there's a real university in Los Angeles, California?"

"Dere's universities here in Lou'siana too." Edward defended his home state.

"Yes, but *everyone* goes to the same schools. Whites *and* Negroes."

"So?"

"Well, what are you gonna do with your life, Edward? Read magazines and play the accordion?" Ann had asked Edward this several times in the past, but Edward never had any real plans.

"It jus so happens, I got a job cleanin up de post office in town after I grad'ate." Ann stared at him, waiting for him to add something interesting.

"Cleaning up the post office?" she grimaced.

"Oh, well I wouldn't make faces, Ann Fruge´, cause wit all yo world wide dreams, you ain't gon nowhe. Yo daddy ain't gon let you."

As much as Ann hated to think about it, it was true. She could never do anything against Papa's wishes. He never asked her for much or made any demands on her but he was adamant about this. He wouldn't let her go.

"Yeah," she pouted silently. Ann and Edward turned into the general store. She carried a sack of salt to the counter and Edward headed for the magazine rack to pay ten cents for the only contact the two of them had with the world outside Basile, Louisiana.

Ann also told Mrs. Thibideaux of her dream to leave Basile, who laughed, "Why de hell you wonna go somewhe else, che´? You tryin to run from us?" Holding some blue gingham material next to Ann's shoulder, she said, "It don matta how you talk or

Leaving Basile

whe you live, no. You always gon be Creole."

"I know that. I'm proud to be Creole. I just want to go to school,"

"Oh yea. You get out de wit dem udda people, and forget all about de way us Creole's live. You forget yo language and yo culture and no tellin what kinda husband you be done picked up. You need to stay wit yo own kind, Ann." She smoothed back her shiny, black hair with her short fingers. Although Mrs. Thibideaux had to be old, no one knew quite *how* old, there wasn't a strand of gray on her head. "I always tought you and dat nice fella Edward, Erma Broussard's boy, would marry. You don like him?" She spread the material out across the table.

"Yes. I like Edward." Ann didn't want to get into that conversation again. Mrs. Thibideaux had been planning Ann and Edward's wedding since they were ten. "But I'm talking about school, Mrs. Thibideaux, not marriage."

"Well, you know yo daddy. And de two might as well go hand in hand, cause you ain't gon to no school nowhe, till you get yo'self married."

That opinion seemed to be unanimous.

Ever since Papa had bought Ann a radio, her favorite pastime was to listen to *Sky King* every Sunday evening at six o'clock. She, Edward Broussard and Dorisse Guillory would line up in front of the radio spellbound, not moving until the last syllable of the show was uttered. They would sit cross legged on the wooden floor, and stare at the radio like it was a guest speaker at a podium. They would lean forward, their eyes widening when the exciting parts came, then relax back, their palms flat on the wood planks, and grin at each other when it was over. Ann loved to listen to the characters' voices. She was intrigued by the way they pronounced their words so distinctly.

Dorisse also listened raptly to the way the announcer spoke each word so loudly and clearly. She too, wanted to leave Basile when she got out of high school. Dorisse had known Edward and Ann almost as long as they had known each other. She lived on the other side of the general store and didn't get to hang out with them as much as she would have liked to. She had lots of household chores to do and spent a lot of time caring for her seven younger brothers and sisters. Ann was her best friend. She had always looked up to Ann, like a big sister, even though they were the same age. To Dorisse, Ann knew everything. She could ask Ann about anything she could think of, and Ann would know something about it. It was from all the reading she did, Dorisse thought. Dorisse was never very good in school. But she was lucky to be able to go to high school at all, with all the work that had to be done at home. She had begged her parents to let her go. She didn't care much for school itself, but it was there that she was able to see her friends, Edward and Ann.

Dorisse's straight, shiny black hair was cut at shoulder's length and her fair complexion was as flawless as a bowl of cream. Her delicate, narrow features gave her face a soft, youthful look. Dorisse was slim and very shapely for an eighteen year old. Many of the young men in town asked to court her, but she didn't go out much. She and Ann would sit and talk for hours about all the things they'd do when they left Basile. Dorisse was also audience to Edward's stories of the sunshine state on the coast. She pictured her slim body stretched out across one of those chaise lounge chairs, almost as brown as Ann was, sipping a pink-colored drink with an exotic piece of fruit wedged on the rim of her glass. She pictured bright, red lipstick painted on, a colorful scarf on her head, and dark, Hollywood sunglasses balanced on the end of her narrow nose.

Each Sunday after *Sky King* was over, the three would gather in the small graveyard behind Edward's house and talk. Ann and Dorisse would usually exclude Edward from their conversations about leaving Basile. He didn't have the urge to leave the way they did. He didn't really understand their desire to move somewhere else. The places in the movie magazines didn't even seem real to him. The people didn't seem down-to-earth and honest like the hard working people in Basile. They only seemed interested in spending money and lying around in the sun. Well, if that was what the girls wanted, that was fine for them, but Edward was perfectly happy living in Basile.

"You know what I want?" Dorisse asked Ann one evening in the graveyard. She and Ann swished their bare feet through dried leaves and dirt. "I wonna be an actress," Dorisse said with her Southern Creole accent. Ann stopped and stared at Dorisse.

"An actress?" Ann looked at Dorisse as if she'd said she wanted to join the circus.

"Yea, an actress." Dorisse smiled up toward the sky . "And a model too. And maybe I can pose for some of them pictures in them magazines, like one of them cigarette ads or something."

"Don't be silly, Dorisse. Anyway, have you ever seen any Negroes in all those fancy Hollywood magazine pictures they take?" Dorisse really was dreaming, Ann thought.

Dorisse stopped and looked at Ann with hard eyes. "Ann, do I look Negro to you?"

They stood facing each other. Ann looked into Dorisse's brown eyes. She had known Dorisse since they were children, and hadn't thought about her looks much, but Dorisse didn't look Negro at all. She could easily be mistaken for a Caucasian, with her fair complexion and sharp features. Ann glared at Dorisse through squinted eyes. "So what *are* you gonna do Dorisse, pass as a white person? We'd still know you were Creole." "I ain't said that." Dorisse snapped, then looked away, but Ann saw the frown on her brow.

"Listen." She hadn't meant to upset Dorisse with her taunting. She tried to speak sympathetically to her. "You can do whatever you want, Dorisse, but if you did, you'd never be able to come home. You'd live in another world. You and I, well, we couldn't be friends anymore."

"Of course we could! We'll always be friends, Ann!"

"Oh, and what would you tell your fancy white Hollywood friends? That we grew up together? Maybe you could tell them I worked for your family or something." Sarcasm coated Ann's words. "Yes, I could show them the callouses I got picking cotton. Hey, maybe I could get a job as your mammy or something." Ann spit the words at Dorisse.

"Shut up!" Dorisse cried. She pushed Ann hard and Ann stumbled backward over a tombstone and fell on top of a gravesite. Dorisse knelt down in the dirt in front of her friend and cried harder. "You think you know, don't you? You just think you know everything." She gripped some dirt between her fingers and leaned in closer to Ann's face. "You, you've always done good in school. You want to go to college. I know you. You could do it. You're smart." She pointed at Ann. "But what can I do?" She patted her own chest and shouted at Ann through her tears. "What can I do, Ann?" Ann leaned away and looked into Dorisse's dark eyes. Fear and confusion was buried in them.

"Well, Dorisse you can do whatever you . . ."

"No I cannot!" Dorisse slammed the dirt back on the ground and shouted at Ann. "If you go away to college in California, and they see your pretty brown skin and your wavy hair, at least they'll know what you are. They'll know you aren't white." Dorisse's voice became dry and bitter. "Did you think it was better to look like this, Ann? Did you think it made things easier for me?" She looked at Ann through wet, questioning eyes. "Is that what you think?" She spoke slow and intense. "Do you have any idea, Ann, how hard it is to be so different from your own people?" She sat up and looked out over Ann's shoulder into the distance. "Did you know that when we was kids, my parents wouldn't let me play with no dark-skinned Negro kids? Especially those Baptists." Dorisse laughed a small, bitter laugh, and looked back at Ann. "Did you know that? Well, I surely couldn't play with those white kids. I was in the middle, Ann." She poked herself in the chest. "But I was a child!" she shouted. "I didn't understand why. I still don't." She wiped her dark eyes with the back of her hand and sniffled. "They didn't even like me playing with you and Edward, really" she said sadly, "but since you all was Creole and Catholics, they didn't really say nothing. Of course, I would *never* be allowed to *marry* somebody who looked like Edward. Why do you think I don't go out with most of the boys that ask me, Ann? Huh? Cause my parents want me to court somebody that looks like I do. But all I know," her voice began to quiver again but she swallowed and continued, "is that here in Basile, the white people know I ain't white. They don't care how light your skin is, or how straight your hair is. You still ain't white." She looked deeply into Ann's face "What would you do, Ann? What would you do if you was me?"

    Ann stood in front of her bedroom mirror early that Sunday morning. She remembered when Papa had first gotten her that mirror. They had never had one before then. Glass was hard to come by. They still didn't have any glass in the window panes in the house. Just old wooden shutters that kept her awake at night when the wind decided to rattle them against the house. The old mirror was scratched and had big gray spots in places, but she could see her smooth, caramel skin well. She peered at her profile out of the corner of her eye. Her soft brown freckles weren't noticeable unless you got up close, but seemed to be placed very strategically on their tan background. Her wavy hair hung loose, spilling over one shoulder like a brown waterfall.

    Once, Mrs. Thibideaux had told Ann that Dorisse Guillory's parents and some other very fair-skinned Creoles had their own social meetings to try to match their young ones with each other. Mrs. Thibideaux often gossiped about the town's people. She had known every one of them for years. Ann didn't pay much attention to some of the things she said, but she would ask Mrs. Thibideaux about it the next time she saw her. Ann was glad she wasn't Dorisse. She had problems of her own.

Ann walked around the wrought iron bed, out into the kitchen and out the back door. She filled a large bucket with water from the pump and put it on the stove to heat for her bath. She cut off a piece of lye soap Papa had made from the chunk they kept in the cupboard as some chickens ran into the house and began pecking at the wood floor.

"Get out!" Ann stomped her foot at them. "Get out *poulet*, before I make you dinner for tonight!" She stamped her bare foot again. Ann guided the trespassing chickens back out into the yard with her feet, then filled a large metal tub which sat in the middle of the back yard half full with cold water and poured the water from the stove in to make it luke warm.

She pulled her flour sack night gown over her head and lowered her thin naked body into the metal tub. Although Ann was almost eighteen, she had a thin, boyish figure and small breasts. She covered what she had of them with her skinny arms and tried to sink her whole body down into the water. Even though it was barely six o'clock in the morning, the bright sun warmed the back of her neck through the waves in her hair. The sun felt so good. She could almost feel her skin turning another shade darker. Every summer, Ann tanned a golden shade of bronze. The color of the way Papa liked his coffee, strong, with just a small amount of cream. In the winter she paled to a mixture of half coffee, half cream, the way the children drank theirs. She relaxed in the morning warmth and let her long legs hang over the edge of the tub. Ann rubbed the bar of lye soap over her body and rinsed it off in the tub.

After she absorbed all the sun she could, she splashed water on her face and stepped out onto the grass. She bent down to start drying her feet, and noticed a red droplet on her foot. Papa must have been slaughtering meat for dinner, she thought, but then another drop landed on her right foot. Ann stepped back into the water. This was it. This was that curse Mrs. Thibideaux had told her about. She thought maybe since she hadn't gotten it yet that she might not be cursed after all. Ann thought about what Mrs. Thibideaux had told her. She said it would come every month at the same time and that she would

15

bleed for a week and then stop. Then she had given Ann a bag of old sewing scraps to put inside her underwear. Well, Ann hadn't seen that bag in years. She didn't even know if she still had it. Now where had she put it?

Ann got out of the tub, stuffed the flour sack gown between her legs and walked to the house naked and dripping wet. Ann searched her room, squeezing her knees together the whole time until she found the rags under her mattress, right where she had put them all those years ago when she first heard that dreadful story about bleeding every month. Why does this have to happen, Ann thought. Maybe, if she was lucky, hers would stop. She had to go tell Mrs. Thibideaux that it had finally come.

Ann started to make *mas-pa* for Papa's breakfast. He had gone out to do some carpentry jobs, probably well before four that morning. Now it was almost seven and he'd be back to eat soon. Ann boiled some milk and a beaten egg in a pot. Then she added flour, a little salt and some cane sugar. She stirred it slowly as it cooked and tried to figure out this bleeding thing again. Why did this happen? Would it last for the rest of her life? Can you bleed to death? It just didn't seem right. She had so many questions to ask Mrs. Thibideaux.

"I thought you said it would happen sooner? Why did it take so long?" Ann had asked Mrs. Thibideaux after she bolted over to her house after breakfast.

"Us'ally do. I guess all that huntin and goin on you do like you was a damn boy or sometin make it come late."

Ann looked perplexed. "Why?"

"Well, cause boys don . . . ," Mrs. Thibideaux took a deep breath. "Dey don have dat, no."

"Well, what do boys have?" Ann was *really* curious now. She honestly had no idea. This was something no one talked about, and Papa had never given her a book on *this* subject.

"Notin." Mrs. Thibideaux's answers became shorter and shorter.

"Then why do we have it?"

Mrs. Thibideaux started fiddling with some fabric. Ann noticed her nervousness and this made Ann even more curious. She moved closer to Mrs. Thibideaux. "Why, Mrs. Thibideaux?" Ann asked again.

"I don know, che´. Jus stay away from dem boys na."

Ann didn't understand the correlation. Why was Mrs. Thibideaux telling her to stay away from boys now? What did that have to do with her bleeding? Sometimes Mrs. Thibideaux was very confusing, but Ann could tell this was one of those times when she definitely didn't want to talk.

"Oh, Mrs. Thibideaux. I have something else to ask you. Do the Guillory's sit in another part of the church on Sunday because they're light-skinned Creoles?"

"Shit." Mrs. Thibideaux relaxed back in her chair. She was glad Ann had changed the subject. "I told you dat a long time ago."

"Why?" Ann was still puzzled about this. "Are they trying to be white?"

"It ain't dat, che´." Mrs. Thibideaux tried to explain it to Ann. "You see che´, back when de white firs settle in Lou'sana, long time ago, dey wadn't no white women here, jus dem In'juns dat was here workin, buildin up de city, an dem slaves dem white people brung over. Well, dese white men had to have somebody to court, you see, so dey courted dese slave women and sometime dem squaws. Den, dem Spaniards come round, and all dese folks had dese chil'ren that look like you and me. Well, since dese babies was bo'n from whites, dey was free. Dey wadn't no slaves, no. Dey had dey own property and had honorable trades and some got to be very wealthy. Why, my own grandmudda was a *modiste*."

"What's that?" Ann had gotten comfortable on the floor. She sat cross-legged and rested both elbows on her knees and her head on her hands

"Well, she was a woman who went aroun and made beautiful dresses out of silk and taffeta for *our* people, Creoles. Dey all had dey own trade. How you tink yo own daddy learn to build so well? Cause his daddy was a carpenter and so was *his* daddy."

Ann's eyes widened and she scooted a little closer. She loved to listen to some of Mrs. Thibideaux's stories.

"Anyway, cause dese people, de *gens de colour*, was treated separate from de white *and* de slave, it was very impo'tant dat dey only sociate wit each udda. Dey refuse to learn English and dey was very strict about dey Creole family lines. If dey had mix wit white or dem slave, dey wadn't no full Creole no mo, you see. Family background is the mos impo'tant ting dere is to a Creole, and after dat is culture and manners. Dem light-skin Creoles is jus tryin to make sho de keep de family Creole."

"What about education?"

"De you go wit dat school shit." Before she got herself mad, she answered Ann's question. "Education jus don mean dat much to us folk Ann. Des mo impo'tant tings in life, in a Creole's life." Mrs. Thibideaux finally freed her hips from her chair. "If you don wonna be Creole Ann, den go head, leave Basile. Cause when you leave you won be Creole no mo. Dat's jus what happens." She waddled toward her kitchen. "Na run off and get ready fa church. I know yo daddy must be waitin fa ya."

Ann stared at her wide frame as she walked away. Mrs. Thibideaux had been around a long time and knew a lot, but there were some things she had to be wrong about.

Leaving Basile

CHAPTER THREE

Ann, Edward, and Dorisse all graduated from high school that June. Edward began his work at the post office. He had not forgotten what Ann had said to him about spending the rest of his life reading magazines, or the disgusted look she had given him when he said he'd be working cleaning up the post office in town. So, without telling anyone, he applied for a job as a mail sorter at the post office in Los Angeles, California. They had told him it might take a while because there weren't any openings at the moment and there were people in Los Angeles who would have seniority over him. If this ever came through, he thought, he would ask Ann to marry him.

Edward still dazzled Ann with his stories of beaches and sunshine. He was desperately in love with her and he wanted to be the type of man Ann had always dreamed about. He knew that if this transfer came through, that if he, Edward, could be the one to fulfill her lifelong dream, Ann would be eternally grateful. She would look up to him with reverence. He could see the cinnamon sparkles in her eyes flicker when he told her, then she'd stretch out her slender arms toward him and wrap them around his neck and place her honey-sweet lips on his and tell him how much she loved him. Edward smiled as he pictured Ann's loving kiss. Ann would be his forever. He was sure about this.

The three sat in their usual spot in the graveyard that Sunday after church. Edward placed his accordion on his knee and closed his eyes as he opened and closed it and pushed the keys with his fingers

"*Soleil apr`es coucher caillette est pas tire' . Les enfants apr`es pleurer, il y en a rien pour manger .*" Ann sang the melody softly as she rocked back and forth. "*J'ai cherch'e tout, j'ai pas pu la trouver. Je connsais pas quoi je v'as faire si caillette s'en revient pas.* "

Dorisse sang the second verse. "*La femme apr`es revenir, elle revient en pleurant. C'est l`a elle m'a dit que caillette 'etait creve'e.*" Her naturally tuned voiced trailed off into a mild vibrato.

The three sat in silence as Ann finished the song about the little calf that had died.

"Guess what!" Ann broke the silence with news of the church. "Papa's building a new church!"

"A new church!" Dorisse smiled broadly.

"Yes. They're going to begin work on it next Spring."

"We need a new church," Dorisse added. "St. Augustine's is so old. It's falling apart."

"We sho do," Edward agreed. All three nodded their heads. "Dorisse," The talk of the new church reminded Edward of something he had been wondering about. "Why you always leave right after church? We always stay around laughin and talkin and eatin. Me, Ann, and some udda kids." Edward asked.

"Cause, my folks won't let me."

"Dey sho is strict, ain't dey."

She and Ann glanced at each other knowingly.

"Yea, Edward. They are." Rising, she picked up a large leaf and began breaking it into tiny bits.

"What you gon do na dat we outta high school, Dorisse?"

"I dunno. Help Mama around the house, I guess."

"You know, David Mouton been askin bout you a lot. You gon let him court you?"

"I don't know, Edward! Stop askin' so many personal questions!"

"Well excuse de hell outta me!" Edward rolled his eyes at Dorisse. The girls laughed.

"Well I gotta go. I betta practice my cojun if we gon have a big celebration fa da new church." The girls waved at him, both eager for him to leave so they could talk girl talk.

"You know what I think I want to do when I leave Basile, Dorisse?" Ann started their usual topic of conversation. "I want to study English in college."

"And then what?" Dorisse could see no reason for studying a language they already knew.

"Then teach it."

"To who?" As far as Dorisse knew, everyone who wanted to speak English already did.

"I could teach it in high school. Just like we had English lessons in school."

"Well you don't gotta go to college for that . . . do you?" Dorisse couldn't see studying beyond high school to teach what *they* had learned about English.

Leaving Basile

"Sure you do. I heard once about a Creole lady, who went to college in New Orleans. Xavier University." Ann said the name proudly. "She became a real teacher. She left Louisiana. Taught out in New York or something."

"You ain't going to no New York are you?!" Dorisse got excited. "Don't leave me Ann." She grabbed Ann's bony elbow desperately. "I'd just die if you left me here." She held on to Ann's arm as if Ann were trying to leave at that moment.

One reason Dorisse didn't want Ann to leave was that she'd be left there alone in Basile. She had no other friends like Ann and Edward and her parents wouldn't allow her to talk to anyone except the other Creoles who looked like them, and those were few. They had already decided that Dorisse would marry Joseph Doucet. He was a fair-skinned Creole boy whose family had been in Basile for generations and Dorisse hated his guts. She'd rather die than marry that boy. She didn't tell Ann about this wedding her parents had planned. She was hoping maybe he'd die before they set a date. Once, she had let him court her. They went for a stroll down by the river, and he kissed her right on the lips. That wasn't so bad, but as they laid on the grass he put his hand on her private parts and tried to lie on top of her. Dorisse felt him grow hard as he pressed himself against her. Well, she scrambled from underneath him and ran fast away from that river. But she turned, looked back and saw Joseph standing there with his private parts outta his pants! She stopped and stared for a minute. She had *never* seen no boy's private parts look like *that* before! Well, she ran home like lightning, too scared to tell what had happened. But she knew she didn't want that Doucet boy courting her ever again! There was one thing she did know; she had to leave Basile before the wedding took place. She didn't know where she would go, but she had to get out of Basile.

"No, no. Let go of me." Ann shook her arm loose. "Listen Dorisse. I want to ask you something." She got close to her and said in a faint whisper, "I got the curse."

"What?" Dorisse said in a regular tone, "The curse? Just now? Why, I've had mine for years."

"Shhh!" Ann put her long fingers over Dorisse's mouth and looked around to make sure they had no eavesdroppers, although they had met there for years and no one else had ever appeared. "I wanted to ask you," Ann was back to her original whisper, "Do boys have the curse, too?"

Dorisse looked at Ann for a moment, then realized she was serious and fell backward in laughter.

"Well? Do they?" She couldn't seem to stop Dorisse's attack of laughter with the seriousness of her question.

Dorisse caught her breath and sat up, still tickled by the look of anticipation on Ann's face. Knowing how smart as Ann was, Dorisse couldn't believe her question.

"What's so funny, Dorisse?" Ann said aggravated by Dorisse's laughter. "Mrs. Thibideaux told me to stay away from boys now. Why?"

Dorisse told Ann the story about Joseph Doucet at the river. This was something she had never told anyone.

Ann listened intently, covering her mouth in shock. "I don't believe it. What was wrong with him?"

Dorisse explained to Ann how she had peeked in and seen her parents at night. Ann's hazel eyes became as big as corncakes as she listened to the details of how people make babies, according to Dorisse, especially when she told Ann where the babies came out. Dorisse had seen her younger sister born and explained it to Ann in detail. *Now* Ann understood why Mrs. Thibideaux told her to stay away from boys. She also understood why Mrs. Thibideaux got so nervous when Ann asked her about it. That was the most disgusting story Ann had ever heard. But why, Ann thought, couldn't God have made an easier way of having babies?

That Sunday, Ann and Edward and Dorisse had listened to *Sky King* as they did each Sunday evening, and *The Shadow* had also become one of their favorite radio shows. Dorisse left soon after *The Shadow* went off, and Ann and Edward sat discussing what next weeks show might bring. The two laughed and talked until Ann stretched out on the floor and yawned.

"I'd better turn in, Edward. Early day tomorrow, you know."

Edward stood up over Ann as she sat on the floor, and peered down at her with a slight smile on his lips. "Ya know Ann, I got a very impo'tant letta in da mail. And it got sometin to do wit you." He pointed down at Ann.

Ann stared curiously at Edward. He had suddenly got a very pleasingly serious look on his face. More serious than Ann had ever seen him look. "What?"

"It done came. It done fin'ly came." Edward was now smiling broadly with his hands spread out toward Ann.

"What!?" She shouted at Edward, and stood up to meet

him. Ann was waiting for an explanation, so she could celebrate whatever had come, with Edward. But what was it? *What* had come?

Edward gripped Ann's shoulders and smiled close to her face. "Da transfa," he said with great joy. "My job done transfa'd me ta Califo'nia." His smile broadened even more, as he waited for Ann's reaction.

Ann's mouth fell open. She put one hand on her cheek and her eyes widened with her mouth. Then, her open mouth turned up into an open smile. She covered it so as not to wake up Papa with her screech of excitement. She grabbed Edward's hands and jumped around on the floor in a small jubilant dance. "Edward, I can't believe it!" She paced around the room, gripping her own hands in joy. "This is fantastic!" Ann shook her hands in repressed energy while grinning at Edward. She pictured the warm, sunny days in California, and Edward, comfortably living and working there everyday. "But, Edward . . . ," she said to him still smiling, "What does this have to do with me?"

They stood staring at each other, smiling, for several seconds, until Ann bobbed her head up and down, pressing for an answer. "Well?" she asked, still waiting.

Edward reached into his pocket and produced a thin, gold ring. He gently lifted Ann's left hand in his. "Dis ring belong to my grandmudda. Na," Edward said softly, "I want you ta have it."

Ann looked down at the ring and frowned in confusion. Could he. . .could Edward be asking me. . ., Ann thought. Could he be asking me to. . .to. . .to *marry him*? She looked up at his face. He stood there, Ann's hand still in his, holding the ring at the tip of her ring finger, a gentle, pleading look in his eyes.

Edward led Ann over toward a chair and sat her down. Then he knelt down on both knees at her feet and situated himself closer to her, never letting go of her left hand. He then pushed the gold ring onto Ann's finger, took her hand in both of his, and looked up into her eyes. "Ann," he paused and swallowed hard, "I want you ta be ma wife and come wit me ta Califo'nia," he said all in one breath.

Ann started to feel dizzy. This was too much for her. Far too much to take in at once. She leaned back in the chair, let her mouth fall open and took a long, deep breath. Ann stretched her legs out in front of her and put her right hand on her forehead as her head rested on the back of the chair.

Edward still gripped her left hand. He wasn't sure what her reaction was...or her answer. She looked like she was going to faint. But he just held her hand and waited. He would give her time to think if she needed it. This was a big step in a woman's life and he understood perfectly if she wanted time to think about it.

California, Ann thought. Me, finally in California? This is real, she thought. I could really go. I could really go to California if I wanted to. All my dreams, she thought. All the things I've always wanted to do. I can't believe I'll finally have the chance to do them.

She then abruptly lifted her head as she remembered Papa. But what would Papa do? She was ashamed to have selfishly forgotten about him. Who would take care of him? Who would take care of the house? She couldn't leave him alone. Could she? She sighed unhappily now and Edward loosened his grip on her hand as he realized she was upset.

"Edward, as excited as I am...I need to talk to Papa first." Ann's eyes dropped to the floor.

"I had planned on askin' him for yo hand. I want his approval too."

"No. It isn't that. I'm worried about who will take care of him if I leave."

"I understan. Well, you can talk ta him firs, okay?" Edward was glad it was only Papa she was concerned about. That meant if Papa told her yes, that he would be alright, then she would accept. "Keep da ring, Ann. I'll see you tomorra." He twisted the ring around and around on her finger a few times, then got up off his knees. Pushing his hands down into the bottoms of his pockets, he walked out the front door.

The next morning, Ann was already up making *crêpes* for breakfast when Papa strolled into the kitchen. Holding the skillet handle with both hands, she sharply flipped the pan up, and the paper thin pancake twirled neatly over onto its other side. She let it grill for a minute or two, then slid it out onto a plate with five other *crêpes* that had been folded into quarters. Ann sat at the table and watched Papa smother them with cane syrup and sweet, fig preserves.

"Papa," In her excitement, Ann didn't waste a minute announcing the news to him. "Edward asked me to marry him."

Papa stopped spooning figs onto his plate and looked over at Ann. A smile soon broke through a mouthful of *crêpes* and he

Leaving Basile

put the spoon down to hug Ann around her shoulders. Papa then sat back down and continued to eat. The proposal wasn't that much of a surprise to him. Ann was a grown woman now. Young and beautiful. And Edward was the only young man Ann ever spent any time with. He had heard the two laughing in front of the radio the night before, as they had done every week for so long. It was just a matter of time, Papa thought.

"But there's something else, Papa." Ann fidgeted with the corner of her kitchen rag, twisting it into a tight point. "Edward's job is transferring him to California. I'd have to go with him." She looked down toward the rag and twisted harder.

Papa stopped eating again. He watched Ann began winding the rag tightly around her finger turning her finger tip a dark red. Her expression was a struggle between happiness and guilt. A tough choice for a youngster, he thought. He stopped eating and swung his chair around next to hers.

"Ann, dis time was gon come soona or lata. I knew dat." He looked at the side of her bowed head. "You worried 'bout me?"

Ann nodded, still looking down at her rag. Now the entire rag had become a crude bandage wrapped so tightly around her hand that all her fingers were red and bulging above it like a cloth tourniquet had been applied. "Papa," she looked up at him and a huge, single tear spilled out of one eye, "what will you do without me? Who will care for you?"

He patted her shoulder and laughed. "You tink you da only person in Basile who know how to cook and clean?"

Ann looked at him in astonishment, wiping the giant tear off her cheek. "But. . ."

"Barbara St. Julian do some light housekeepin and cookin for extra money. I got plenty a money save for dis, Ann. I knew you wadn't gon be here foreva."

"Papa, the money I saved under my bed. . ."

"Das yours." he waved his hand and laughed. "I got all ma carpentry money save for dis. Yo ain't got nuttin to worry 'bout, Ann." Ann wrapped her arms around him and hugged him tight. He rocked Ann a few times and looked down at the top of her head. The early morning light had come in through the back door and shimmered off of each wave in her hair like the sun off of the swells of water in the ocean. He smoothed his hand across them and each bounced back into place after his hand passed over it. It would be the hardest thing in the world to watch his little girl go off to a place so far away. California. Why,

25

Papa thought, would anyone want to go to a place like that so badly? He had heard Ann talk many times about California. About the schools and how different things were there. Papa knew how different it must be from Basile. He wondered how a girl like Ann would get along there. A girl from a place like Basile. He would worry about her. Worry himself sick if he didn't watch out. At least she wouldn't be alone, he thought. He felt a little better that she was marrying Edward. At least people in town wouldn't talk, with Ann being married and all and Edward would take care of her. Bu the only time Papa would see Ann was when she came back to visit, because you would never get *him* to visit California. Papa would stay in Basile until he died. But he knew he couldn't keep Ann there. So if she wanted to go, he would give her his blessing.

He finally pried her thin arms from around him. "Na, you go tell Edward yo ansa. I gotta go ta work." Papa rubbed the top of her head briskly and gently pushed her away.

Right after breakfast that morning, Ann ran over and told Edward that she would marry him. They planned for the wedding to be in October after the new church was built. She was so excited about moving to California, that she hadn't even thought about becoming Edward's wife until he grabbed her and kissed her on the lips when she told him that she accepted his proposal. It was a strange feeling, him kissing her that way. Their faces had gotten so close to one another, that she could feel the heat from his body. She had backed away afterward, and put her hands on top of her lips. They sort of. . .tingled when he put his lips on them. She tried to lick the feeling away, but she could only taste his breath on her tongue. It made her feel a little nauseated at first, and glad he had done it quickly. She looked at him, wondering why he had done such a thing, but he just hugged her and whispered, 'thank you' in her ear, so she hugged him back.

Ann supposed if she ever was to marry anyone, it would be Edward. She always liked him more than any other boy she knew. But she wasn't quite sure how she was supposed to feel about him now. Should she like him more now than she did before? Shouldn't she have enjoyed the kiss he had so happily planted upon her lips? But it must be natural for her to feel uncomfortable. Yes, it must. She had never had a husband before. It was new to her. She *thought* loved Edward. But how was she to know for sure, since she had never loved anyone

Leaving Basile

before? Well, she loved Dorisse and Mrs. Thibideaux, and Papa . . . and she loved Edward. Ann smiled. Of course she loved Edward. She loved him very much.

Mrs. Thibideaux was more excited than Ann *or* Papa when she heard the news. "Fa dis," she had told Ann, "I ain't gon make you no dress, no." Ann's face dropped into a frown. She knew if anybody, Mrs. Thibideaux could make the most beautiful wedding dress there ever was. But as Ann opened her mouth to protest, it fell wide open when Mrs. Thibideaux said she would take Ann to Lafayette and *buy* her a wedding dress . . . from a store! This would be her wedding present to Ann.

Ann got up early that Saturday morning to get ready for her and Mrs. Thibideaux's shopping trip to Lafayette. Ann was so excited she could hardly eat breakfast and hadn't slept a wink the night before. They rode the bus to Lafayette and when they stepped off, it was like stepping into another world. Motor cars were all over the place. People were all dressed up in hats and shoes like it was Sunday or something. The streets were paved in cement and they even had cement walkways along side the streets! Ann's eyes moved a mile a minute, trying to take in everything she saw all at once. Mrs. Thibideaux dragged her along by the hand like a toddler as they turned into a dress shop where Mrs. Thibideaux greeted the lady inside with a hug. She had known the White lady for many, many years and she sent Mrs. Thibideaux packages through the mail of beautiful fabric whenever she was over stocked.

"Dis young lady here is lookin fa a weddin dress." Mrs. Thibideaux smiled proudly, her dark mustache spread out along her lip, as she pushed Ann's frail frame forward.

"Well let's see how we can help her." The petite, well dressed lady disappeared into the back and reappeared with a handful of white frilly material over her arm. She separated the stack and hung up five of the most dazzling creations Ann could ever have imagined.

"Well, Ann?" Mrs. Thibideaux smiled widely and folded her arms under her large busom. All Ann did was gasp. "Maybe she wonna try one on. Which one you like, che´?" Mrs. Thibideaux waited for Ann to recover from her shock.

Ann walked along the wall and looked each dress up and down, taking in every detail as she had done the city outside. She finally went back to the second one and still speechless, she pointed.

Mrs. Thibideaux paid fifty whole dollars for the dress. An amount of money that was unimaginable to Ann for a garment. Ann held the dress like a newborn infant on the bus home and decided she would sleep with it until the day she wore it when she married Edward.

The new church was named Holy Trinity, and it was just as beautiful as Ann knew it would be, with Papa working on it. It was a small, brick building, rather simple on the outside, but the inside was something the town's people had never seen. Beautiful, shiny wood pews lined the tiled floor, two black, iron candle racks stood in front and a life sized crucifixion hung over the altar. Holy Trinity church was finally finished, and plans for the celebration were underway.

* * *

Bright and early the following Sunday morning Ann helped Mrs. Thibideaux load the foods she had prepared on the cart and their mare pulled them to the church. All the town's women had cooked wonderful dishes. A cow was killed for the occasion, they couldn't afford this luxury too often, but they'd have roast beef for this celebration. It would be the party of the year for the town's people. Ann had helped with the decorations and she and Papa had gone hunting. Ann made a big pot of gumbo with the blackbirds she shot. Mrs. Thibideaux made some *boudin* sausage and fried chicken, and other women in town brought fig, sweet potato, and pecan pies. There were also plenty of fish, duck and quail for the opening festivities. Edward was going to play his accordion and Dorisse would sing. The Indian summer sun reflected softly off the church's gold painted steeple. The yard in front was lined with tables covered with delicious dishes and treats. The soft breeze carried the savory smells throughout the town, inviting all to the church reception.

After Ann had helped prepare the tables, she went back home to get cleaned up and changed. She walked along the edge of the road back to the house she and Papa lived in. Ann pictured herself walking up the aisle of the new church, gowned in that magnificent creation Mrs. Thibideaux bought for her, with Papa at her side and Edward waiting for her at the alter. She suddenly felt like an adult. Like a woman. Even more than when she got the curse. She and Edward would even have a family of their own one day. Papa would be grandfather to a little boy or girl of theirs. She smiled at the thought of taking the child to visit

Leaving Basile

Papa, and watching him lift it into the air and teaching it to fish and hunt just like he did with Ann herself. She was glad that she was going to be married. She couldn't wait until her wedding day.

Ann turned into her yard with a smile still on her lips, envisioning a small child with caramel skin and curly hair, and freckles like Edward's. But her smile disappeared as she looked toward the small wooden house and saw Papa sprawled across the front porch. Her heart began to beat heavily and loudly. "Papa?" Her voice was thick with dread. As she slowly walked closer to the porch, her body began to tremble uncontrollably. Papa's face was an ashen color and his mouth hung loosely open against the porch's wood panels. His thin body lay abnormally positioned on the hard surface with one arm twisted underneath his body. Ann dropped to her knees and grabbed Papa's shoulders. He felt flaccid, like a cloth doll that needed more stuffing. She brought his twisted arm forward and began shaking him back and forth and crying. "Papa," she screamed into his expressionless face. She waited for him to answer and shook him again when he didn't. "Papa." She cried out so loudly this time that her voice echoed over the farm, frightening the chickens into cackling hysterics. Some saliva dripped out of his open mouth and his head fell to one side. Ann straightened his head and tenderly cradled it in her arms. She pulled him close to her chest, rocking him, and crying softly now. "Papa," she said quietly, as her tears fell silently onto his face.

CHAPTER FOUR
Port Allen, Louisiana

    The autumn leaves colorfully carpeted the church lawn as Ann and Edward emerged from the doors of Holy Trinity Church, man and wife. She looked like a golden angel in the dress Mrs. Thibideaux had bought, but she had walked up the aisle to meet Edward alone. Papa's death had hit Ann like a sledge hammer. She had never thought about a time when he would no longer be around. She somehow felt he'd be there for her forever. He was all the family she had. Edward had been very comforting to her after Papa's heart attack. He never left her side and listened to her talk about Papa for hours on end. She was so grateful to him for being there for her when she so desperately needed someone who loved her.
    When Edward had gotten that glorious letter from the U.S. Postal Service about his transfer, in his excitement he hadn't clearly read exactly where his transfer was sending him. They had explained in the letter that there were still no openings for him in California, but there was an opening for a custodian in a town called Port Allen about two hundred miles away and about twice as big as Basile — which made it another small town in Louisiana. When Edward had broken this news to Ann, she had been so devastated by Papa's death and so appreciative of Edward for letting her lean on him, that she was happy to move anywhere. She just wanted to get away. Plus, Edward would get a raise and he explained to her how this town had a real department store and a real movie theater nearby, and that he was sure the transfer to California would come up in no time.
    Ann and Edward rented a place for thirty-five dollars a month that was near the post office where he'd be working. It was a small apartment joined to a circle of other apartments that formed a small village. Ann was delighted. Even though it was tiny and didn't have a huge yard as she had back home, there was a faucet with hot and cold running water in the kitchen *and* in the bathroom! There was a bathtub and a working toilet inside the house. No more going outside to use the outhouse,

Leaving Basile

although Ann would miss taking warm baths under the sun. There were painted walls and floors squared with patterned tiles. The windows weren't just holes in the walls like back home. They were filled in with real glass that Ann could press her face against and look out at the rain without getting wet. The only furniture they had was the big wrought iron bed that had belonged to Ann. The rest of the small apartment was empty.

A year had passed since Papa's death, and Ann and Edward had became comfortable and happy with their new life. They sat on the bed of their new apartment talking one night, when they heard a small, hollow knock on their front door. When Edward opened it, there stood Dorisse with a paper sack on one hand and a little canvas purse in the other.

"I couldn't stay there another minute," she said looking at him sadly. Ann ran to the door and stared at Dorisse silently. Dorisse looked at both her friends with a begging gaze. "Can I stay? Please?" Her bottom lip hung down and began to quiver. Edward and Ann looked at each other and both began to smile. They embraced Dorisse, smothering her at their doorstep and finally led her into the apartment. The three sat down and began to get caught up on the past year. The three were together again.

Ann and Dorisse couldn't wait to venture out into the town together. They were so excited you'd think they were in California, but there were so many things in Port Allen they had never seen. They caught the bus to town and walked slowly down the street, switching their glances from one side of the street to the other, and there it was, as huge as they had imagined, a real department store, just like Edward had said. Ann was thrilled. She'd never wear homemade clothes again. That day, she bought herself a gold corduroy suit with gloves and a hat to match. Dorisse bought a navy blue dress that buttoned up the front, just like the women she saw on the fashion magazine covers, and they each bought a pair of nylon stockings. They were ecstatic. Dorisse couldn't wait to buy cosmetics, so when they left the department store she and Ann went to the five and dime and Dorisse bought mascara, eyebrow pencil, and a bright red lipstick. When she put them on, she felt like a movie star in Hollywood. Cosmetics didn't interest Ann much. She was happy to be able to buy groceries at a real supermarket, all picked and cleaned and everything. She and Dorisse walked along Main Street together carrying their packages proudly. They held their heads up and tried to appear as if their shopping spree was an everyday occurrence. But their casual demeanors disappeared when they saw the giant white movie marquee across the street. They stood side by side and stared up at the huge black letters as if the movie stars had appeared on the marquee in person.

"We're gonna go, Ann," Dorisse said without taking her eyes from the marquee. "We're gonna go to the show."

"We sure will, Dorisse." They slowly pulled their eyes away and began walking, looking back every few seconds.

"Why did you leave Basile, Dorisse? I mean, why now?"

"My parents had me all set up to marry Joseph Doucet. They set the date for next month. I would've just died if I had to marry him."

"Do they know where you are?"

"No. I left 'em a note. I told 'em was going away to be an actress. I know they think I just totally lost my mind."

"They probably blame me for it. Everyone knew I was the one with all the crazy ideas about leaving Basile. I never made that a secret." Ann thought about Papa for a second. What would he think about her leaving Basile? What would he think about her moving to Port Allen and wearing store-bought clothes and buying her food at a grocery store? Well, he'd be happy she was married. What would he think about her selling the house, Ann thought? She'd had to sell it. Ann knew she would never go back to Basile. She knew the minute she and Edward left that she would never live in Basile again. Never. Papa would have understood, Ann decided. Papa would be happy.

"Well I don't care if they like it or not. I had to do what I wanted. I couldn't spend my whole life doing what pleased my parents. If it were up to them, I'd be married to Joseph Doucet now, and still living in Basile. I didn't love him, Ann. I didn't even *like* him. I would've died if I had to marry him. I would've just died." She looked at Ann and shook her head and the two stopped and sat on a bench.

"Ann," Dorisse scooted close to Ann on the bench and smiled a devilish smile. "When you and Edward, you know, first did it . . . what was it like?" Her eyes expanded, awaiting Ann's response.

Ann sat forward and looked up and down the street before answering. She shrugged her shoulders and smiled modestly.

Leaving Basile

"I dunno," she said shyly.

"What do you mean, you don't know? Did you like it?"

"Dorisse!" Ann blushed and looked up and down the street again.

"Well? Waht was it like"

Ann took a deep breath at Dorisse's persistence and shrugged again. "He just... you know... kissed me... then," Ann waved her hand in circles trying to gesture the rest of the story, "you know, he...,"she elbowed Dorisse a few times.

"What, what?" Dorisse edged her on to finish.

"Well... he... he...," she rolled her eyes in circles to keep from finishing the story verbally. Then they both sat on the very edge of the bench and leaned forward. "He put it in," she whispered.

Dorisse and Ann's eyes both widened at Ann's graphic description. Dorisse gasped, sucking in a huge, vocal breath of air, and covered her grinning mouth. "Well, did you like it?" She and Ann were face to face now.

"Shhhh!" Ann said at Dorisse's repeated question. "I don't know! I didn't like it or dislike it." Ann shrugged again. "I just did it." They both relaxed back on the bench.

"Well I guess you're all grown up, Ann."

"Yes," Ann liked the sound of that, "and speaking of being all grown up, what are you gonna do for money, Dorisse?"

Dorisse looked at the ground for a moment as they stood up and began walking again. Then, she stopped and lifted her head as if she had just made a decision. "I'm gonna get a job, Ann."

Dorisse was so fascinated with the department store, that she went back the next day in her new navy blue dress, all made up like the models in the magazine ads, and went to apply for a job.

Dorisse sat with her shapely, stockinged legs crossed, as Mr. Gifford, the manager at the department store in town, spoke to her. She looked at the obese man as he talked. He had a pink face and magenta cheeks. His eyes bulged slightly out of his head and their bloodshot sclera matched the color of his cheeks. A protuberant belly spilled over his belt and sat in his lap like a sack of flour. His short legs dangled from the chair and parted to make room for his belly. He waved around a short, smoldering cigar as he told Dorisse about the job in his heavy southern drawl.

"It's impo'tant to look presentable while you all work cause the young ladies who shop here like to be waited on by someone who looks nice." He looked Dorisse up and down, holding the cigar between his yellowing teeth. "You'll get a discount from the store so you can be properly attired." Dorisse smoothed down her navy blue dress. She couldn't wait to use that discount Mr. Gifford was talking about and buy more new clothes. She was getting more and more excited. "Oh yes, don't spend too much time on them colored women," he added. "They don't never spend no money nohow, so it's a waste of time. Plus, we don't really want to encourage them to shop here anyway." Dorisse stared at the white man. Those colored women, Dorisse thought. He thought Dorisse was white.

"Anyway, the pay is fifty dollars a week," he continued, "so if you want the job, you can start tomorra."

Fifty dollars! Fifty dollars . . . every week, Dorisse thought. Why, she'd be rich!

"Tomorrow?!"

"Yes. Be in here at nine o'clock sharp tomorra mo'nin."

"I'll be here!" Fifty dollars a week! Dorisse couldn't believe it! That was more than she ever dreamed she could make. She couldn't wait to tell Ann and Edward she had a job.

To celebrate Dorisse's new job, Ann, Dorisse and Edward all had dinner out and went to the theater in town to see a movie that had just opened that day called *Blackboard Jungle*. It was Ann's first time wearing her new suit out and she felt like she was going to a Hollywood premiere. Each row of the theatre was packed with people sitting down or hurriedly making their way to their seats before the lights went out. The three followed the sign that read *Colored Section* up to the balcony and found seats.

The screen was so big to Ann, it didn't seem possible that the images walking and talking on the huge screen were real people. Ann watched the moving black and white pictures like she was watching a miracle in progress. The best part of the movie was one of the characters, a Negro. A Negro movie star! Just knowing that it was possible, that a Negro could do something as wonderful as make moving pictures made Ann want to move to California a hundred times more than before. And this man was so handsome and debonair, with his enthralling voice and hypnotic eyes. He stood tall and masculine and spoke his lines so eloquently and strong. Did

Leaving Basile

men like that really exist, she thought, who spoke like him and were movie stars? Was he real? She begged Edward to take her to see the movie again, but he explained that they couldn't afford to go every night. Eventually, Edward gave her the money and she and Dorisse went two more times before the movie left town. She asked to go again and again and he thought she had gone crazy.

"Ann, you done already seen dat movie three times, be'. You know all de words by heart." Edward told her. "Anudda movie gon come next week. Maybe we can go again in two mo weeks." But Ann knew that Sidney Poitier probably wouldn't be starring in the next one.

Ann cooked and cleaned while Edward was at work. She had learned how to make new dishes like spaghetti and meatballs and hamburgers and was enjoying doing things the way the other wives did. Each time Ann went to the supermarket, she stopped by the theater to see what movie was playing, and later begged Edward to take her. He knew she was getting bored at home all day, with Dorisse working now, but he wanted to support his wife alone. He didn't want her to have to work, so he worked extra hours at the post office and had been recruited to play his accordion at *zydeco* dances in town. He had made suggestions to Ann about having coffee with some of the other wives in their apartment village in the afternoons, but that seemed incredibly boring to Ann. She preferred to read alone at home or go out with Dorisse on her days off. Ann spent most of her days grocery shopping, cooking and keeping house.

At least Ann had plenty of time to read. She read Port Allen's newspaper everyday and bought plenty of books from the used book store. When browsing through the *Port Allen Times* one day, an ad caught Ann's eye about registration deadlines at the university. There was a real university in Baton Rouge that Negroes could go to. Baton Rouge was only a short bus ride from Port Allen. Ann got so excited that she almost caught the bus there that very day. Instead, she waited until Edward got home from work to tell him.

"Edward," Ann approached Edward excitedly as soon as he walked in the front door that evening. "You won't believe what I've found."

Edward slowly walked into the kitchen and began washing his lunch bowl out in the sink. "What, be'?" he said without looking up.

"There is a university in Baton Rouge." She paused and looked at Edward closely. She knew he would know what she wanted. "Edward, can I please go? I have the money for the first semester's tuition from my savings . Please. I want. . .I *need* to go." Ann had walked up to Edward with her hands clasped together, and pleaded with her eyes. She was fully prepared to kneel down on the tiled floor if it convinced Edward of how desperately she wanted to go to school.

Edward dried his hands on the dish towel and walked Ann over to the sofa with his arm around her shoulder. "Ann, I'm so glad you found a school nearby. I'm sho it's a good one, but I bet the schools in Califo'nia is even better."

"Well, there *are* some better schools there, I bet." Ann thought for a second. "But I can't wait. We've been waiting for this transfer for so long already. We may not ever get to California. What will I do, wait forever?"

Edward saw how difficult it was for Ann to be patient. And now, knowing the university was so close, he knew it would be even harder for her. "I'm sho we'll be movin' soon, Ann. Den, you can enroll in da best school in Califo'nia." Edward said encouragingly. "And by den, we'll have save enough money so you won't have ta worry about how ta pay for da rest of da semesta's. Dis will give us mo time ta save fa it."

Ann looked at Edward and took a deep breath. She tried to push a smile through her disappointment, but really felt like crying. Of course Edward was right. But Ann would think about the university everyday. Wonder what it looked like, what kind of people were there, what it would be like to actually be a student there.

She continued reading and taking care of Edward and tried to forget about the university for a while, but she knew one day, if she could just wait, she would be a real student.

Dorisse stood behind the counter at work, folding soft lace handkerchiefs into decorative fans to place in their display case. She loved her job at the department store. She had bought some new dresses and a pair of high-heeled shoes and loved dressing in the morning for work in all her new clothes. Mr. Gifford had quickly promoted Dorisse to his assistant in the women's apparel department and she had managed to put away some money in a savings account. Dorisse spent most of her time at the store arranging displays and putting new arrivals

Leaving Basile

out on the floor. Dorisse did miss Ann and Edward. Ever since she had started working she hadn't seen much of her two friends. Mr. Gifford kept her very busy at the store each day.

"Dorisse?" Mr. Gifford waddled across the room and summoned her from behind the counter. "Can I speak with you in my office, please?" He smiled at her. Although he was a hideous looking man to Dorisse, he had been very kind to her since she had began working at the store and he had recommended that she get a generous raise with her promotion.

"Yes?" Dorisse stepped into the doorway of his small, cluttered office in the back of the dress department. He picked up a fifth of bourbon about half empty from his desk and held it toward Dorisse, offering her a drink. She shook her head and smiled slightly. He took a short, thick glass from his desk drawer and filled it with bourbon for himself and took a heavy swig.

"I have something for you." He said after he grimaced over the strength of the alcohol, and handed her a thin box with a gold lid. "Just a bonus for all the excellent work you've been doing here."

Dorisse opened the box gingerly as Mr. Gifford downed the rest of the bourbon in two more large gulps.

"They're silk stockings." He said, smiling at her even more broadly now. Dorisse peeled them from the box and held them up. The delicate material flowed over her fingertips like a soft breeze.

She layered them back into their box and looked up at Mr. Gifford grateful but a bit embarrassed at such an intimate gift.

"Mr. Gifford, I'm very flattered," she said slowly, "but . . . I couldn't possibly accept these."

"I told you it helps sales if you're well dressed. I'm sure they'll enhance your outfits." She looked back into the open box irresolutely. "Go ahead Dorisse. I want you to have them." He smiled a yellow smile at her.

"Well," she looked back up at his wide, grinning face, "If you insist."

Almost a year had passed since Ann had read about the school in Baton Rouge and it had been on her mind a lot lately.

"Have you heard anything about your transfer?" She asked Edward over dinner one evening.

"Well, I put in fo anudda reques and I get news back in about a mont." In reality, Edward had long since lost hope of being transferred to California. He guessed that there were many sophisticated men in California, whom they'd much rather have for the job. He saw the way Sidney Poitier spoke so handsomely on the screen that day. All the men in California were probably like him. Who wanted some old accordion-playing country hick working at their fancy, big city post office? They probably wouldn't even want him cleaning their floors let alone handling their mail for them.

    Ann was about to tell him how tired she was of waiting, but he looked so pitiful and pathetic she couldn't bear to hurt his feelings. She knew how he must feel putting in for that transfer over and over again, worrying that she might be losing her patience. He tried so hard to please her, to keep her happy. He gave her all the money he earned so she could buy things she wanted and go to the movies. He was the kindest, most thoughtful man she had ever known. She nodded at his plea for her to be patient for yet another few weeks, knowing that those few weeks would turn into months and those months would turn into years. The past year had dragged on like a lifetime for Ann since they had moved to Port Allen. Although she tried to hide it, Edward could see the disappointment on her face. He placed his arms around her neck and held her close to him as he stroked her long, dark hair and worry swept across his face. He didn't want to lose her. She rested her cheek on his shoulder and the same look of worry swept across her face. She felt as if time was running out. She wouldn't tell him, but tomorrow morning Ann would get on the bus and head for Baton Rouge to sign up for classes. She hadn't touched her savings since she deposited the money she got from she and Papa's house, which she had sold when she moved to Port Allen. She would use some of that money to pay for her first semester of tuition. She couldn't wait any longer.

    The next morning Ann was up early fixing breakfast for Edward. He entered the kitchen dressed and sat down at the small dinette set they had bought at the used furniture store in town.

    "So what you gon do today be´?" he asked her.

    "Oh, nothing. The laundry needs to be done." She faced the sink rinsing out pots as she talked. "You'd better hurry. You don't want to be late for work." She kissed him and hurried him out the front door, trying not to be too obvious. She then bathed, pinned her long hair up, put on her gold corduroy suit with the

Leaving Basile

matching hat and gloves and caught the bus to Baton Rouge.

Ann couldn't have imagined that the "small" college she had read about up in North Baton Rouge would be so huge! It seemed to cover acres and acres of grassed land interrupted by large concrete buildings and tall shady trees that had grown in just the right places. She walked along a cement path and stood in the middle of the campus like a lost child in the supermarket. She made a slow three hundred and sixty degree turn, steadying her pillbox hat and trying to find a sign or an arrow or something to direct her to . . . to . . . She didn't even know where she should go. She saw a building in the distance with lots of bodies entering and exiting just like at the department store in town, so she headed toward it, knowing she could at least ask someone for directions. As she got closer to the building the smell of hot food penetrated her nostrils. With the long ride on the bus that morning, and skipping breakfast, the aroma made her temporarily forget about what she was looking for and she headed for the wonderful smells ahead. She followed her nose to the double doors which opened into the school's cafeteria. There, a luscious smell of tomato sauce and garlic crept underneath the doors and up to Ann's taste buds. Her mouth watered like a faucet and her stomach made a few noises like one of those old motor cars that drove in town. Ann put her hand to her stomach to muffle the sounds and licked her lips trying to turn the smell to a taste in her mouth.

"Can I help you with something?" A voice spoke closely behind her.

Ann answered without turning away from the cafeteria doors, "Yes. *What* is that glorious smell?"

"Well, why not let me buy you lunch and see," the young man said peeking around Ann's face, trying to see her completely. Ann turned around to face a young man, somewhere in his early twenties and quite handsome. He reminded her of the men she saw in the movies. He had black, shiny curls and a soft, creamy complexion. She noticed his good looks immediately, but quickly responded to his suggestion with an unfriendly, "no thank you." He eyed her from head to toe and his expression remained unchanged from the friendly, confident smile he had greeted her with.

"Hey!" He put his hands up in defense. "I'm sorry if I offended you," he said seriously, then smiled again, "but is there some place I can help you find? I saw you in the courtyard looking pretty lost a few minutes ago."

"Well yes. As a matter of fact I want to take some classes . . . that is . . . I want to enroll in the university."

"Oh. You're looking for the admissions office. It's in the administration building. Room A236." Ann stared at him blankly.

"Come on," he said smiling again, "I'll take you."

"Well . . ." Ann didn't know this man. He could be one of those lunatics who hung out on college campuses and preyed on new students like herself. Ann eyed him suspiciously.

"I'm a student here. This is my second year. I'm a sophomore. My major is business." He looked at Ann with puppy dog eyes. "Okay," Paul pulled his wallet from his back pocket. "Here's my student I.D." It was him on the picture all right. Paul Fontenot. Sophomore.

"Well . . ." Ann looked at him and back at the picture again. "I guess this is really you," Ann said reluctantly. His sad eyes turned up into a smile and he put his arm out directing her to lead the way. He joined Ann at her side as they walked through the courtyard on the gray path toward the administration building and introduced himself as they walked.

"I'm Paul Fontenot," he stretched out a hand to her.

"Ann," she said seriously. She shook his hand still peering at him through squinted eyes. He took Ann's hand in both of his and held it softly while staring into her hazel eyes. She gripped his hand hard, shook it, quickly removed it from hers, and looked straight ahead as she walked.

"You have a very pretty face, Ann."

"Yes, my husband thinks so too." Ann smiled and squinted her eyes at Paul. She turned and walked into the building he lead her to. Paul took her to each department she needed to go to and she spoke with a counselor in the English department. Ann and Paul sat down and he helped her pick out her classes, fill out all the proper forms for registration and got her all the information she needed. Ann had no idea it would be this complicated. She was admittedly leery about him when she first met him. He was so handsome when he smiled to one side as he did. He probably was used to girls falling all over him, Ann thought. Well, she wasn't about to do that. She had Edward at home waiting for her. This was one girl Paul would not have to worry about. There was something cocky about him. He was far too confident. He'd play the villain if he were in a movie, Ann

Leaving Basile

thought, with his dark, shiny hair, unilateral smile and eyes the color of the old wood burning stove she and Papa had in Basile. Although he was somewhat of a pest, flirting with Ann every chance he got, he was very helpful and it wouldn't hurt to have a friend at a place like this. By the time they finished Ann was famished. The whole process had taken the entire afternoon.

"Thank you so much Paul. I would've been totally lost without you," she said sincerely as they walked out of the administration building. "I'll have to return the favor someday."

"How about today?"

"OK," Ann put her hands on her hips and smiled. "What is you want?" She looked at him out the corner of her narrowed eyes.

"Don't be so suspicious. Just let me buy you some lunch. You must really be hungry by now."

"Now *that*, I couldn't turn down if I wanted to." They smiled at each other and walked quickly back toward the cafeteria.

"So where are you from?" Paul asked Ann over lasagna.

"Port Allen."

"Originally?"

"No. I'm from Basile."

"Louisiana?" Paul asked with a disgustingly surprised expression.

"Yes. Is there something wrong with Basile?"

"No. It's just that you don't seem like one of those *bayou* girls."

"And just what are *bayou* girls?" Ann asked, insulted.

"Well, they kill alligators, and wade in swamps and they talk like this," Paul spoke in a mocking southern accent and laughed afterward.

"And what makes *you* so great, Mr. *Baton Rouge?*" Ann used a regal French accent.

"Oh. *Parler vou Francais, mademoiselle?*" Paul asked in terribly spoken French.

"*Oui. Couramment!* That means fluently, in case you didn't know."

"Well that's not real French anyway. You only speak that back woods, leftover French," Paul said.

"Whatever it is, it's part of my heritage, and I'm proud to speak it. And who do you think you're descendants of, Mr. *Fontenot.*" Ann's frown thinned her lips. Paul was obviously Creole too, with his slightly tanned skin, soft black curls and dark, deep set eyes.

"Oh I'm just teasing you. Don't get all upset," Paul laughed it off. "Finish your lasagna."

"What is this called?" Ann distorted her face.

"La-san-ya," Paul annunciated each syllable loudly.

"I'm not deaf. I've just never had it before."

"Don't s'pose they sell much lasagna in Basile, do they?" Paul said using his country accent again. Ann's face began to tighten.

"Oh, don't be so sensitive. I just would never expect to meet anyone from Basile here in Baton Rouge, especially here at the university. I suppose you're a very unique girl — very different." He smiled a slight, crooked smile and looked at Ann, fascinated by her. "Your husband should be proud of you."

"He is. But more importantly, Paul, I'm proud of myself."

By the time Ann got home it was dark and Edward was home from work pacing the floor wondering where Ann could be — no note or anything. He was terribly worried. Ann hadn't even thought about how late it was or that Edward must be worried sick, until she stepped off the bus, walked toward their door and saw Edward looking out of the window at her walking up the step.

"Where you been!" he asked running toward her taking her hat and coat, checking her up and down to make sure nothing was wrong with her. He still imagined something terrible must have happened to make her stay out this late. Maybe something had happened to Mrs. Thibideaux and she had to take the bus back to Basile or something. Instead of stuttering around with a lie, Ann told him the truth.

"I went to the university . . . to enroll. She looked at him closely for his reaction. She wasn't quite sure what it would be. He stood perfectly still, her hat and coat in his hand.

"Well, why you didn't tell me dis monin you was gon dere, be'?" The look on his face was not anger. It was a hurt look.

"I'm sorry, Edward," she leaned toward him. "I didn't tell you because, well, I don't know why. I didn't think you'd want me to go. I knew you wanted me to wait until we moved and all, but I was impatient." Ann was sorry now that she hadn't told him she was going first. "I wanted to go so bad. I'm sorry for lying to you." Edward slowly laid the hat and coat on a chair and took Ann by the hand.

"You didn't lie to me." He kissed Ann on the lips and hugged her tight around her waist. Although he didn't want her to go to school, he was relieved that there was no bad news. He was just happy she was home. Ever since they had been married, he had always been insecure about their relationship. Ann had such a mind of her own and if she went to school it might just pull them apart. The thought was so scary he quickly dismissed it from his mind. She was back now and she was sorry for what she had done. He pulled her into the bedroom by the hand and tenderly set her down on the bed. He sat down next to her and took her slim hand in his and rubbed it softly, then kissed it while looking into her baby-brown eyes.

"Ann, whateva you wanna do is alright wit me. I jus want you to be happy." And that part was true. He really did want her to be happy, because he was so afraid that if she was unhappy she'd search for happiness elsewhere. He gently lowered Ann onto the bed and made love to her. Afterward they lay in bed in each other's arms.

"You should see the university Edward. Its so big. Its like a little city in itself. There's a huge grassed area in the middle with trees surrounding it, and there's the student union where everybody hangs out and the food is real good. Its like eating in a fancy restaurant." She left out the part about meeting Paul. There was no need in getting Edward dreaming up things that didn't exist. He had already agreed that she could go, so she just wanted him to know that she'd be safe and happy there, and Ann felt from now on, she would be very happy.

CHAPTER FIVE

September seemed to take forever to arrive, but Ann's first semester finally began. She could hardly sleep the night before her first day of school. She tossed and turned and dreamt of the huge grassed areas and the concrete paths that connected each building. It was sunny and warm that morning, so Ann dressed in her black capri pants and short sleeved top. She slipped on her flat sandals and let her wavy hair hang down her back. She was nervous but very excited. Ann, a real college student. Something she had been planning for and thinking about for all those years was finally coming true. She stared out the bus window on her way to school and daydreamed. She saw herself walking in black cap and gown with a rolled up diploma in one hand. Over a loud speaker she could hear her name. A smile came upon her face as she pictured herself throwing her tasseled hat into the air with a thousand others.

"It must be a very pleasant thought," someone said, startling her away from her graduation ceremony. It was Paul.

"What? Where did you come from?" Ann said, embarrassed at how she must have looked, smiling all alone.

"I'm sorry. I didn't mean to interrupt such a wonderful dream. Was it about me?"

"I don't think so!" Ann said angrily. Paul's smile broadened at his ability to anger her. "What are you smiling at . . . and what are you doing on this bus?" Paul sat back and relaxed in the seat next to her.

"Well, I'm going to school, of course. I'm moving into the dorms today. And look who turns up on the same bus!" Ann turned toward the window and rested her chin on her elbow. Why was Paul such a pest? He could be so nice sometimes and so obnoxious at others. Ann certainly didn't need any distractions from what she was going to school for, to learn, and to get her degree.

Ann's first day was wonderful. She sorted through her syllabuses at her lunch period, highlighting tests and important deadlines, and organized her notes. She had signed up for the

Leaving Basile

freshman English classes and some basic education classes and couldn't wait to go to the university bookstore to buy her books and supplies. The bookstore was such a grand place, she thought. The whole school was. It was such a wealth of knowledge all in one place. She loved everything about it. The library, the bookstore, the cafeteria, she even loved her statistics class. That was her first class of the day. Eight o'clock. Although it was an introductory course, it was her hardest class. She shared this class with Paul. Everyday Ann sat in the same desk in the front row so she wouldn't miss a word of lecture, and everyday Paul plopped himself down in the desk next to her. One thing they did have in common was their interest in school and their knowledge of just how difficult it was. Paul was still a pest to Ann, but she was delighted to know someone who got as excited as she did about Econ and History and even Statistics.

"What's the difference between discrete and continuous data?" Paul asked Ann as they left class one morning.

"You're going to have to start paying attention in class, Paul," she reprimanded him.

"It's so hard with such beauty seated next to me." He made a poetic gesture and smiled. Ann stopped in the middle of the courtyard and placed her hands on her skinny hips the way she always did right before she said something she thought was important.

"I will not tell you the difference between discrete and continuous data. You go to the library and look it up." Ann extended her arm, pointing a long, thin finger toward the library. Paul bowed and playfully pouted like a scolded puppy. He looked up at her with charcoal black eyes and smiled and she pounced him on the head with her notebook. They laughed as he ran off toward the library.

He turned and shouted back at her, "Okay. You'll see. I'll give you the answer tomorrow." Ann waved him off toward the library, shook her head at his silliness and headed to her next class.

Paul found a quiet corner by the window in the library and spread his books out to study. He peered outside and saw Ann walking across the campus to her next class. What a strange girl she was, he thought. She didn't seem like she was from a town like Basile. She was rather naive, but she was smart, well spoken, and assertive. She was very confident and sure of herself. She must have been very determined to come from a town like Basile to Baton Rouge to enroll in college. One thing Paul did know about Creole people was that this sort of thing was very rare. He smiled to himself. She was a very strong woman. He liked that. The girls Paul was used to going out with were usually nothing like Ann. The last girl he had dated, Irlene, was smart, and pretty too. Irlene had been a lot of fun, for the time being, but she had started to get far too attached and Paul had to let her go. She had started talking about marriage and settling down after they had only been dating for three months. Paul was by no means ready for that, so he broke it off with her. She had called him all hours of the night, begging him to see her again. Poor Irlene. It had taken awhile, but she finally got over it. Thank goodness. Paul had been afraid he would never get rid of her. He hoped she didn't hold grudges. He might even want to call her up again sometime. Irlene was a nice girl. Just too needy. Ann didn't seem that type at all. She was . . . interesting. He liked talking to her. She had actually become a good friend, and Paul had to admit, she was the prettiest friend he had.

The only friend Ann really had was Dorisse, and they hadn't seen much of each other since Ann started school, so she thought it would be nice to have another friend, especially one like Paul. He was so silly. He made her laugh all the time, even when they studied statistics. They had become very close. She hadn't ever met anyone like him, so clever and witty. She certainly had never met any one from Basile like him, and he was so handsome. Those dark, mysterious eyes, and brilliant, white smile, that curled up at one corner. He even could give Sidney Poitier a run for his money, well . . . almost.

The semester was moving fast and Ann's classes were going well. She studied hard and spent hours on top of hours preparing her assignments to turn in. One afternoon, Ann walked over to the bookstore after class to look for a study guide for her speech class. As she scanned the dozens of shelves in the bookstore, she heard Paul's familiar voice. "Aisle seventeen, top shelf, ma'am."

Just as Ann was about to ask him how he always seemed to appear wherever she was, she turned and realized that he was speaking to someone else. Ann noticed a name tag on his lapel. He worked at the bookstore. Paul spotted Ann and she tried not to look as impressed as she really was. She never pictured Paul doing anything serious, but he was very helpful to

Leaving Basile

the other student and seemed to know the bookstore backward and forward. "Need some help young lady?" He finally said to her.

"Yes, as a matter of fact I do. I'm looking for a book."

"Well then you're in the right place." For some reason she saw Paul in a different light. He looked so smart in his cardigan sweater with his name pinned on the lapel. He had answered that other student's questions so professionally and confidently. Ann was somehow . . . proud of him.

"I didn't know you worked in the bookstore." Ann smiled at him and for the first time her eyes sparkled with the smile. Paul noticed the change immediately.

"At your service." He clicked his heels and saluted. They laughed together. Ann leaned into her laugh and Paul lifted her up by her shoulders, bringing her face an inch away from his when she lifted her head. They stared at each other silently as their laughing ceased. Paul gently pulled Ann toward him and softly kissed her lips. Ann had closed her eyes and lifted her chin into the kiss before she even knew what she was doing. Her muscles relaxed as a chill went through her entire body. Paul ran his tongue across Ann's lips and she slowly allowed them to part. He just barely traced the inside of Ann's lips, then placed his lips on hers before their faces backed away from each other. They stared at each other silently before Ann dropped her eyes to the floor. She realized that maybe all that she just felt was showing and she softly tugged away from his grip. Could he see, she wondered, how that kiss had just taken her and sailed her through the sky and back down to earth within a matter of seconds? Paul lifted her chin and she stared back into his eyes. She no longer felt like she was just looking at him. Her glance felt like a stare. A deep stare-not into his eyes, but straight through them, into his mind, his private thoughts. Paul's coal black eyes melted into the hazel of hers. They stood motionless until Paul spoke. "Can you come back, Ann . . . when I get off?"

"What time?" Ann said still staring magically into his eyes.

"Nine tonight. Meet me here."

"I'll see you then," she said. Paul smiled a crooked, happy grin and walked into the back. Ann still stared at him as he walked away. He turned back and smiled at her once more before he disappeared underneath the "Employees Only" sign.

Mechelle Randall

Ann stood in that spot and thought nothing of Edward, or Port Allen, or the study guide she had come to get, or even of Sidney Poitier. Only of Paul's kiss and what it had done to her.

Ann took a deep breath and tried to orient herself back to the present. She had forgotten she was in the bookstore and what she had come to get. Suddenly it dawned on her-nine o'clock?! Ann couldn't meet Paul at nine o'clock. She was supposed to be home by then! What had she been thinking? She couldn't meet him. Meet him for what? She had already done too much. They had already done more than they should have. She had to let him know. He would be disappointed, she was too, but she just couldn't. Nine o'clock?! No, that was too late. She couldn't meet him.

"Can you give this to Paul Fontenot, please." Ann handed the note she had written to the cashier at the bookstore who later handed Paul a sealed envelope with his name written on the front. Paul read it slowly.

Paul,

I cannot meet you tonight at nine o'clock, or any night. I don't know what happened to me today. I don't know why I kissed you. I shouldn't have. I'm a married woman and I love my husband. I don't think we should see each other anymore. Please understand. I don't want to fall for you and I feel I may if I see you again.

Love Ann

Paul held the letter in his hand. Her handwriting was stressed. He felt her fear in the paper it was written on. She feared she may fall for him? Well, he feared he already had. How on earth had this happened, Paul thought. Of all the hundreds of women on campus, he had to fall for a married woman. He couldn't figure it out. What had happened? There was something about Ann. Something that he had to have. He tried to convince himself before that he only liked her as a friend. But now, with this letter in his hand, he felt he cared far more for Ann than he had known. Maybe he had fallen for her when he first laid eyes on her, maybe when they kissed, or maybe right now, when he read her letter. He wasn't quite sure when it had happened, but it had. He couldn't let her go with the simple excuse of her marriage. He had looked into her eyes when she talked about her husband, which wasn't often, and he had looked into her eyes when they kissed. He had never seen that look in her eyes before. He had to know if she felt the same

Leaving Basile

for him as he did for her. He had to find out for himself, face to face. So that next Saturday morning, he got on the bus and rode to Port Allen to the address on the copy of Ann's class schedule she had given him.

"Oh yea. Ann really seem to be enjoyin her school." Ann could hear Edward talking in the living room. "Did you say something, honey?" She shouted at him from the bedroom.

"Ann," Edward shouted back, "Dere's somebody here to see you, be'." Ann casually strolled into the living room, totally unsuspecting Paul to be standing there next to her husband. She stopped in her tracks when she saw his handsome face. A flush went over her body as she struggled to overcome her surprise.

"Oh!" Ann tried to react normally. "Paul!" She smiled nervously and looked back and forth between Paul and Edward. "Hi." She waved an awkward hello.

"I came by to bring you the notes you asked for . . . from Stat."

"Oh the notes!" Ann said overacting. She looked at Edward, her nervous smile still intact.

"Well, ya'll two scuse me," Edward said. "It been a real pleasure Paul. You be sho to come back na." They shook hands and Edward retreated into the bedroom. As soon as Edward disappeared, Ann turned to Paul and her phony smile disappeared.

"What are you doing here?" Ann whispered through her teeth.

"Ann I know you care for me. I can tell. I can hear it in your voice." He gripped her narrow shoulders in his hands. Ann shrugged away from him.

"Don't talk like that, please," Ann pleaded quietly. She looked back toward the bedroom.

"Just tell me you don't care, that you don't feel anything for me," Paul whispered much too loud for Ann's comfort, "and I'll never bother you again." Paul's eyes begged for an answer.

Ann looked back toward the bedroom again, sure Edward could hear this whole conversation. "Please, just leave." Ann shielded her face from him and stared at the ground. "Just leave." Paul knew she felt the same as he did. Her hand shook as she held it over her face. She was in pain. This hurt Paul, seeing her like this, denying her feelings to herself. He felt her pain in addition to his own, but he understood her decision. He stood and watched her delicate hand try to conceal her anguish. Then, when he couldn't watch anymore, he turned and walked out the door. Ann took a big gulp as she heard the door close, and tried to swallow the lump that had formed in her throat, but it remained like a giant pill refusing to go down. She walked to the kitchen and ran a glass of water. As she quickly poured the water down her throat, Edward walked into the kitchen.

"Paul studin dat English too?" Edward asked pleasantly, wringing his hands together as he spoke. Ann finished gulping the water but held the glass motionless at her lips. She removed it for a second to respond "yes", then quickly placed it back at her lips without turning around.

"Oh. Dat's nice. I'm gon down to Baker's house to practice my cojun." Edward had his accordion strapped on. "I ain't gon be long." He touched the back of her hair gently and Ann heard the front door close at her back as tears trickled down into her glass.

By the time Edward returned from Baker's house that night, Ann had taken her bath and gotten into bed. "In bed already?" Edward leaned over and kissed Ann on the lips.

"Yes. I had a lot of homework to do."

"Aw. Po baby," Edward looked at Ann sincerely.

"It's alright. I just need a good night's sleep."

"Den dat's just what you gon get. Want some warm milk?"

"That sounds great, honey." Ann looked up at Edward's honest face. "Come here." She reached up toward Edward and pulled him close to her. "Thank you for being here," she said. Edward kissed her on the forehead and went into the kitchen. Ann lay thinking. Why did she feel that way about Paul? What had happened? The feeling was very strong. Her heart began to pound when she thought about him. Was it lust? Paul was the most handsome man Ann had ever laid eyes on. Six foot one, he had told her when she asked him one day, and a tall perfectly proportioned frame. Slightly broad shoulders, a solid, but slim waist and long masculinely shaped legs. And a smile, oh, like a child's, playful and friendly. Mischievous. A smile that sparked a flame in her. A smile that could melt every drop of resistance she had ever had in her. She tried to shake his face out of her mind. Ann lay in bed and physically shook her head back and forth, trying to eradicate Paul's image, but it stayed, floating over her head, hovering, haunting her. She felt his lips on hers,

Leaving Basile

pressing against them. She felt his moist tongue gently slide inside her mouth. Ann closed her eyes tight and covered her face with the covers. Why was he doing this to her? Why was this happening? She just wanted things to be normal. She had even started liking Port Allen and being a wife. Now these feelings were making things very difficult for her. Edward entered with the milk as Ann lay with her head under the covers. "Ann. Here yo milk," he said softly.

"Turn the light off, honey. Thank you." Ann didn't want Edward to see her face. He'd know something was wrong. It would show. Ann was never good at hiding her feelings. Her face told a story like a book, and Edward could read it fluently. He turned off the light and snuggled up to Ann's back. He molded himself into the shape of her curled up body and kissed the back of her neck. Edward slowly turned Ann around to face him. He held her close and slowly began to caress her shoulders, her arms, her back, and down and over her round bottom. He softly stroked the back of her thigh up and down with the palm of his hand. He traced the crease of her thigh with his fingertips underneath the elastic of her panty. Edward rolled her onto her back and began to make love to his wife, and there Ann lay open-eyed, staring into the darkness at a vision she couldn't seem to erase from her mind.

CHAPTER SIX

Ann purposefully slept through her statistics class on Monday morning. She didn't want to see Paul. She couldn't face him. She finally got herself dressed and to school in time for her second class. The lump she had felt in her throat the day before was back. She kept asking herself why she felt so terrible. Had Paul upset her so much by coming to her house? Did she feel guilty for kissing him in the bookstore? Ashamed for cheating on Edward? Afraid that Edward had known something was wrong? Could she actually be in love with Paul? Ann drifted through each class that day. She signed her name to show that she was present in each class, but only physically. Her mind was elsewhere. On her way home she stared out the bus window, lost on a winding road of emotions.

"Whas de matter Ann?" Edward asked her over dinner that night.

"You seem a little . . .worried. Sometin on yo mine?"

"No. I . . . I'm . . . school is getting very difficult. That's all."

"Oh, you smart. You gon do real good. You been doing good so fa ain't you?" He smiled encouragingly at her.

"Yes, but it's still hard. It's not easy to get good grades, Edward. Don't you see how much I study?" He looked at her as she talked, but said nothing. "Oh, you wouldn't know." Ann looked down into her plate and stabbed her peas with her fork.

Edward felt left out. She's right, he thought, I wouldn't know. Ann's new college world was so foreign to Edward. He couldn't even imagine what it was like. Maybe her new friend Paul knew what it was like. Maybe *he* understood that stat homework he brought to her. What the hell was stat homework anyway? Edward didn't even know what stat was, let alone what it was like to have homework in it. She was right. He didn't know.

"I'm sorry Ann. I hope it get bedda fa you." He didn't have the guts to tell her he was jealous of her friend and their both knowing what stat homework was, plus he didn't want her to think he was angry or jealous. He wanted her to think he was understanding and wanted her to go to school, to do what made

Leaving Basile

her happy. Well, he hated it. Ever since she had started school she seemed more and more distant. At first he was glad she was so excited about it. She'd describe the school, which he had never been to, and tell him funny stories about her teachers and classes. He even began working more double shifts, so she'd have money for the next semester, but the stories became less and less frequent and now she hardly talked about school at all. She just came home, sat practically silent through dinner, bathed, and went to bed.

For the next two weeks conversation was scarce between them. Ann still hadn't attended her statistics class. Each evening she'd say to herself she would get up and go the next day. But when morning came she'd start thinking about what she'd say to Paul when she saw him. Would they sit in their same seats next to each other in the front row? She'd think about the way he used to talk to her during class, asking her to explain things and how she'd shush him quiet. Then each morning she'd fumble around the house until it was too late to make it to the class on time.

She'd already missed one midterm and was way behind in class. School was more important to her than anything in the world. She had to pass this class. So Monday morning, she got up, dressed, and caught the bus to her statistics class.

About five minutes after class had begun, Ann snuck in the back door of class, which was already underway. She knew her instructor started promptly, so she quietly sat down in the last row at the first seat next to the door. She opened her notebook and began to listen to her instructor, who was lecturing on standard deviation. She had reviewed where they should be in the text before class and was glad to get some instruction on this foreign topic. As Ann listened intently, her heart started beating wildly as she saw the back of Paul's head in the front row. His shiny, black curls were unmistakable. She stared blankly at the back of his head and her mind began to wander to their kiss in the bookstore. Just then, he turned around and looked straight into Ann's face. His coal eyes opened wide and he stood up in the front row and bolted toward the back of the lecture hall where Ann was sitting.

Oh my God, Ann thought. She wanted to run out of the back door. She tried to gather her books fast but he was standing in front of her desk before she could move.

"Ann, where've you been?" Paul said, his voice loud with

distress. Several members of the class turned around to listen to their conversation and see what had gotten Paul out of his seat in such a hurry.

"I don't want to talk." Ann tried to whisper.

"Why haven't you been to class? Was it to avoid me?" Paul said in not as much of a whisper. A few more class members turned. To avoid a scene, Ann gathered her books and left the class because now Professor Larousse was looking in their direction. Paul followed closely behind, leaving his belongings on the desk in the front row. Ann walked quickly down the hall with Paul at her side trying to look into her face, shuffling quickly beside her.

"Please talk to me," Paul pleaded. Ann walked quicker. She walked out of the building and turned the corner behind the student union looking straight ahead. Paul finally grabbed her arm and held it tight. Ann looked him in the face. They both stopped cold in their tracks facing each other. Ann's chest heaved up and down and she held her thin lips tightly together breathing audibly through her nose.

"Ann." Paul's expression pleaded with her. Ann fought the tears that welled up in her eyes as she looked into his. "Why are you doing this?" he began to shout at her. "Why haven't you been to class? Talk to me, Ann. I know you've wanted to see me. Look at you." Paul saw the tears welling up in her eyes. He lowered and softened his voice. "What's the matter, Ann?" He held on to her shoulders firmly.

"I can't," she said shaking her head slightly as the tears spilled over.

What do you mean, you can't see me? Why? Because you're married?" Paul tried to look into her bowed face. "Ann," he shook her once gently to try to get her to look at him, "you're not in love with your husband."

Ann looked up quickly. "I am!" Ann shouted at him. "I love Edward." She wiped some tears from her face and continued to try to fight the new ones that formed. "He's a wonderful man."

"*That's* what you mean. He's a wonderful man. Not that you're in love with him. I'll bet he *is* a wonderful man, Ann, but he's not for you. He's not like you. I could see that. You two are like night and day. I know that after meeting him one time. Why are you trying to convince yourself that you're in love with him?" His voice raised with fervor.

"Because he's my husband!" Ann shouted back.

Leaving Basile

Paul stared at her desperate expression for a moment. "That's not a good reason, Ann," he said quietly

Ann took a deep breath and closed her eyes tightly. She didn't want to look into Paul's eyes, or to see his face. She didn't even want to hear his stupid voice. How dare he tell her that she wasn't in love with her own husband? What made him think he knew so damn much? Who did he think he was, a mind reader, or did it show so much, she wondered? Could he look into her crying eyes right now and see how she felt about her husband? Was it that clear to him? If Paul could see it, could Edward? Ann tried like hell to hide her feelings, but it wasn't working. It never did.

"Ann," Paul said quietly to the ground between them. He waited for her to speak but she sniffled in and stared at the cement in silence. Paul looked at the top of her head. Her soft waves fell over both shoulders shielding her face from him. She took another deep breath and shook her head. "I don't know, Paul. I don't know anything any more," she renounced.

Paul lifted her feminine jaw in his strong hand and he knew he had been right. Her eyes surrendered to him. He softly kissed her lips . She gently turned her head to one side. "Please," Ann pleaded. She could feel herself weakening. She could feel her resistance diminishing. Paul slowly pulled her chin up more, forcing her to look at him. When they looked into each other's eyes, Paul slipped his arms around Ann's thin waist and she helplessly strung her long arms around his neck and they kissed, long and hard. Their tongues intermingled within the warmth of their mouths. She stroked the back of his neck, twirling his soft, short curls around her finger. He felt her let herself go in his arms. Paul hung on to the smallness of Ann's back and pulled her closer. He could feel the heat building up between them. Ann's body tingled inside and the hair on her arms stood on end. Her stomach burned with excitement. Their lips parted but stayed a millimeter apart. Ann kept her eyes closed. It felt so good not to fight. It felt good just to feel what she really wanted to feel. Paul's body felt so natural against hers, like it belonged there. Ann let her mind relax with her emotions. Paul slowly backed away from Ann's warm body and took her hand. That desperate, pleading look she had worn was gone. She stood with a soft, dreamy look in her eyes and a very slight smile on her thin lips as he led her down the cement path behind the student union, through the chain-link gate, and up the

Mechelle Randall

walkway to Lincoln Hall, his dormitory. He led her up the stairs and opened his room door with a key. Ann had not said one word but followed him in a silent trance, hoping she would never awake from this wonderful dream. It seemed that after she had told herself that she wasn't in love with Edward, that everything had fallen into place, just that fast. Now, she knew what she wanted. She wanted Paul.

Paul set her down on his bed and stroked her long brown hair, pushing it away from her oval face. How beautiful she was, he thought. He picked up one of her tan hands and kissed her slender fingers one by one. Ann looked at his profile as he sensuously slid each of her fingers into and out of his mouth. Ann's mind floated through each motion. He kneeled down on the floor in front of her and kissed the back of her hand like a handsome prince. He looked up from the floor into her cinnamon-colored eyes. She breathed deep and smiled at him a little, still in a daze. Ann's mind wasn't moving in a hundred directions as it had been the past few weeks. It just hovered weightlessly in space.

Paul slowly parted Ann's legs and pressed his chest against the inside of her thighs. His hands traveled under her dress and he hugged her bare hips underneath. He then easily slipped her panties down, past her knees, over her ankles and off over her shoes. He parted her legs wider and kissed the insides of her thighs softly. Paul softly buried his face under Ann's dress. When Ann felt the same warmth she had felt kissing her lips underneath her dress, she fell back on her elbows and dropped her head back. Her eyes rolled into the back of her head and her mouth fell open. She had never felt this way before. It was . . . it was like . . . heaven on earth!

Leaving Basile

CHAPTER SEVEN

Ann and Paul resumed their front row seats in Professor Larousse's class. Ann quickly caught up and got even higher grades on her exams than she had gotten before. Professor Larousse let her take the midterm she missed over and on the next one she got the highest score in the class. Ann had never felt so confident in her life. She had always felt she could do whatever she set her mind to do, but those things had seemed so far away, as if they would never happen. Now she had all the opportunities to do whatever she wanted.

She and Paul had lunch together every day and studied together during lunch. Each day after they studied, they went back to Paul's dorm room and made incredible love, as Ann never had before. After the first time it was difficult for her to go home and face Edward. She had called Edward from school and said she had to stay late at the library to study. She stayed at Paul's and got home around midnight when she knew Edward would be asleep. Soon she was so happy and content she practically skipped home after school. Edward immediately noticed the difference. She even talked about school again. She ran home and showed Edward her straight "A" papers and talked about projects she was working on or papers she was writing.

Edward was happy for her. Happy she was happy again. What he wasn't happy about was their sex life. At first, Ann seemed a little unenthusiastic about sex. Then, she began making excuses not to have it. Soon she just always managed to come home when Edward was already asleep. They hadn't had sex in a month. Later, Ann attributed it to her final exams. The semester was drawing to a close and Ann studied for her finals every night. Many nights she came home far after midnight. Ann called home one evening around five o'clock to tell Edward she was staying at the dorms with a classmate so they could pull an all night study session. Edward was innocent and somewhat naive, but he wasn't stupid, he thought. Edward gave her a calm "Okay," hung up the phone and got on the bus that headed toward this school he had heard so much about. "It's about time I seen dis university fo mysef," he said.

The ride was anxious for Edward. He wasn't sure what he might find, but if he had to search every corner of the library and every classroom on campus, he'd find out what the hell Ann was up to. The only classmate Edward had ever met was that Paul. He and his sophisticated city good looks made Edward feel like a hillbilly. Also, Paul and Ann had school in common, which was Ann's whole life now. Edward knew absolutely nothing about any of it. Although Edward listened attentively to Ann as she spoke of her experiences at school, most of the time she may as well have been speaking a foreign language. She got so excited when she talked about her classes, that she never even noticed the blank stares he gave her when she went on and on about multiple choice exams or class credits or grade point averages. Edward just tried to be enthusiastic whenever she was and pretend he knew why.

The bus let Edward out in front of a village of buildings and a maze of sidewalks. He wandered into the center of the courtyard and stood there just as Ann had her first day at the university. Darkness had overcome the winter sky and Edward stood feeling bewildered, not knowing where to start his quest, which now he wasn't quite sure he should have taken. He stood twisting his hands in each other as he focused in on each of the few people that walked the school's sidewalks. Edward had no idea where to start looking for Ann. He had almost decided to turn and head back toward the bus stop, when he spotted Ann across the courtyard turning behind one of the huge buildings. He yelled out her name, but she didn't reappear. He ran to the corner of the building and looked around, but she was no where in sight. His eyes searched frantically for her familiar walk, when he saw the arm of her sweater disappear through a chain-link gate at the end of the path. Edward opened his mouth to call her name again but stopped short. Instead, he followed her quietly through the gate. She walked quickly and entered a building with the words "Lincoln Hall" written over the front door. Edward watched her arms swinging happily as she walked with a small bounce in her step. As Ann entered the building, Edward crept up the path and peeked into its glass doors. He saw Ann enter the elevator and the doors close behind her. He entered the lobby and watched the elevator dial stop at the third floor. He headed for the staircase and got to the third floor in seconds, three steps at a time. Just in time to look down the hall and see Ann knocking at one of the dorm doors. Edward had a plain view of Ann's back and the door she was knocking on, so whoever answered... Edward had formed a picture in his mind of Ann falling into another man's arms. Ann stood in front of the door tapping her foot, whistling. Still in her happy mood, Edward thought. Well now the truth would come out, finally. Edward's heart began to pound. He couldn't believe he had gone there. Ann knocked again, but with no answer. She took a piece of paper from her bag and wrote Paul a note.

She stuck the letter in the side of Paul's door and instead of walking toward the elevator, decided to take the stairs down. Edward practically fell down the staircase trying to get down before she saw him. He made it from the third floor to the second floor in three steps. He stood on the outside of the staircase on the second floor until he heard her walk by. Then, he tiptoed to the first floor, slipped out a back door of the dormitory and watched Ann exit out the front. Edward re-entered the building and climbed back up to the third floor. He looked back and forth up the hallway like a secret agent before he took the letter from the door and read it. It said:

I was here at about 7:00 p.m. Sorry I missed you. I'll be at the library in the reference section. When you get back, come get me. I have the whole night free tonight.

Ann

Edward put the note back. Didn't he feel silly. Well, of course Ann was going to be studying all night in the dorm room. She was going to the library to wait for her friend. Here Ann was, planning to stay awake for the rest of the night studying that really hard stuff she did, and he was jealous. Now he felt even more stupid than before. He thought he'd better get out of there before she saw him and asked him what on earth he was doing there. Edward walked through the campus and picked up his pace as he saw the bus approaching. Paul didn't recognize Edward when he ran past him toward the bus, but Edward recognized Paul. As the bus pulled away, Edward watched Paul's handsome frame walk toward the city with the cement paths where his wife would be for the rest of the night.

"You are the most beautiful woman I've ever met," Paul said as Ann lay in his arms that night.

"And you are the most beautiful man." They grinned at their corny compliments in the dark and kissed.

"Paul, do you love me?" Ann listened in the dark for his response.

"Of course," Paul said casually.

"No. I mean . . . do you really love me?" Ann turned her head on her pillow this time to face him.

"Yes. I do." He answered her firmly.

"Well . . .," Ann took a breath then paused, "I'm going to ask Edward for a divorce." Ann had thought about this for a long time, "You and I can be married as soon as its final." Paul's expression froze in the dark room. He thought about what Ann had just said so conclusively. Married?

"Ann," he was momentarily at a loss for words. "I don't know if that's such a good idea."

"What!" Ann sat up in bed, leaning back on her sharp elbows.

"Well, I just think you need to think about this."

"What is there to think about?" Ann paused and looked at Paul's silhouette trying to read his mind. She was glad it was dark so he couldn't see the frightened look on her face. "I don't love him, Paul. I love you."

"I know but . . ."

"Paul if you aren't in love with me just say so. If you don't want me. . ."

"I want you, I want you!"

"Don't let me force you to say anything you don't really mean." She was beginning to get angry now. Oh sure, Paul was so in love with her last night, and the night before, when he knew she'd be returning home to her husband afterward. Oh what a great life for him, she thought. She got angrier as she thought about it. A built-in lover and tutor all rolled up into one but without the hassles or costs.

"You're just using me aren't you?" Ann sat straight up in bed and faced Paul straight on.

"Using you? For what?"

"Oh don't play dumb with me, you. . .you, gigolo!"

Paul looked up at Ann, who was now facing the window kneeling up in bed. The moonlight outlined her frame against the darkness. Her hands were on her naked hips. Her skinny elbows stuck straight out. Her thin lips pressed tightly together. Her eyes squinted and he was sure he saw steam coming from her nose. Although Ann was furious, Paul couldn't help smiling at her and soon broke out into laughter.

Leaving Basile

"Gigolo?" Paul said as he curled up in laughter.

"What the hell are you laughing at!" Ann said, still quite upset.

Paul sat up and pointed up at her but fell back onto the bed laughing hysterically. Ann dropped her hands from the bone of her hips and her lips poked out. "This isn't funny." She pouted like a two year old. Paul stopped laughing long enough to notice Ann's immature expression. He slowly ceased his laughter but still found the situation quite funny.

"I'm sorry, sweetheart." He put his arm around her and pulled her back down onto the bed. She rested her head on his arm and he held her slender shoulder. "Listen Ann, I knew you were married when I met you. That was...very disappointing for me. But it was a reality, so I dealt with it. I had to. I didn't have any choice."

"Well now you have a choice. I'm giving you one. You don't have to deal with it anymore." Ann tried to convince him to be happy about it, but he didn't sound very happy to her.

"Ann...," Paul took a took a deep breath and a long pause before saying what he had to say, "...I don't know if we should continue this."

Ann's heart dropped to the bottom of her stomach. She should have known it was coming. She had been so happy. She should have known it was too good to be true, but she didn't move. She stayed packed in his arms.

"It's not that I don't love you," he continued, "I do. It's just that I'm not ready for a serious, permanent relationship. I've loved spending every moment we've ever spent together but I'm...I just couldn't do it right, and you wouldn't want me to half do it. Would you?"

Ann looked into Paul's sparkling ebony eyes. How she had been drawn into them, so quickly, so deeply. She had sauntered into his heart as if passing through an open door. Invited in to visit, then trapped. No windows, no doors. No visible means of escape. Committed to remain forever. "No Paul. No. I wouldn't"

The next day, Ann drifted around campus. A constant frown wrinkled her forehead. A slow, sick throb grasped her heart with each beat. She wished she had never met Paul. She thought about what she could have done to prevent this from happening but she never dreamt it would have gone this far. She remembered when she thought of Paul as a pest. When she was just happy to have a friend at the university. Why couldn't it have stayed that way? Why did she let this happen? Why did she let herself fall in love? She carried herself through each class, ill from emotion. Ann had never felt this bad in her entire life. She felt nauseous and faint. She hadn't eaten anything all that day. Ann's fatigued body was no longer functional enough to carry her around. She finally dragged herself to the student health center, searching for some sort of remedy.

"I'm what!" She cried out to the doctor.

"Your HCG test was positive. You're pregnant." Ann stared at the woman in the white coat as if she had told Ann she was terminally ill. "Yes ma'am." The doctor said and put her hands in the pockets of her lab coat. "Congratulations." She smiled professionally at Ann.

"Thank you, doctor." Ann tried unsuccessfully to force a smile.

"We need to talk about prenatal care and planning for the delivery. Put your clothes on dear and meet me in my office two doors down." The lady doctor patted Ann comfortingly on her shoulder and exited the room.

Ann dressed quickly, left the examination room and walked past the doctor's office door. Ann didn't want to talk about any prenatal care. She didn't want to talk about anything. She left the student health center and headed toward the bus stop. She had no idea what her next move was. Pregnant? She couldn't have a baby. Not now. What about school? She couldn't possibly continue now. What about Edward? But more importantly to Ann, what about Paul? How would he feel about her carrying his child, especially when he didn't even want to marry her? Ann had never been so overwrought with confusion in her life. She stared out of the bus window lost in despair. She had no idea what she would do now. She headed home to Edward, the one person Ann knew cared more about her than anyone on earth.

"Dorisse, can you meet me when you get off of work? I need to talk to you."

"Sure," Dorisse said on the department store telephone.

"OK. I'll meet you at work."

"No!" Dorisse said nervously, then tried to sound calm. "Meet me at the coffee shop at the corner, then maybe we'll catch a movie."

"Okay. I'll see you there at five."

Leaving Basile

Dorisse sat quietly as Ann told her the story of her affair with Paul and now the news of her pregnancy. Dorisse could hardly believe what Ann was saying. Dorisse wasn't so surprised that Ann was sleeping with a man other than her husband. She knew Ann would always do exactly as she pleased. She almost envied Ann for having so much excitement in her life, and the way Ann described Paul, she could hardly blame her. Dorisse had never met a man like that. Dorisse hated to see her friend in so much distress. Ann was obviously very confused and torn between what to do. Dorisse also felt sorry for Edward. She knew how he felt about Ann. What would he do when he found out about Paul? Would Ann tell him? What a mess Ann was in. Dorisse didn't have any suggestions about what she should do, but she knew one thing that would make Ann feel better, at least for the moment. The two walked over to the theater, sat upstairs, and watched Sidney Poitier and Tony Curtis dazzle the audience from the silver screen in *The Defiant Ones*.

As the two left the theater Dorisse put her arm around her friend, "Now, don't you feel better?" Ann nodded but she still felt sick with worry. "Don't worry Ann, things'll work out."

Dorisse's boss eyed the two women coming from the colored section of the theater and peeked at them from behind the exit doors as they walked out onto the street. He watched Dorisse stroll up the street with her hand on the young colored woman's shoulder.

Ann walked into her empty apartment. Edward was working late again. Another double shift so Ann could continue going to school. She couldn't do this to him. She picked up a pen and paper and began her letter to Edward as she sat in their dark bedroom.

My dearest Edward,
I'm finding it difficult to tell you what I'm feeling right now. I don't even really know myself, but I'll try to put it into words for you. Edward, when I married you I thought you were the most thoughtful, the most considerate man alive. I still think so. You don't deserve anything less than the best. I haven't been the best wife Edward. I know you love me, but I haven't earned your love. I don't deserve to have it. No matter what happens Edward, you'll always be very, very dear to me and close to my heart, but now, Edward, I must leave you. I need to find out who I am and what it is I want out of life. I don't want to ruin your life in the process. I'm moving to San Francisco. I'll keep in touch

63

Mechelle Randall

with you, I promise.
   With all my heart, Ann
   Ann packed her essentials, toiletries and four or five changes of clothes, gathered all the cash she had and got on the bus toward school. She began her second farewell letter as she headed to the bus station in Baton Rouge. The bus left Baton Rouge for California at six the next morning and she planned to be on it.

Leaving Basile

CHAPTER EIGHT
San Francisco, California

Ann stood in a telephone booth at the San Francisco bus station, her suitcase at her ankles, and phoned every motel in the book looking for the cheapest possible rate. Her money was scarce so she planned to stay at a motel for the night and look for a cheap apartment the next day. But for that night, she hailed a taxi in front of the bus station to take her to the Waterfront Inn on Fisherman's Wharf. Three days on the bus with terrible morning sickness had left her exhausted. All she wanted was a good night's sleep. The Inn didn't look too bad from the outside but it wasn't quite on Fisherman's Wharf and the neighborhood didn't look great. Ann looked around carefully before stepping out of the taxi cab. It was late and two dim lights barely lit the dark street. Ann was in very unfamiliar territory. It was strange for her, being in a city like San Francisco. Although Baton Rouge was a big city, San Francisco was very different. She could tell that just from her short ride through the city. Ann paid the driver and quickly slipped into the motel office. An elderly man sat behind the counter watching an old black and white television. The volume was up to its maximum capacity.

"Seventeen dollars per night ma'am," he said when he saw Ann walk in. "How long will you be here?" he asked very loudly, although Ann stood less than a foot away.

"One night."

He handed her a key. "To your right. All the way down at the end," he shouted at her. "Third door. Check out time's at eleven a.m."

Ann took the key and picked up her single piece of luggage. She walked to the doorway and stretched her neck looking for any strange city characters who might be lurking on the street. The coast seemed clear. She looked back at the hearing-impaired clerk who was, once again, staring at the old black and white. He'd certainly be no help if anything happened, Ann thought, and walked to her room.

The room was dark and cold, but it seemed to be clean. It

Mechelle Randall

had a stale, dry odor though, as if it had been empty for a while. Ann walked into the bathroom and stared at herself in the mirror. Dark circles hovered underneath her hazel eyes. Blue veins showed through her tawny skin. She looked pale and sallow. A queasy feeling came over her all of a sudden, and she leaned over the toilet to vomit. Instead she just gagged and retched a few times. That was worse. At least when she threw up she felt better. Now she still felt nauseous and her stomach muscles hurt from heaving. Ann laid on her back across the hard mattress and stared at the stucco ceiling. What a mess she was in. Two thousand miles away from anyone or anything she'd ever known, in an empty motel room, alone and pregnant. Well, the first thing tomorrow she had three things to do. Look for an apartment, a job, and an obstetrician.

    Ann showered, slipped into her nightgown and slid underneath the stiff, white sheets. As she drifted off to sleep, a pair of eyes stared at her through a crack in the thick drapes.

Leaving Basile

CHAPTER NINE

Edward sat on the couch holding Ann's letter in one hand and a glass of whiskey in the other. He slouched back and stared straight ahead. His head was spinning, half from the whiskey and half from reading and re-reading Ann's letter. He could hear her quiet voice saying the words in her perfect diction, meaning them. Ann's image popped in and out of his head. He remembered her soft, freckled complexion and how her long, wavy hair draped over her thin shoulders. He remembered the way her hazel eyes sparkled when she was happy and how she squinted them and held her tiny lips tightly when she was mad. He pictured her thin, supple body, so fragile and petite. He could feel her delicate hand in his. He felt her long feminine fingers. Edwards emotions were numb. His insides felt dry and empty. Nothing seemed important to him except to sit on the couch and refill his glass. What had he done wrong, so wrong that she could do this?

Edward had tried to be everything Ann wanted him to be. He worked like a dog to help pay for her schooling and he never said anything about her late hours. Whenever she wanted to go to the movie show, he took her, or gave her money to go. He tried to think of what else he could have done or what it was he had done that had made her want to leave him like this. He saw her small face in his mind again. He recalled how happy she had been lately and the times when school had gotten so hard for her that she barely spoke a word to him. He thought about that ridiculous trip he had made to the school out of insecurity. He thought about when they first moved to Port Allen. It hadn't been California, but she had been so excited about the department store and he remembered how much she loved that very first movie she had seen. He remembered how they used to sit on her porch in Basile and the time he had given her his grandmother's gold band which now sat on their Formica table in the kitchen where she left it. He remembered their wedding day and how beautiful she looked in her white dress. She looked like a princess, an angel. Edward smiled as if he were there again, as if he could see her gentle smile right now as he gazed into her golden eyes. As Edward gazed, his eyes focused on a crack in the pale yellow wall and the emptiness in the room engulfed his body. A wretched ache gripped his lungs and he took short, shallow breaths trying to fill the painful space in his chest. It didn't work. He began to feel dizzy and sick. His head throbbed. He tried harder to fight the pain but it only moved through his body down to his abdomen. There it stewed and bubbled like a parasite gnawing away at him, leaving him feeling like a raw, hollow shell. There on that couch, he felt he had met his end.

I can't die here, with this glass in my hand, Edward thought. He stood up and threw the glass at the crack on the wall and it shattered into tiny slivers. "And I won't," he said aloud. The next day Edward packed his bags, got on the bus and headed for San Francisco. He had no idea where she was or how he would find her, but if he had to, he'd spend the rest of his life looking. And when he found her, he swore to himself he'd make her happy, whatever it took.

CHAPTER TEN

Ann could sense a presence. She opened her eyes from her heavy sleep and lay still listening intently. The room was pitch black except for a ray from the streetlight entering through a crack in the curtains. She turned her head toward the beam and saw a pair of eyes peering into her room. She froze. Oh God. What should she do? She had heard stories about the city. How people were killed and mutilated for no reason by psychopathic maniacs. Maybe she could scream. No one would come help her, certainly not the old man at the desk. He would never even hear her. She'd die alone in this motel room in San Francisco. No one knew where she was. They wouldn't find her for days. Her decomposed body would be unrecognizable.

Ann's heart raced as she slowly lifted her head to look back at the eyes. They suddenly realized she saw them and quickly moved away from the window. Ann immediately jumped up and ran to the window, swung back the thick curtains and saw a figure disappear into one of the other motel rooms a few doors away. Something odd was going on. It looked like . . . a woman. Ann was sure she saw the tail end of a pink robe trail into the door. Although Ann was still frightened, now she was curious. Why was this woman spying on her? What could she want? Maybe she wanted to break in Ann's room and rob her. She was a drug addict, yes. Ann had heard about these people. They'd do anything for their drugs, she had heard. Ann checked the lock and chain on the door. She peeked out the curtain and looked over at the door the woman had run into. It remained closed. Ann pulled the drapes tightly together and sat back the middle of the full-sized bed. She pulled her knees to her chest, rested her chin on her knees and stared at the blank television screen. Ann sat still in the room listening for a break in the silence.

When a knock on the door woke Ann it was morning. She glanced over at the clock which read ten forty-five. It must be the deaf desk clerk, Ann thought. She must have really been tired to sleep straight through to checkout time. She walked to the door and opened it as far as the chain would allow. There stood a rather robust young woman with highly ratted red frosty hair, and a shiny hot pink robe trimmed in pink ostrich feathers. Black, smudged eyeliner surrounded her large blue eyes. The door down the hall from the night before was left half open.

"Um," the woman stumbled around with her words as she addressed Ann. She looked more nervous than Ann was. Although the woman now seemed harmless, Ann was still uncomfortable. This was the woman who was looking into her room and she *did* look a little bizarre with her shocking pink robe and smeared make-up.

"Can I help you?" Ann stood behind the partially opened door, peering around it through the small opening the chain left.

"Yes. I . . . I saw you come in last night alone. You looked kind of sick."

She spoke in a tiny, high-pitched voice with a very slight lisp that made her sound like a five-year-old. "Are you okay?" She pulled on her shiny robe and folded her arms to keep it closed.

"Why, yes." Ann was still puzzled.

"That was me looking in your window last night. I thought you might be real sick or something but I didn't want to disturb you. I didn't mean to scare you or anything." She looked at Ann, silently asking forgiveness.

Ann looked back at this poor soul She looked pitiful. The hem hung out of her robe and she held a half smoked cigarette butt between her fingers.

"My name is Elizabeth, but everyone calls me Liz."

"Ann," Ann said relaxing after seeing Liz's apologetic expression. She took the chain off the door and opened it. Liz relaxed too.

"You did frighten me. I'm new in town and I don't really know anyone here. Plus this doesn't look like the best neighborhood in San Francisco."

"No, it isn't. Hey, where are you from?" Liz started chewing some gum she had pulled from inside her jaw.

"Louisiana."

"Oh. I'm new here too. . .kinda. I moved into this motel two months ago."

"Here?" Ann couldn't imagine having to stay in this place for two months.

"Yea. I got the room monthly because I couldn't afford to get a real apartment on my own yet. You know, with first and last, and then they want a deposit and everything."

"Well, I'm going to look for an apartment today," Ann said, "and a job."

"I'm a waitress at a coffee shop over on Vanness. We have an opening. It's at night, but if you can get good tips it pays the bills."

"That sounds great!"

"Do you have any experience? Have you ever waited tables before?"

"No."

"Lie."

"OK." They laughed. Ann was so happy to have met someone. Even though Liz seemed a bit eccentric, Ann felt one hundred percent better. She didn't even feel nauseous this morning.

"Oh. There is one other thing you can help me with," Ann said to her new friend. "I need a doctor."

"Why? What's wrong with you?" Liz touched Ann's arm and looked at her closely, as if she might be dying.

"I'm pregnant," Ann sighed.

Ann got the waitress job at the twenty-four hour coffee shop where Liz worked. She worked from eleven at night until eight in the morning. She and Liz found a one bedroom apartment and split the rent. At first Ann was totally exhausted from working the graveyard shift, but soon she got used to sleeping during the day. Since Liz worked from eight to five it was quiet while Ann was home sleeping, and Liz got her privacy at night.

Ann didn't see very much of Liz because of their schedules. When Ann got home in the morning, Liz was in her uniform ready to leave. On the rare evenings when Liz didn't have a date. she and Ann would meet and have dinner together. More often, Liz came home, showered, and dressed in one of her flamboyant leopard skin outfits or brightly colored dresses, heavily accessorized with costume bracelets and pearls, and headed out for the evening. Most of the guys Liz dated were nice, she said, but there was no one serious. "Still looking Mr. Right", she would tell Ann. Ann wanted to suggest to her sometimes that maybe she could dress differently. Maybe she could wear a little less make-up, and she'd look a lot nicer. But Liz seemed so proud of herself as she stood in the mirror, chewing her huge wad of gum, that Ann didn't have the heart.

She probably wouldn't believe her anyway. Ann liked Liz a lot, with all of her eccentricities. She was often depressed though, over some relationship that didn't work out. Ann thought she just picked the wrong kinds of guys. Since Liz dressed so provocatively, she attracted a certain kind of man. Even at work, Liz wore her push up bra, and her uniform was as tight as her shiny orange stretch pants. She often returned from dates early. On Ann's night off, she kept her up telling her about how her date took her to some sleazy bar, bored her to death telling her how he won his last bowling game, and then suggested they go back to his apartment after buying her a few drinks. Many weekends Liz would refuse to go out altogether and walked around the house wallowing in her depression. She'd lie around in her robe both days eating and crying on and off, feeling sorry for herself. She wasn't a bad looking girl either. She was rather full-figured, quite the opposite of Ann. Even in her pregnancy Ann's limbs remained thin and dangly. Only her abdomen had begun to swell. Liz had a full, chubby frame and an extra chin and she was sure to accent her figure with each outfit she chose. But on those melancholy weekends, she would let her red, frosted hair lie unteased and the actual beauty of her features showed through when her face wasn't covered with cosmetics. Liz continued trying to meet Mr. Right in spite of her many unsuccessful attempts.

 When they first met, Liz had told Ann about a pregnancy clinic run by the county. Ann went in for an exam and found she was eight weeks pregnant. Her baby was due on July 28. Her stomach had begun to grow and her doctor said she was doing well. It was difficult for her, working full time and on her feet all day, but it kept her busy, and it did, as Liz had told her, pay the bills. The clinic charged on a sliding scale, so she paid according to her income. "How did you end up living in a motel?" Ann had asked her one night after another failed date.

 "Well, I was living with my boyfriend Sam, and we weren't getting along. Sam had a lot of problems," Liz said in her mousy voice. "He drank too much, but he was really a good person deep down inside. We used to have so much fun, the two of us. We'd go down to Ocean beach practically every weekend. I'd lie out on my beach towel and Sam would rub sun tan oil on my back. We'd buy those great hot dogs from the boardwalk and walk in the sand for miles. I was in cosmetology school and Sam worked at the dock, you know, loading and unloading boxes and crates and stuff. He really hated that work. He was frustrated. He got into a fight at work one day, and they fired him. Whenever her was mad at someone else he'd always get into it with me when he got home. Sometimes he'd hit me, you know, slap me or something." Liz's voice began to quiver. "The day he got fired, he came home and I was cooking dinner. He started yelling and screaming and trying to start a fight with me. Well I just ignored him. He was crazy. I don't know, it happened so fast. I was standing at the stove and he just snatched my arm you know, and the hot oil spilled all over my arm." Tears rolled down Liz's cheeks. "He didn't mean it. He just wanted me to listen to him. I didn't know what it was like to have to do something I hated every single day. And he was doing it for me, so I could go to cosmetology school. Well, I guess he just couldn't take it anymore. He swung his arm back and hit me. The things before, the bruises and black eyes, I always went back to him afterward. But this was the first time I was scared, I mean really scared. He usually stopped right after, and told me he was sorry. You know, made me an ice pack or something. I knew he didn't mean it. But this time, when he got fired, it was like he lost it. My arm was all blistered from the oil, and he kept hitting me and hitting me." Ann listened to Liz's story in horror, tears in her own eyes. "I ran out of the house and started running down the street, holding my burnt arm in my other hand. I didn't turn around. I just kept running until I fell on the ground. The next thing I knew, I was at the hospital. Well they patched up my arm, but the police told me I'd better get out of that situation before I wound up dead. So I went to the motel with nothing but the money in my purse and the few clothes I could gather up before he came home." Liz wiped her eyes and straightened up. She looked at Ann's wet eyes. "And then I met you." She smiled at Ann. They reached out for each other and Liz squeezed Ann so hard and long Ann could barely breath. But she held Liz's cushiony body tightly until she let go.

Ann had made one last stop before she had gotten on the bus in Baton Rouge She stopped at the university just long enough to leave Paul a note.

Paul was shocked when he read Ann's letter. He knew she was upset after that night but he never dreamed she'd take off. He sat in his dorm room and read her letter again, word for word.

Dear Paul,

Mechelle Randall

I've never had to make such an important decision in my life, but today I found out I was pregnant. You are obviously not ready for a family, and I need for my child to be raised in a loving, stable environment. So, I'm leaving my husband anyway. Not for you, but for the baby. I don't love Edward, so this is best for everyone involved. I'm moving to San Francisco. I love you more than you'll ever know. With all my heart, Ann.

He did love her, but she was right. He wasn't ready for a family. It frightened him to think about marriage, let alone having a child, but it was too late anyway. Ann was gone and she was having a baby, their baby. He was too young to be having a baby, he thought. He didn't know anything about being a father, and he knew even less about being a husband—a good husband anyway.

Paul had read Ann's note over and over the past few weeks. At first he thought her leaving was for the best, especially with her being pregnant. How could he, with a part-time job, and half a college degree, care for a baby? But now he was beginning to miss her, to worry about her. What was she doing? How was she supporting herself? Did she have a decent place to live? Ann was not used to being in a city like San Francisco. The people out there were different. They took advantage of people like Ann. She could get into all sorts of trouble out there and she was carrying their child. What was she thinking right now? How must she feel, all alone out there, with no one? What must she think of him? She must think I'm a jerk, Paul thought, He sure had begun to feel like one. How could he do this? Paul called the bus station. As soon as he could, he would leave for San Francisco to look for Ann. He would do the right thing. He'd search every inch of that city until he found her, no matter what. He knew he'd find Ann. Now he realized how much he really loved her.

Dorisse stacked boxes on the top shelf of the storeroom at work. She had stayed late for inventory and was almost finished. Dorisse had practically run the dress department alone for the last few months. Mr. Gifford had been called upon to organize one of the departments in a new store they were opening in New Orleans. He had been gone for several months but had come back two days ago. Dorisse had been uneasy around Mr. Gifford ever since he had given her the stockings. It wasn't so much the gift itself. It was the way his tiny bloodshot eyes seemed to ogle at her, as if he were trying to picture how the stockings might look on her. Rubbing the back of her neck, she slowly climbed down the small stepladder. Two hands suddenly gripped her waist and Dorisse turned sharply into Mr. Gifford's grinning face.

"Mr. Gifford!" She placed her hand against her chest in surprise.

"I'm sorry, Dorisse. I didn't mean to startle you." He lowered her smoothly to the floor. She could smell he had been drinking. He stunk of bourbon.

"Oh. Oh, well . . . thank you." She laughed nervously and looked around the cramped store room for space as he stood between her and the door.

"Are you finished with the inventory?" he drawled, as he folded the ladder and leaned it against the wall.

"Yes, Mr. Gifford. Pretty near." She stood in the middle of the small room. "I just have a few more things to do."

"Good." He arranged some boxes on a shelf as he talked. "Would you like to have a drink with me in my office, Dorisse? You've had a long day. It'll help you relax." He smiled a cigar-stained smile at her again.

"No, no thank you, sir." Dorisse stuttered. "I should be getting home."

He remained in the small area between her and the storeroom door. "You know Dorisse, you've done good work here in the department."

"Thank you sir." Dorisse replied apprehensively. "I appreciate you giving me the job." She picked at her short fingernails.

"You should, Dorisse." A callousness came through in his voice as he looked at her. "You lied to me, didn't you?" he asked her. His face turned into a wicked mask, his sharp eyes piercing into her widened ones. "You lied to me. Didn't you!" He snapped at her viciously and Dorisse flinched at his accusing outburst.

"I . . . I . . . I don't know what you mean, sir." Dorisse leaned away.

"You know damn well what I mean, nigger."

Dorisse swallowed hard and slowly backed against the wall.

"I should've known you were one of them Creole's trying to pass." His hot breath smelled of sour bourbon. "I should've looked at that dark hair of yours," he walked toward her and touched Dorisse's face with the back of his fat hand, "and that smooth, creamy skin of yours," He glared at her lecherously as she turned her head to one side and stared at the store room floor. "Yesss," he dragged the word out as his fingers traveled onto her neck, down the front of her chest over her wildly beating heart, and drifted over one of her breasts. Dorisse instinctively slapped his hand away. Mr. Gifford shoved her by the shoulders against the wall and held her there brutally. "Listen to me nigger, you are working here under false pretenses." He spoke invectively. "I could have your ass put in jail. Did you know that?" His blood vesseled eyes bulged out at her.

"I never said I was White," she whimpered.

"What!? I wouldn't allow no nigger run this department! What the hell made you think that? And there's no way in the world a nigger'd ever make the kind of money you make." He released Dorisse's shoulders from his grip but she stayed pressed against the wall. "I know you don't want to go to jail, Dorisse. Why, a pretty young thing like you, all locked up?" He smiled an evil grin at her. "Why, I wouldn't mind if you continued to work here. It'd be our little secret. "Just you...," he touched her on the chest, "...and me." "How about that drink, huh?" He stood close to her and slightly pressed his groin against her dress. Dorisse slowly looked up at his bloated face. She saw saliva fill his mouth and heard him swallow hard. She worked up a slight smile and looked him up and down. She tried to force a sexy look in her eyes as she said to him, "Okay, Mr. Gifford. I'd like that."

He took Dorisse softly by the hand and lead her out of the storeroom. They walked toward his office door and he turned to look at her face in the dim room. As they passed in front of her work counter, Dorisse stopped and smiled sensuously at him. "I think I'd like a cigarette with my drink." She pouted her lips at him and he grinned lustfully. Dorisse gently released her hand from his grip and got her purse from behind her work counter. She stared at his disgusting frame for a few seconds before she bolted for the front door. Dorisse moved like a frightened gazelle, darting between clothes racks and counters skillfully on her high heels, as Mr. Gifford ran behind her. His heavy body knocked over displays and racks clumsily. He moved as fast as he could trying catch her before she reached the front door. She heard his heavy breathing and fat footsteps moving up quickly behind her and everything in the store jumped off the floor an inch or two each time he landed. Dorisse felt as if she were moving in slow motion, the way the suspenseful part of a movie was dragged out to make it even scarier, to let the terror build up. She ran for her life. She could hear Mr. Gifford cursing as he stumbled along behind her. He was a foot away from her as he reached out and grabbed the collar of her dress. It tightened around her neck and swept her off her feet onto the floor with Mr. Gifford right behind her. He hit the floor with a loud, hollow thud and landed at her feet. The two lay on the floor, Mr. Gifford panting and sweating profusely, and Dorisse almost in shock from fear. She looked toward her feet and Mr. Gifford lay there beyond her black pumps, staring into her terrified eyes. Dorisse stared at his corpulent body, lying on its side like a wounded animal, the trail of fallen clothes he had knocked over, leading up to him like footprints in the jungle. He had her.

His teeth began to appear slowly as his lips curled up into a smile. His red eyes seemed to glow and his face took on a gargoyle-like appearance as he spoke. "I got yo ass now," he said.

This was the part in the movie when the audience held their breath, Dorisse thought, when their hearts beat hard and fast, like hers was. This was the part when the suspenseful background music got louder and louder until it deafened the audience, when the heroine had to fight for herself. Fight she thought, you're the heroinne, Dorisse, fight. Dorisse bent one of her knees up to her chest and kicked Mr. Gifford in the face as hard as she could. The tip of her spike heel landed directly into one of his beady eyes and he screamed out in agony. Dorisse pulled her leg back and felt it dislodge from his socket. He lay on the floor howling out a sound iike an animal's mating call as blood seeped out from between the short fingers that covered his eye. Dorisse stared in horror, at what she had done to Mr. Gifford. She watched as thick, red blood oozed out and began creating a puddle beneath his head as he squirmed and writhed on the floor. She looked at the same thick blood on the bottom of her left heel, then scrambled to her feet and ran out the front door.

CHAPTER ELEVEN

Ann and Liz sat in their living room one sunny Saturday, morning. The May sun had come up bright and warm that spring day, something she had only seen a few times in San Francisco. Ann folded some new baby clothes she had bought at a second-hand store. Liz sat wrapped in her old fushia house robe and fuzzy high-heeled slippers, holding an unlit cigarette between her lips. She always carried a cigarette around for an hour or so before she lit it. She sat slouched in the arm chair, polished toes peeking out from under their furry shoes resting on the ottoman, the cigarette barely hanging onto her bottom lip, complaining as she always did when she was in this mood.

"What's wrong with me, Ann?" This was how she always began her, "why can't I find a boyfriend", speech.

"I mean, I know I'm a little overweight, and maybe I complain a little too much."

"No," Ann said sarcastically, "not you!"

"At least I realize it. Nobody's perfect you know," Liz said feeling sensitive.

"Oh, I'm just kidding." Ann smiled and got up to pat Liz on her back, but suddenly bent over in pain. She held her abdomen and grimaced as a sharp pain shot down through her pelvis. Liz jumped up onto her slippers and led Ann back to the couch.

"What's wrong? What is it?" She held Ann's hand tightly. Ann caught her breath but stayed bent over, clutching her stomach.

"If I'm not mistaken," Ann said with much effort, "I think I'm in labor."

Liz screamed loudly and her unlit cigarette fell to the floor. "Ahhh! Labor?! But, but it isn't time!" Liz looked panic-stricken. "What'll we do?!" She let go of Ann's hand and began to pace the floor. The heels of her slippers clicked across the tiled kitchen floor. She held her arms folded to close the faded robe which had lost its buttons long ago.

We should start timing the contractions," Ann breathed deeply recovering from the pain. "and call my doctor."

"Oh my God!" She looked at Ann as if Ann had just said they should jump off the Bay Bridge. Liz got another cigarette to hold and resumed her pacing.

"Liz, get the telephone, okay?" As Liz ran to get the telephone Ann felt a trickle of wetness between her legs. She reached down to look under her dress and all of a sudden a giant eruption of fluid gushed out like a tidal wave. "Oh my God," Ann said. "It's too early." She began to cry. "Liz!" she cried out. "Liz, hurry!" She sat on the couch soaked in clear amniotic fluid. "Please hurry," she screamed as another sharp pain ripped through her abdomen.

Liz ran in with the telephone, her hands shaking. She placed it down and fumbled with the receiver.

"Liz my water bag broke. Call Dr. Jackson and tell him. The number's taped to the phone. Then call a taxi." Liz dialed frantically and did exactly as Ann instructed. Dr. Jackson's secretary said she'd page him and he'd meet them at the hospital. Liz screamed at the taxi dispatcher to come right away.

"Now what?" She stood in her robe and looked at Ann helplessly.

"Get dressed, Liz," she tried to speak calmly to keep Liz from losing it. Liz was her only hope. She had to handle this. "I'll be all right." Liz ran toward the bedroom and emerged in seconds in an orange tank top and black mini skirt, tripping over her black sling-back shoes holding some clothes and a box of chocolates.

"Here." She handed Ann some dry underwear and one of her maternity dresses. She helped Ann pull the wet dress over her head. "Don't worry Ann. Everything's gonna be just fine." Liz tried to reassure Ann but her face was frozen in a terrified expression. Ann held her large abdomen as Liz finished dressing her. Liz grabbed her purse and the chocolates and the two walked outside just as the cab pulled up.

"Oh my God," Ann mumbled as she and Liz sat in the back seat of the taxi on their way to City hospital. She rocked back and forth with her legs wide open and squeezed Liz's hand as the contractions came and went. "I can feel the baby coming," Ann cried. A stream of blood flowed from her crotch. "Please hurry!" The pain seemed constant.

Long streams of tears flowed down Liz's face. She held her forehead, trying, but unable to handle the situation at hand. She cried uncontrollably and squeezed Ann's hand tightly in hers. Ann felt the baby's head slowly moving toward her vaginal opening.

"The baby!" Ann cried. Liz looked over and cried even louder after seeing the blood trickling from under Ann's dress. The driver wove in and out of traffic and kept his eyes on the road. It seemed to Ann he got stuck behind every slow moving car and red light on the road. Ann felt a tremendous pressure on her pelvic floor. She rocked back and forth trying to relieve the pain caused by this immense weight. Liz still sobbed loudly. The baby's head was making its way toward the orifice. Ann felt the tissue begin to tear. She sat soaked in fluid and blood and was numb from the pressure. She held her hand between her legs with her hand on the crown of the baby's head, literally holding it in. She was terrified. "Oh please," she thought. "Please God. It's coming. My baby is coming!"

Leaving Basile

CHAPTER TWELVE

The last few months had not been easy for Edward. He was still finding it difficult to deal with the fact that Ann was gone. Although he had been suspicious about Paul, he truly believed Ann had left him because his transfer to California never materialized, and she was afraid she'd be stuck in Port Allen forever.

On his arrival in San Francisco, he checked into a motel and began to go through the telephone book. He got the names and addresses of all the colleges in the area. Edward planned to travel to each and every one of them, until he found the one Ann had enrolled in. He first checked the universities, then junior colleges, and trade school. He checked under both her married and maiden names. He called the university in Baton Rouge. They said Ann hadn't had her records transferred anywhere. Edward filed a missing persons report at the police station and checked with them everyday.

Every time he passed a girl on the street who in any way resembled Ann, his heart began to pound. He followed girls for blocks with dark brown wavy hair only to find himself following some stranger, who was usually quite disturbed by his approach. After Edward had depleted all his avenues, he just walked the streets, day after day, looking into every face that passed him. Every day he sat in the bar across the street from his motel, peering out of the window at passersby, expecting to see Ann's face at any moment. He planned how he'd react. He'd tell her he'd do anything to make her happy and beg her to return. They could stay in San Francisco if she wanted, together, the two of them. He pictured how she'd fall into his arms, ecstatic to see him, telling him how she had missed him and holding him as tight as her thin arms could.

Edward sat in a bar in the Tenderloin District of San Francisco, whiskey in hand, drunk at three o'clock in the afternoon. His money was running out and so were his plans to find Ann. Edward had applied for a job at the post office in San Francisco but with no luck so far. He had left them his phone

81

number at the motel and they said they'd call him as soon as something was available. That hadn't happened so far. Emotionally, Edward was going downhill fast. He had put every ounce of energy he had into finding Ann, and so far, he had failed. Physically, he looked terrible and he constantly felt sick. His stomach ached worse every day. He had aged years in the past few months. The daily drinking had taken its toll on him. His eyes were sunken, his hair was dry and dull and his skin was pale and yellow. At the age of twenty-three, he looked twenty years older. Each day he tried and tried to imagine where else she might be, or any other means he could use to find her. He had used all the resources he could think of. Edward had very little money left and even less energy. All he could do now was sit in the bar, and stare out the window. He took the crumpled letter Ann had written him from his pocket and looked at it. He kept it with him at all times, taking it out periodically to look at her familiar handwriting. He re-read the part where she said she'd keep in touch with him. She promised. Edward had phoned Mrs. Thibideaux and given her the number and address of the motel where he was staying. Edward checked the desk at the motel everyday for messages, either from Mrs. Thibideaux or the post office, but no messages ever came. He waited and watched from the bar window every day, aging another year as each day passed.

Leaving Basile

CHAPTER THIRTEEN

Paul had plenty of time to plan how he'd find Ann by the time he left for San Francisco in the Spring. He knew she would have to have an obstetrician, so he'd just get the telephone book and call every OB/GYN in the city. As soon as Paul rolled into San Francisco, he checked into a motel, got settled and proceeded with his plan.

"Physicians, physicians", he checked the yellow pages. "Neurology, neurosurgery . . . obstetrics and gynecology." He dialed the first phone number.

"Doctor Abbott's office," a female voice answered.

"Yes, hello. My wife has forgotten when her next appointment is with Doctor Abbott. Can you give me that date and time please?"

"What's your wife's name, sir?"

"Ann. Ann Fruge´." He knew she'd use her maiden name.

"I'm sorry. We don't seem to have a patient by that name. Are you sure she. . ." Paul hung up.

He spent most of his first day in San Francisco phoning doctors. There must be a million of them in the city, Paul thought. He went to sleep that night only up to the G's.

The next morning Paul resumed his quest.

"Yes, hello. My wife has forgotten when her next visit is with Doctor Jackson. Can you give us that date and time please?" It had taken him most of the day to get to the J's. He had repeated this speech so many times he wasn't even really listening to the answer. He knew it as well as his speech. There must be some mistake, they'd always say.

"Ann Fruge´?" She repeated the name Paul had given her. "Oh my, Mr. Fruge´!"

"Yes, what is it?" Paul stood up.

"It seems Ann is in labor at City Hospital right now. Dr. Jackson's on his way to meet her there."

"She's in labor? Now?" Paul dropped the phone and grabbed his coat. City Hospital. He ran outside and hailed a taxi. His calculations must've been wrong. He hadn't figured her to be due yet. But his plan to find Ann had worked. He was on his way.

Ann's taxi cab finally swung into the emergency room parking lot at City General Hospital. The driver got out, ran into the building and emerged with a woman and man, both in white, pushing a gurney. The two lifted Ann onto the gurney and wheeled her in through the emergency room entrance. Liz jumped out the other door of the cab and chased after the gurney. The driver forgot about his fee and the mess in the backseat and ran after Ann and Liz into the hospital. As all five of them ran up the hall of the emergency room Liz held on to Ann's hand tightly and ran alongside the moving gurney. Ann breathed deeply through the contractions and looked up into Liz's face, now puffy from crying. "Thanks for being here with me," Ann said.

"Well where else would I be silly?" Liz said in her little voice. The both of them smiled for the first time since the whole ordeal began. They wheeled Ann into a room and Liz waved with one hand and clutched her purse and the box of chocolates with the other. For the first time, she noticed the cabbie beside her. "Want a cream filled?," she offered. He accepted.

The pain still writhed inside of Ann. She saw her blurry reflection inside the giant metal lights on the ceiling. They stripped her naked and put her legs up into stirrups as Dr. Jackson's face appeared between her legs.

"Don't worry Ann," he said far too calmly for her. "Just do as I tell you, okay?" He ran his gloved fingers around the bottom of her vaginal opening. "I'm gonna have to cut you a little. You've torn some and I don't want the tissue to tear anymore, okay?" At this point Ann didn't care if he cut her whole body in half. It already felt like somebody had done that anyway. She just wanted this baby out of her. She saw him take a pair of surgical scissors and felt him cutting her. But it didn't hurt. There was too much pressure and pain elsewhere to feel whatever it was he was doing down there. She felt the baby still trying to move out. It felt like a fifty pound lead weight hanging in her uterus, trying to pull every other organ in her body out with it. It seemed as though her abdominal muscles were pulling apart, like a giant hand had reached inside of her and yanked all her insides from the abdominal wall.

"This baby wants to come right now," someone said. Who were they telling? She could've told them that, but the only

Leaving Basile

sounds she could make now were primitive moans and groans. Ann wanted to jump from the table and strangle Dr. Jackson and the taxi driver and Paul and every other man that ever lived. This was their fault. All they ever did was give pain. They had no idea what pain was. Paul was to blame for all of this. And that stupid Edward, country hick. Why couldn't he be ambitious? If he were, maybe she would've loved him and maybe he'd be here right now. Stupid husband. Everyone was stupid. Ann hated everyone.

"Ann. I want you to take a deep breath now and push, okay?" Dr. Jackson instructed her. Ann inhaled and turned a bright shade of red underneath her sweat-soaked face as she pushed. "Good Ann. Push again." Dr. Jackson sat at the foot of the table, "It's coming. One more push Ann." Ann bore down as hard as she could and let out a loud scream as the baby's bald head squeezed out. The nurse suctioned the baby's nose and mouth with a green bulb.

"Okay, Ann. Push some more. You're doing wonderfully." The baby's pale, rubbery body popped out and it let out a funny, newborn wail, moving its limbs around rigidly.

"Congratulations, Ann," Dr. Jackson said, smiling between Ann's open legs. "It's a girl!"

CHAPTER FOURTEEN

Dorisse sat in her apartment crying. She had never been so frightened in her life. She trembled like a lost kitten as she sat huddled in the corner of her bedroom. She had run all the way home from the department store and seemed to hear Mr. Gifford's screams for blocks, it seemed. He'd send the police and she'd end up in jail. They'd never believe what really happened — that it was self defense. They'd just take her straight to jail, no questions asked. Or worse, Mr. Gifford would come after her himself. She could still see him easing up behind her in the store, suddenly strangling her off her feet. She could smell the putrid odor of digested bourbon mixed with perspiration exuding from his pores. She could see his pupils like amphibian slits on their red backgrounds and that ghastly, sardonic smile. She could feel her heel like a pestle mash his eyeball to useless pulp.

Dorisse covered her face with her hands and cried into them. What could she do? Everything was wrong. Ann had left. Then Edward, in his despair, up and left without telling anyone. Dorisse didn't even know he was gone until she went to visit him just the other day. The apartment manager told her he had moved to California, and left no forwarding address. They had left her all alone in Port Allen, just like they had left her in Basile. She wished Ann was here right now. Dorisse felt so alone. She didn't have anyone to turn to. She didn't know what to do. She had to run, she knew that. She had to leave Port Allen. She threw her clothes in a suitcase quickly and headed for the bus terminal without looking back. She had no choice. She had to leave. Dorisse bought a ticket on a bus leaving for Los Angeles that night. She was going to Hollywood.

CHAPTER FIFTEEN

Ann felt like a can that had been kicked for ten miles. Her back ached, she could feel where they had put the stitches in, and she felt totally drained of all energy even though she had just awakened. How long had she been asleep? Hours? Days? She lifted her head slightly, trying to focus on a clock across the room. She felt someone's presence.

"Ann," a male voice said softly.

She looked up into a face that was so familiar to her but. . . Slowly she brought the man's features into focus. She forgot about how uncomfortable she was as she realized those midnight eyes could belong to no other. Her tired eyes frowned in perplexity, staring at Paul like a ghost from her past. She tried to stop and gather her thoughts. Had she been dreaming? Was she dreaming now? She shifted her confused glare from Paul's face and glanced around the room. Yes, she was in the hospital. That whole ordeal in the taxi and her grueling delivery suddenly resurfaced. She remembered feeling the tissue tearing between her legs, then the doctor later cutting it even more. The pain throbbed at the incision and this incredible sight of Paul at her bedside took a backseat for the moment.

"Can you get my nurse please," she said to him, eyes closed, grimacing in discomfort.

Paul stepped from the room and returned with a heavy set lady in a white polyester dress and nurse's hat. She was as solid as a piece of furniture and stood filling the doorway in her white dress like a blank movie screen. She walked to Ann's bedside.

"My baby," Ann asked, "How's my baby?"

"She's in the intensive care nursery. We can go see her soon. I'm going to give you a little something for pain. Okay hon?" She placed her chubby hand on Ann's shoulder and smiled sympathetically. Ann nodded, her posture guarded. The nurse injected something into Ann's I.V. "You have a good rest now, Okay?" She left Ann and Paul alone.

He pulled a chair up and sat next to Ann's bed taking her

hand.

"Paul . . . ," she sighed. Her eyes were beginning to get heavy from the medication. She fought to finish her sentence but Paul interrupted her, taking advantage of her drowsy state. He rubbed her hand like a small pet.

"Close your eyes, my love," Paul said, "Sleep well and we'll talk when you wake up." He slowly placed her hand at her side when she drifted off to sleep. He pulled the blanket up over Ann's body and tucked it under her chin Even after all she had just been through, Paul thought, she was still as beautiful as he remembered. He decided, at that moment, that he would ask Ann to marry him.

As Edward lay sprawled across the motel room double bed, the telephone began to ring. He stirred slightly after several rings, but only enough to move the empty bottle of whiskey from his fingers. The phone continued to ring several more times, but Edward was too hung over to react to the ringing. He lay motionless in a deep, drunken sleep. The post office in San Francisco had been trying to contact him for several days and had left several messages. But Edward hadn't remained sober enough in the past few weeks long enough to answer the phone, let alone to work, and he hadn't checked the office for messages. After that call, they gave up.

Ann awakened feeling a lot better. The drill sergeant nurse helped Ann wash up and put on her own clean pajamas Liz had brought from home. She sat in a wheelchair waiting to be taken to the intensive care nursery to see her little girl. Ann tried to forget about Paul. He only complicated matters. What did he want? Why was he trying to make things difficult for her? She had moved two thousand miles to get away from him. Now, here he was, in San Francisco. The whole thing was insane. Ann began to feel anxious. The hefty nurse entered, placed her hands on her wide hips, and stood with her fat legs apart. She cocked her wide, motherly face to one side and smiled sweetly when she spoke to Ann. "Ready to go see that little darling of yours?" Ann smiled and nodded.

Ann peered through the plastic, see-through beds the tiny infants slept in, as her nurse wheeled her through the nursery. Ann spotted her daughter from across the room. A tiny pink cap hugged her elongated head as she stirred slightly and smacked her tiny lips. Ann's eyes filled with happy tears as she watched the infant shift inside the papoosed blanket. Her beautiful baby skin was a creamy shade of tan, and she blinked coal black eyes at the ceiling. The nurse removed the baby from her transparent chamber and placed her gently in Ann's arms. Ann held her firmly and touched her tiny face with a fingertip. She looked up at Ann with newborn eyes, and seemed to recognize her mother immediately. Tears fell from the corners of Ann's eyes onto the flannel nursery blanket.

"You're so teeny," Ann sniffed. "I can't believe you're mine. My little girl." Ann played with her delicate fingers. "Don't you ever worry little one. Mommy will never, ever leave you. You're all I have in the world. You are my whole family." Ann looked up from her daughter's jet eyes into an identical pair. Paul stood pressing his palms against the outside of the nursery window, smiling sadly, and waved a childlike wave. Ann saw the regret on his face. He had traveled across the country so she could see that look, Ann thought. She wondered how, on earth, he had found her and her daughter, in a city as big as San Francisco. But there he was. The same man she fell in love with in Baton Rouge, Louisiana. A lump formed in her throat. Paul stood there like a boy in a pet shop window. She stood up carefully, carried the baby to the window and held her up for Paul to see. He leaned into the glass, trying to reach through it, and pressed his entire face against it. He waved a small, scrunched up wave to the baby.

"Say hello to your daddy," Ann found herself saying. Paul's brow began to wrinkle as he held his fingertips up, frozen in their tiny wave. Ann's nurse approached from behind.

"Well, I see you're walking ok. Let's get this little one back into her incubator."

"Is she going to be all right?" Ann hated to give her up. She could hold her twenty-four hours a day.

"Her lungs are doing quite well, for a preemie, but she'll have to sleep in the incubator so she won't get cold. Does she have a name so I can stop calling her little one?" The nurse leaned her large head to one side.

"Yes." Ann stared at the tiny bundle. "Her name is Miette." Ann couldn't help but cry. She tried not to, but she had never felt this way about anyone or anything. The warm infant looked at Ann as if she knew she was crying from happiness. Ann looked up at Paul again. A tear was trickling down his face and onto the nursery window. The nurses eyes began to water. Everyone was crying except Miette.

"Let's get little Miette back into her bed." Ann hesitantly handed Miette back to the nurse and watched her daughter drift off to sleep. The nurse pulled out a hanky and walked away, blowing her nose loudly. Ann turned back toward the window, but it was empty. Paul was gone.

Ann walked back to her room slowly, with her nurse's help. She couldn't have run any marathons but she felt much better. As soon as she got comfortable in bed, a shadow appeared in her doorway. Liz's patent leather skirt picked up a reflection from the window as she entered the room. "Liz!" Ann beamed.

Liz put her hands on her patent leather hips, "I met that gorgeous creature Paul." a lustfully mischievous smile on her face. "What a handsome hunk of man! Where have you been hiding *him*?."

"Oh, its a long story Liz."

"Oh, like part of that same long story about why you came here in the first place?"

Ann nodded guiltily.

"Well?" Liz waited for elaboration, "Did you talk to him?"

"Not really. He showed up in the nursery, then disappeared just as fast. He hasn't changed. He still can't handle responsibility."

"You're wrong Ann," Paul's voice announced from the doorway. He walked in. "And I've come two thousand miles to prove it to you, to be the best father our daughter could have, and to ask you to be my wife. Paul kneeled down next to Ann's bed and looked straight into her pale-brown eyes. Ann stared back and tried like hell to fight the thoughts that were going through her head. The time they used to spend together, laughing, talking, playing. The intense love they used to make, carnal, sensual, like no other. The things he used to do. The way he smelled. His touch on her body. The way she used to run her thin fingers through his dark curls. She remembered every inch of his body, every strong, muscular curve. Then, Ann pictured the tear that trailed down his cheek outside the nursery when he saw Miette for the first time.

"If you need to think about it Ann, I understand. You can reach me at this number." Paul placed a phone number on Ann's nightstand as Liz looked on from a corner of the room. "I love you Ann," Paul said from the doorway, and left.

Ann sat up in bed, placed her head in her hands and bent her knees up under the blanket. Liz stood still in the corner for a minute waiting for Ann to react. Ann finally looked up and the two women stared at each other until Liz finally spoke. "He loves you Ann. Can't you see that?" Liz walked over and grabbed Ann by her skinny shoulders and smiled a huge lipsticked smile. "Are you insane girl? Marry the man!"

They both laughed and hugged each other, Liz smothering Ann in her bosomy chest.

"There's only one thing, Liz," Ann said pulling her way to the surface. "I'm already married."

Liz released her bear hug on Ann and paused for a moment to think of a solution. "Well that's easy. Tell him you want a divorce."

Ann thought about facing Edward after what she had done to him. What must he think of her, running out like that. She could have at least talked to him, not left him something as impersonal as a note on their kitchen counter as if she had gone to the supermarket. And now after all this time, he'd finally hear her voice, asking him for a divorce. It would probably kill him. She wondered what Edward had done when he got her letter. Maybe packed up and moved back to Basile. She wondered what he was doing right now.

Loud fists banged at Edward's motel room door. He could hear them, but he couldn't respond.

"Yea?" Edward said, faintly. The banging continued. "Yea?" he said a little louder.

"Open up Broussard. You're rent's overdue buddy," the motel manager's voice barreled inside Edward's head. "I want you outta here by noon, Broussard!" Edward's pounding head turned toward the alarm clock which read eleven fifteen. His body felt like an elephant had stepped on it and his head like the elephant was still standing on it. His bulging stomach ached terribly. Edward had spent his last few dollars on the bottle of whiskey that lay next to him, now empty. Ann's face flashed through his mind for a split second. He smelled the scent from her hair for that second, then it disappeared. He thought about taking a shower. It had been several days. He buried his face in the bed for what seemed like a minute. Again, banging at his door awoke him. "Broussard?" Edward turned toward the clock again. Twelve thirty? He must've dozed off again. "I'll use my key if you're not outta there in ten minutes." Edward heard him walk away.

Edward sat up in bed and took a deep breath, trying to

muster up enough energy to stand. He rubbed his hand over his forehead and down over his face. After several minutes he lifted himself from the mattress laboriously. He grabbed his suitcase by the handle, strapped his accordion over one shoulder and stepped out the front door.

The sun was bright and blinding as Edward drug his drained body down the street. His insides felt as dry as tumbleweed and his brain pounded through his eye sockets with each step he took. Edward stumbled down the city streets for hours before even stopping to think where he was going. Edward looked around and discovered he had traveled into another neighborhood. The streets were littered and gray. A man stopped and asked him if he wanted to buy drugs. A hooker winked her false eyelash at him. Edward turned into a dark, narrow alley, trying to escape the pedestrians he had just encountered. His round belly throbbed from the inside. Despite the pain he wanted a drink. He couldn't even remember the last time he had eaten, but it didn't matter. What he wanted was a drink. He wanted a drink terribly.

Edward stopped in the alley, placed his suitcase and accordion down and sat on the ground next to them. He opened his suitcase and paddled through it, looking for some money he may have missed. None there. He closed it and scraped the bottom of each of his pockets. First, the front pockets of his trousers, then the back pockets. Then the side pockets on his jacket, then the breast pockets. All he recovered was a hardened Kleenex, and the softened, blurred remains of Ann's letter. He held it in his hand tightly, laid his head down on the suitcase and drifted off into a weary sleep.

CHAPTER SIXTEEN

Liz sat with Miette the nights Ann worked. She had just looked in on the baby before Ann came home from work one morning. Miette was sleeping soundly. Liz met Ann at the front door as she came in.

"Ann I have some news."

"What? Where's Miette?" Ann looked around for her baby daughter.

"She's asleep. Ann. . .," Liz hesitated for a moment, "I'm moving back in with Sam."

"What?!"

"Yea. He called me. We talked for a long time. He. . .he's gotten himself together, Ann. He wants me back. He still loves me. He wants to try to start all over."

"Liz . . . he abused you. What makes you think he's changed?" Ann was worried.

"He got help. He stopped drinking. He's dry. He says he didn't want to call me until he knew he was better. He hasn't had a drink in over a year."

"Well that's great . . . if it's really true. How do you know he's changed?"

"I can hear it in his voice. We talked for a long time. He's changed, I can tell Ann." Liz smiled. She wanted so much for Ann to support her decision to return. "Wish me luck Ann. I really want this to work. I want to have a real family like you and Paul."

Ann knew that was at the root of all this. She even thought that perhaps Liz called Sam herself. But she could hardly blame her. She and Paul and Miette had been so happy. Paul was crazy about Miette and he wanted Ann to be his wife. He had traveled two thousand miles to find her. A fairy tale reunion. Paul coming to the hospital like that. Ann still could hardly believe it. But she still hadn't answered Paul's proposal. She still loved him, that much she knew for sure, but she was afraid. Afraid she'd begin to trust him, believe what he said, and that she'd get hurt like she did before. Ann sure hated to see Liz go.

She had the same fears for Liz as she had for herself. But if Liz could make herself trust someone who had betrayed her, give them a second chance, who was Ann to say that was wrong? Ann wished Liz all the best, kept her fingers crossed, and told her to keep in touch.

Miette slept soundly in her crib one Saturday evening as Paul and Ann got comfortable on the couch to watch an old Sidney Poitier movie on television. The two cuddled together in front of the screen.

"You know Ann, I've been on pins and needles waiting for your answer." He looked at her profile. "You know I love you and Miette. You two mean everything to me now. You're my family."

A family. Something Ann wasn't sure she'd ever have again. Paul had never spoke these words to her before. She never dreamed she'd hear them come from his lips. He loved Miette, that was for sure. Miette had become such a beautiful baby. Ann would watch her daughter sleeping in her crib every night before she left. She was very sharp for an infant and she looked as much like Paul as she did like Ann with her pitch black eyes and tawny complexion.

Paul couldn't really blame Ann for being hesitant. She sometimes looked at him as if wondering why he *really* wanted to marry her. She was so suspicious. Why couldn't she just believe him when he said he wanted to be with her and Miette. Paul had enrolled at the University in San Francisco and cared for Miette at night while Ann was at work. The evenings he spent with Miette had been the happiest time in his life. She usually slept right through the night. But if she didn't, Paul would play with her for awhile, then rock her in his arms until she fell asleep. Then he would slowly carry her to her bed and cover her up with her baby blanket. He always stood at her crib and stared at her while she slept. He could never have imagined how much a baby of his own would mean to him. She was the most important thing on earth to him now. She was his own flesh and blood. She meant everything to him. He couldn't wait until she started talking, and when she started school. He would teach her so many things, and watch her grow up into a beautiful young woman. His little girl. Paul knew Ann's answer was only a matter of time. She just had to learn to become more confident with their relationship. He could see it in the very near future.

Ann had no response for Paul. She still didn't fully trust Paul. She also avoided his proposal because she was afraid to

Leaving Basile

call Edward. She dreaded the confrontation. She still couldn't face him, even over the phone. She took a deep breath and lay her head on his shoulder. He knew she was in deep thought because she no longer paid attention to the screen. Paul slid his hand onto the back of Ann's neck and separated his fingers through her wavy hair. He rubbed the back of her scalp with his fingers as she closed her eyes in thought. Ann let her body relax into his hand. Paul draped Ann's hair over her other shoulder and softly kissed the side of her neck. He smelled her feminine fragrance and took small nibbles around her hairline down to her shoulder, sucking up small areas of skin along the way. Ann groaned softly and let her head fall to one side. He pushed a wavy lock from her face with his other hand and noticed a quiet, easy look on her face. Paul swept Ann up in his arms and carried her into the bedroom like a knight in shining armor would have, and gently placed her on the mattress like a sleeping beauty. She opened her eyes as if she had already been given the magic kiss.

  Paul disappeared into the bathroom and emerged with some of Miette's baby oil. He slowly turned Ann over and began to rub her narrow back under her blouse with the oil. The soft baby scent permeated her nostrils, and Paul's hands played a sweet song over her body. Ann closed her eyes and breathed heavily with each stroke. Paul removed her clothes and his hands glided around her shoulder blades and down her slender arms. His firm, tactile pressure moved along Ann's smooth body like skis on a snow bank, sliding over each even slope with ease. He straddled her prone body, spilling more oil into the arch of her back, kneading it into the pores of her skin. Ann kept her eyes closed to the red shadows of the dark and totally surrendered herself to his touch. He spread the oil from her long neck down to her hands, and milked each finger down to it's tip. He smoothed the oil around her small bottom, over her hamstrings and down to the balls of each toe as Ann lay still, hypnotized by his dextrous trance. Paul stroked Ann's thighs rhythmically, then tunneled his oiled hands between them as Ann tingled with pleasure. He rested his bare chest on her calves as she surrendered to his digital manipulation until she nearly ripped the wooden headboard off the bed in pleasure. But at that point, Paul flipped her over on her back like a rag doll and begin to make love to her, as in all of their attempts, he never had. It was only a matter of seconds before both of them were surged into spasms of satisfaction, instantly rushing the blood through their bodies. Their intermingled sweat beaded up on the oily surface of their bodies. They lay there, in the wet comfort of each others arms, their systems slowly returning to normal. There was no energy for spoken words for several minutes, so they lay in the dark, hot silence as their hearts slowed to their average rates, their temperatures lowered to normal and their breathing was finally quiet again.

"Ann," Paul slid Ann up to his eye level while they lay on their sides. "Be my wife... please" He said it as if it were his last plea.

Ann stared into his eyes and wipe some sweat from his browbone. "Paul . . . I'd be delighted."

Edward walked slowly up Market Street, dragging his feet behind him. He was awaken by the crisp San Francisco wind that swept through the alley and underneath his corduroy jacket. He had found a half eaten corned beef sandwich in a white plastic garbage bag in that same alley. But his luck really began when he found a bottle of bourbon with at least two swallows still inside its pint sized bottle. He felt better immediately but the alley was still a frigid wind tunnel, so he hiked throughout the city searching for an alley that blocked the Pacific Ocean winds sweeping over his body like an icy hand.

During his quest for shelter, Edward had found a much warmer and more comfortable park to sleep in, and had been there for the past week. City Center Park had a gazebo that almost made it feel like he was indoors. Other people slept in the park too, and they hadn't been shooed away by the police yet as Edward had been several times in the alley. But each day Edward gathered up his suitcase and accordion and probed the alleys in search of any spirited beverage or delectable goody he could find if he was lucky.

In spite of Edward's good luck, his stomach had continued to ache more each day. He *had* focused more on collecting the bottles of minute amounts of alcohol then he had on collecting food. Edward hadn't had as much luck in the past two days though, with food *or* drink. His lassitude was at its greatest as he tried to make it back to the park. He had gotten a bit confused in his directions and stepped onto a rocky path that seemed to lead out onto another street. One rock gave way and he went plummeting down the side of a hill, his suitcase and accordion tumbling every which way behind him. When he reached the

Leaving Basile

bottom he lay there for a minute, leaves and dried branches tangled in his hair and clothing. As Edward pulled himself upright, he felt a wave of nausea and vomited on the ground. Before he had a chance to open his eyes to see the bright, red blood that ejected from his throat, he passed out.

"He what?!" Ann almost dropped the telephone when Mrs. Thibideaux told her Edward had been in San Francisco for the past year. After Ann found their number in Port Allen disconnected, she had phoned Mrs. Thibideaux in Basile. If Edward had phoned anyone, it would be Mrs. Thibideaux. All the times Ann had asked him when they could move, all the stalling he did, and it took something like this to make him pack up and leave Port Allen. Ann held the piece of paper with the phone number to the motel Mrs. Thibideaux had given her. Edward, in San Francisco? Ann pictured him in his overalls, with his accordion strapped across his shoulder walking through the congested streets downtown, looking up at the skyscrapers as he bumped into people. Poor Edward. Ann felt sorry for him for a moment, but it was difficult because she was so happy herself. She and Paul were in heaven together. It seemed too good to be true. She could hardly wait to be Mrs. Paul Fontenot, and she, Paul and Miette would be as happy as any family could be. She picked up the telephone and dialed the motel number.

"I'd like to speak to a tenant there. A Mr. Edward Broussard?" Ann asked the voice that answered the phone.

"Broussard?" The voice yelled back at Ann. "Yea he was here. But he ain't now. . .and he skipped out on his rent! You know where he is?"

"Well as a matter-of-fact, I was looking for him."

"Oh, owes you money too, huh? Well if you see that drunken so-and-so, tell him I want my money!" The phone slammed down in Ann's face. Drunken? Edward? He used to have a drink now and then. Of course he always smelled like liquor when he came home from band practice. But drunk and not paying his motel bill? What kind of trouble was Edward in? Ann got nervous. She didn't know what to do now. Call Mrs. Thibideaux back? There was no need in worrying her too. Mrs. Thibideaux obviously thought Edward was still at the same motel. Well, Ann had given Mrs. Thibideaux her phone number at home. Hopefully, if anything came up, Edward would contact Mrs. Thibideaux and she'd let Ann know.

Paul was not happy with this news at all. So *no one* knew how to contact Edward? Not that he thought Ann was lying, but how convenient that after all the time he waited for Ann's answer, she finally said yes, then she couldn't find her husband to file for divorce. Well, Paul didn't have any suggestions for finding him either, so all he Ann, and Miette could do was wait.

Leaving Basile

CHAPTER SEVENTEEN
Los Angeles, California

Dorisse couldn't believe her eyes when she saw the words LOS ANGELES written in big white letters on the green freeway sign over her head. The city ahead, was lit up like the Land of Oz. Long, endless beams of white light moved back and forth across the night sky. The tops of the buildings disappeared into thick clouds and colorful, flashing lights spelled out the names of restaurants and nightclubs. And the motor cars! Not pickup trucks. Shiny, long, automobiles with chrome bumpers you could see your reflection in clearer than any mirror Dorisse had ever looked into. She pressed her nose against the bus window, steaming it up with her gasps. Hundreds of people walked up and down the street. Thousands, it seemed to her.

Dorisse stepped off of the bus and stretched her stiff muscles out before she walked into the station and looked around. She walked over to the man at the window inside.

"Where can I catch a bus to Hollywood?" she asked him

"Outside the door, walk up one block and cross the street. You'll see the bus stop sign."

It was dark out, but the colorful city lights lit up the street like a circus. Dorisse crossed the street and saw a bus coming. The word HOLLYWOOD was printed on the front of it in bold letters.

Dorisse climbed on the bus and gazed out the window at the people and streets of L.A. She sat right up front by the driver so she had a clear view of the sites. She thought she was dreaming when she saw the giant, white Hollywood letters on the side of the hill. She was really in Hollywood, California! They traveled up Sunset until they got to Hollywood Blvd. and Dorisse got off.

She walked up the street, her mouth open in amazement, looking all around as she walked. Everything there was a sight to her. She stopped and looked up. Wow! She was standing in front of the Bank of Hollywood where all the stars kept their money! And the Hollywood bookstore and . . . Oh my God . . . the Brown Derby! Dorisse walked with her mouth open the whole time, passing by dozens of other people. None of them payed any attention to Dorisse. She was glad. That meant she blended in, just like a real Californian! A tall cylindrical building stood out in the distant with the name Capital Records around its top. She turned the corner and headed straight for it. Dorisse stopped in front of its glassed in lobby, looked down on the ground in front of the building, and saw a star plastered directly into the sidewalk with someone's name on it . . . and there was another one, and another one. Dorisse followed the marble-like stars along the street, reading each one carefully, gasping with excitement when she read a name she recognized. She stopped in front of a huge lilac building and stared into the display windows at the manikins in amazement. They all had on little, teeny, tiny underwear so small Dorisse had to squint to see them. Fredrick's of Hollywood, Dorisse read to herself. Dorisse continued her sightseeing and saw two lovely women on the street dressed in brilliant gold outfits, with boots past their knees and coats made of fur and brightly made-up faces. They stood chatting with each other, laughing and swinging their arms about as they talked. Dorisse walked over to them.

"Hi!" She smiled at them. "Are you all show girls?"

They looked at each other then back at Dorisse. One of them responded, "Yea. I guess you could say that. We certainly show something alright." The two broke out into hysterical laughter, slapping their fishnetted thighs. Dorisse smiled, disappointed that she had missed the joke, but continued .

"Do you know where *I* can get a job as a showgirl?" She stood up straight.

"Oh, you want a job, huh?" They looked Dorisse up and down with their lips turned up. "Not bad for a white girl, huh?" one said. "Daddy'd like her wouldn't he?" Dorisse thought their father must be the man in charge. She hoped he liked her.

A young man with neatly cut short hair, a white shirt, blue jeans and a brown tweed jacket approached them from behind. "Excuse me Miss," He addressed Dorisse, "May I speak with you please?" He pulled Dorisse away from the two girls and lightly held her elbow as he spoke. "I'm sorry for intruding Miss, but these two aren't . . . showgirls." Dorisse looked at him in puzzlement. "You aren't from around here, are you?" He asked Dorisse. She shook her head.

She hadn't said anything stupid, had she? How did he know already that she wasn't from California?

"I didn't think so."

"Hey, mind your own fuckin business," one of the girls said to him loudly.

"What's your name Miss?" Dorisse liked the way he kept calling her Miss.

"Dorisse."

"They're hookers, Dorisse." She looked at him blankly. "Hookers, you know. Prostitutes. Whores." Dorisse got a shocked expression on her face and felt as stupid as she must've sounded asking them for a job.

"You can take that old country bitch outta here if you want to. She's probably too stupid to turn a trick anyway." They both laughed hysterically again.

"My name is Mike. Mike Branigan." He held out his hand to Dorisse and she shook it. She had never felt a hand that soft on a man before. He obviously had never picked cotton. He touched her elbow again and they began to walk away from the hookers.

"I . . . I feel so stupid." She looked at the ground. "Here I was thinking I'd blend in with everyone else and I must've stood out like a two headed calf." Mike laughed.

"Are you laughing at me?" Dorisse got defensive.

Mike's laugh trailed off but left a smile on his face, "No, no." He lifted his eyebrows over his pale blue eyes. "I've just never heard that expression before.

"Well . . .," Dorisse liked this Mike. She had already forgiven him for making fun of her, "I guess you did get me out of a whole lotta trouble I could've gotten myself into." Dorisse tried to imitate Ann's English to disguise her southern accent.

"It was an honest mistake, Dorisse. Actually I thought they were showgirls too at first."

"So how'd you know they were . . . hookers?"

"Well, I knew there was no way in the world anyone could dance in those thigh-high boots. They'd kill themselves." They both laughed. Dorisse liked his laugh. It was an honest laugh. Not the cackling the two hookers did. The two walked slowly up Hollywood Blvd. together.

"So what're you doing in Hollywood, Dorisse?"

Mr. Gifford's howling face flashed through her mind for a moment. "I just moved here. I want to be an actress."

"Is that right?"

"That's right."

Mechelle Randall

"Well, I suppose you're pretty ambitious, Dorisse. It's a tough business, I understand."

"Yea," she stared at the ground. "But you know, Mike," she looked over at his profile as they walked, "you have to do what you really want to do with your life. Not what other people want you to do, or don't want you to do. Otherwise, you may never be happy."

"That's a very wise philosophy, Dorisse." He smiled at her simple wisdom. "Have you had dinner yet?" Mike asked.

"Dinner? Yea, I ate that at noon. You mean supper?"

"Uh . . . yea. Supper, that's what I meant." She really wasn't from around here, he thought.

"Nope." Dorisse looked into his pale eyes and smiled.

"Like steak?"

Dorisse nodded. Mike looked both ways, took Dorisse by the hand, and the two ran across the street. She couldn't wait. She was starved.

Leaving Basile

CHAPTER EIGHTEEN

The sunlight illuminated the red inside Edward's eyelids as he lay on the ground at the bottom of the hill. He tried to move but his joints felt painful and arthritic. He had been lying on his right arm and as he pried it from underneath his body, it flopped forward limp and paralyzed from the pressure. He lay still on the gravel and tried to pull himself to his feet. The sun beamed painfully through his closed eyes as he made a forward movement to hoist himself to a sitting position. He sat with his head in his hands, trying to conjure up energy from somewhere to get him to his feet. What would he do now? He had no place to live. He had no more money, no job. Maybe he could play his accordion on the street for money. Where was his accordion? He tried hard to remember what had happened. He had fallen, he remembered. His accordion must be somewhere around him. He cracked open his eyes and stared at the hillside. The bright sunlight blinded him as he tried to focus through its rays. His accordion and suitcase lay below. His suitcase was sprawled open with his belongings scattered down the slope of the hill. He looked beside him where a puddle of old blood had browned in the sun. Had he cut himself? He didn't remember. He couldn't remember anything. Things popped in and out of his mind. The man at the motel banging on the door, him staggering up the gray streets. He even thought he saw Paul go by in a car once. He had to get help. He was going crazy, he thought. He crawled to his feet and stumbled out onto the street. Two cars barely missed him as he crossed to the other side. He walked into a corner liquor store and leaned toward the man behind the counter, blood encrusted on the side of his face.

"Scuse me, sir," Edward said, then collapsed on the floor.

"Yea," the liquor store man said into the telephone receiver, "There's some bum here who needs an ambulance. And could you hurry, he's blocking my doorway."

Dorisse had never been in a restaurant so fancy in her life. Mauve, linen tablecloths flowed over the edges of the small round table and soft classical music played in the background.

Dim red lights warmed the atmosphere. The waiters wore little black jackets and spoke like they were addressing royalty. And Mike, he was just like the men in the movies. He was wonderful.

"So, exactly where are you from?" He had asked her over dinner.

"Bas . . . Baton Rouge. Baton Rouge, Louisiana." she answered, trying to sound convincing.

"Ah, Baton Rouge. I've been there once. It's a beautiful city."

Dorisse looked up at his face. "Yes, it is," she changed the subject quickly, "and where are you from?"

"I'm from San Francisco. As a matter of fact, I'm just here in L.A on business."

"Oh," she shoveled a forkful of rice into her mouth. "I have a friend in San Francisco," she said after swallowing half of it.

"Do you?"

"Yea," Dorisse smiled as she thought about her friend Ann. "We grew up together in Bas . . . in Baton Rouge."

Mike nodded with a mouth full of food.

"How far is San Francisco from here?" Dorisse asked him.

Mike finished swallowing and wiped his mouth with the cloth napkin. "A little over four hundred miles. About a six hour drive."

Dorisse nodded. "When are you going back?"

"In a few weeks. As soon as I've finished the project I'm working on."

"Oh," Dorisse said softly and looked back into her plate Mike looked at her at an angle as she pushed her broccoli back and forth. She was very beautiful, he thought. She had a lovely, exotic look about her. She looked like a cross between Sophia Loren and Elizabeth Taylor. A face like he'd never seen before. She was dressed very plainly, but he couldn't have imagined her more beautiful if she had on a million dollar ball gown.

"Well, what would you like to do now?" He tilted his head a little, peeking underneath her bowed head.

She looked up blankly. "Like what?"

"A movie maybe?"

Dorisse thought for a minute. "You know what I really want to do?" Mike smiled at her innocence. "I want to see the movie stars. Yes, I want to see all the movie stars."

"Well then, Miss, that is exactly what we will do!"

Mike and Dorisse spent the whole evening at the

Hollywood wax museum. Dorisse couldn't believe the figures weren't real! It was incredible. She and Mike laughed and pointed all night until Dorisse opened her mouth into a huge yawn.

"You tired?" Mike asked.

"Yea. I was having so much fun, I forgot." She laughed through another yawn.

"Have you found a place to stay yet?"

"Well, I haven't made any arrangements."

"I have plenty of room in my suite. I'm staying at the Hilton Hotel in Beverly Hills" She looked at him with uncertainty. "There's an extra room in my suite."

"You don't have to worry. I'll be a complete gentleman." He smiled slightly, and very gentlemanly.

"You already have been."

"And I promise I will be for the rest of the night." Dorisse smiled at him. She wouldn't really mind at all if he wasn't.

Mike's suite was like a palace to Dorisse. She had to keep herself from gawking, but she was amazed. It was on the twenty-second floor and overlooked the city. The two sat in the living room, gazing out the window, and talked half the night. He told Dorisse about his parents and brothers and sisters and what it was like growing up in San Francisco. And Dorisse talked about her dreams of becoming an actress. They talked until Dorisse nodded off on the sofa. Mike placed a blanket over her curled up body and kissed her on the cheek. Before he turned the light off and went to the bedroom, he turned to look at her pretty face once more and saw a smile on her sleeping lips.

The next morning the two had breakfast in the hotel coffee shop.

"I have some business to take care of for the next few evenings, but Saturday night I'm free, if you'd like to go out?"

Dorisse nodded.

"So what'll it be? Magic Mountain, Disneyland, a tour of the movie stars' homes?" Dorisse smiled at Mike. She was so happy he wanted to spend Saturday evening with her. She really wanted to see him again. She trusted him, felt safe around him. Even before last night. She knew it would be all right to stay at his suite with him. He looked like he couldn't tell a lie if he wanted to, like he had been unaffected by life in the big city.

"I need to find a place to stay first of all," she answered

"Listen Dorisse," Mike said to her as he finished his coffee. "I'll have lots of work to do while I'm here but you're welcome to stay at the suite while I'm in town. I have plenty of room."

"No. I couldn't. I need to find a place of my own." She shook her head at his hospitality. She was eventually going to need an apartment of her own and didn't want to be homeless when Mike left.

"If you really want to, but I have it for the entire time I'm here and the job is paying for it." He looked at Dorisse trying to convince her to stay. "*And* I'd love to have you as my guest." That was the best reason he could have given her and she agreed to stay.

Dorisse lounged around the suite all day Saturday and rested up for their evening out. She picked out one of the fancier dresses she had bought in the department store in Port Allen and applied her make-up meticulously.

Mike picked Dorisse up at the hotel in his red sports car and took her to a Chinese restaurant, a first for Dorisse. There weren't any Chinese restaurants in Port Allen. Then they went to see a musical full of lively dance numbers and brilliant, extravagant costumes. After that they went out to a small club and danced the rest of the night away in each others arms. She felt so content as they swayed on the dance floor to the soft ballads the band performed. They moved so well together. It seemed she had known Mike for years. Like he had been there waiting for her all the time. It had to be fate for Mike to be in L.A. on business the very same time Dorisse decided to leave Louisiana and move to California, which was the biggest step she had ever made; even bigger than leaving Basile. Someone, somewhere had brought the two together. For Mike to be there, on Hollywood Boulevard, the same time she was, and for him to overhear her conversation with the hookers and walk over and rescue her. It must have been fate. That night, the two danced together slowly, embracing under the California sky until the band ran out of songs.

They finally stepped back into the hotel at about three a.m., hand in hand. The two collapsed onto the sofa and Dorisse kicked off her shoes and began massaging her stocking feet.

"I haven't danced like that since . . . I don't think I've ever danced like that!"

"No?" Mike slouched on the couch and folded his arms

Leaving Basile

"No. There weren't any places like that in Port Allen." Dorisse said before remembering to incorporate her lie.

"Where's Port Allen?" Mike asked casually. Then Dorisse realized what she had said.

"Mike?" She stopped rubbing her feet and looked straight in front of her. "I'm not from Baton Rouge." She looked over at his relaxed posture and he looked back, expression unchanged. She continued. "I'm from a town in Louisiana so small it would disappear inside of Los Angeles. It's called Basile. Basile, Louisiana."

"So, where's Port Allen?" he asked her.

"Not too far from Baton Rouge. I moved there when I left Basile," she looked at his still slouched body. "I've never even *been* to Baton Rouge." Embarrassed, Dorisse looked down at her lap.

Mike looked at her frowning profile and smiled very slightly at her scheme to try to impress him. "So, why'd you leave Basile?"

"Well, its sort of a long story."

"I have time."

Dorisse continued to stare at her lap and then spoke. "Living in Basile was like living hundreds of years ago. There were so many things going on outside of Basile that we weren't even aware of. There were things that weren't that far away but weren't available to us. There were certain things that we just didn't talk about or do. Tradition, Mike. That's what Basile was all about — tradition."

"But tradition can be good, Dorisse. It keeps parts of our past alive."

"Yea, but there are some things that may have made sense a hundred years ago, but don't today. Things change, Mike. You know, my parents were very strict. Certain things were very important to them. Things that shouldn't have been anymore. Things that were difficult for me to understand and just made life more difficult for me. I couldn't see anything good coming from it."

"Well, you're young Dorisse. It's hard sometime for us to understand things that people thought before we were around."

Dorisse shook her head and played with a button on her sleeve. "And some people *still* think," she said. She looked like she was near tears.

Mike sat up straight from his slouch, slid over next to

Dorisse and placed his arm around her shoulder. He faced her and lifted her chin to tell her not to worry about the past, but instead, when he looked into her sad eyes, he instinctively kissed her soft, rosy lips gently, and she kissed him back. He tilted her head slightly and pulled her torso toward his and the two kissed each other. Mike felt her supple breasts pressed against his chest through their clothing and stroked the velvety skin on her arm as they explored each other's mouths. Dorisse grasped Mike's sturdy shoulders and tasted his sweet breath mixed with hers. She sighed into the lengthy kiss and reveled in the pleasure it gave her. Dorisse didn't remember Ann describing it to her like this. Her entire body tingled with excitement as his soft hands fondled her skin. As their lips parted, Dorisse looked back and forth between Mike's sky blue eyes and began to unbutton his cotton shirt from the top. She slipped her hands underneath it and slid it off, over his broad shoulders, then easily pulled her own dress over her head and dropped it to the floor next to the couch revealing her white, lace slip underneath. She pulled his body back toward hers and they kissed again, caressing each other's bare upper bodies as their lips remained pressed together. Mike lifted Dorisse's head back gently and kissed the front of her smooth neck. She smelled the soft scent of his shampoo as his lips traveled onto her chest, where he peeled her dainty slip off of her body and exposed her young, naked form to his delighted eyes. He rubbed his face against her milky skin as she played lightly with his baby fine hair. He looked up into her lovely face, gently laid her back onto the couch, slid up her body and lay on top of her, face to face.

"I think you are the most gorgeous, fascinating woman I've ever met." They gazed at each other.

"No one's ever told me that before, Mike."

"I find that very hard to believe."

She blushed and smiled softly. Mike ran his fingers over Dorisse's smooth face and she closed her eyes to his tender palpation. He brushed back her dark eyebrows with his thumb. He smoothed her hair back around the edge of her face and continued around the back of her ear. He traced Dorisse's lips with his fingertip and she let her lips fall open, sensuously circling his finger with her tongue. Dorisse slipped her arms underneath his and locked her arms around his waist. "I'm crazy about you, too." she said. "But there are a lot of things you don't know about me, Mike."

Leaving Basile

"And I'm sure there are lots of things you don't know about me."

"Yea, but I . . ." Mike placed a silencing finger over her pink lips.

"So, are you gonna sleep on the couch tonight?" he asked her, smiling devilishly.

"Do you want me to?"

"I can think of a much better place."

"Well, only if you promise *not* to be a perfect gentleman."

Mike held up a swearing hand. "I promise." He stood up and lead Dorisse into his bedroom suite and closed the double doors behind them.

Ann stared closely into the bathroom mirror at her reflection as Miette toddled at her feet. Ann's once bright eyes were red and drooped down at the corners with heavy shadows hanging beneath them. She looked tired and worn out. Both working and caring for Miette were taking their toll on her. Paul had moved in with Ann after Liz moved out. The two decided that since Paul was closer to getting his degree, he would go to back to school full time during the day and care for Miette at night while Ann continued to work the night shift at the coffee shop. Then, when he finished, Ann could go back and finish her degree. Well, the plan wasn't working out quite like Ann had expected. When Ann got home in the morning after working all night, Miette was wide awake, full of energy and ready to play, and Paul was on his way out the front door, and by nightfall when Paul came home, the baby was worn out from the day and slept soundly while he studied or slept himself. It didn't seem fair that Paul was able to pursue his education while Ann waited tables in some coffee shop in the middle of the night then sat with the baby all day long. It was getting to be too much for her, and Paul couldn't seem to understand why she was upset. He got *his* eight hours of sleep every night, and during the day he was doing what he wanted to do while Ann waited on strangers hand and foot. She walked away from the mirror dragging her right leg behind her as Miette hung on to it. Her feet were still sore from the night's work. She'd love nothing better than to sit and soak them in warm water for awhile, but she couldn't do anything while Miette was awake. She'd have to wait until she settled down for her nap. She detached the child from her leg and swung her up into her arms. Miette had become the most beautiful little girl Ann could ever have imagined. Her baby soft skin was a shade or two lighter than Ann's, somewhere in between her and Paul's. The color of a cupcake lightly browned in the oven. Ann brushed back her silky black hair with one hand and placed the active child in her high chair for breakfast. The money Ann made was hardly enough to support three people. She had to learn to stretch her money as far as it would go. Prepared baby food was far too expensive so Ann mashed up rice and milk in a bowl with a little sugar for Miette's breakfast. She spooned the mixture into her daughter's eager mouth as the baby bounced around in her high chair, already anxious to get out and play. Ann hummed to settle the child and switched to the lyrics when Miette stopped and looked at her mother in silence.

"*Gardez donc, ch`ere be´be´ quoi c'est y a eu. Par rapport `a tout ca que mon je t'ai fait. Je connais je va's jamais, jamais te revoir. Je va's mourir avec toi dedans mon coeur.*" The sad words to Ann's song captured Miette's attention and Ann repeated some of them aloud in English.

"Look, dear baby, what's happened. All because of what I did." Ann sat with her slim face in her hands and watched as her daughter turned back toward her bowl, grabbed a handful of the mixture with her round hand, and squished it until it oozed out between her dimpled fingers. This isn't going to work, Ann thought. She knew she couldn't last much longer.

When Dorisse awoke in the large hotel bed, Mike was in his bathrobe wheeling in a cart with fancy, silver hoods on it and delicious smells coming from underneath them.

"What time is it?" She moaned and stretched as she sat up in bed.

"Almost one." Mike began to pour her a cup of coffee. "Sugar and cream?"

"One?!"

"One sugar?"

"No! One o'clock! It's one o'clock!?"

"Well, we were up past five a.m."

"Oh." Dorisse smiled remembering the night before. "We were, weren't we?" Mike poured himself a cup and relaxed in the bed next to her. He handed Dorisse a plate with a warm cinnamon roll and fresh fruit on it.

"I really had a good time last night, Dorisse," Mike said sweetly. He munched on a roll.

"Me too." Dorisse took a sip from her hot coffee and placed it on the nightstand. "But there really are some things you don't know about me."

"What? Do you have a husband and ten kids back in Basile?" Dorisse laughed and shook her head. "Ten husbands and one kid?" She smiled at his good humor, then looked away and took a heavy breath.

"Mike . . . I'm not white, you know." He turned his head toward her and she looked at him as she talked.

"I'm a Negro." She paused for his reaction. "My parents are Creole." He looked at her. His expression was the same and he remained quiet for a moment.

"Is that your deep, dark secret?" he said finally.

She still wasn't sure *what* his reaction was and looked at him wide-eyed. "Do you still like me?"

"Dorisse," he shook his head at her ridiculous assumption. Mike sat straight up in bed and faced Dorisse. "If I told you I weren't white, would you still like me?"

"Well of course I would!"

"What if I told you I were. Would you?"

"Yes." She pouted

"It wouldn't matter, would it?"

She shook her head and looked down at her fidgeting hands and began to cry. Heavy tears fell from her eyes as she sniffled and sobbed audibly. She leaned over Mike's shoulder and he patted her on her back, surprised at how emotional she had gotten over the subject. She whimpered and snorted, drenching his shoulder with moisture as he smiled to himself at her childlike way of crying. He had wondered about her unique looks. Creole. From Louisiana. He pulled her off his shoulder and smiled at her juvenile appearance.

"Are you alright?" She wiped one eye with the back of her hand and nodded.

"Well, thank goodness." he said, "I thought I had said something wrong." She shook her head and tried to pull herself together. "Good. Now go wash your face and get dressed. We have more sightseeing to do today." Mike gently pulled Dorisse to her feet and patted her bottom toward the bathroom.

"Go on, now, " he said.

Dorisse went into the bathroom and stepped into the hot shower. Mike was like an angel. She couldn't believe someone like him existed, and here he was, with her. He was like all the movie stars she had ever seen all rolled up into one. Except he wasn't a movie star. He was just a regular guy, and he thought

Dorisse was wonderful. He had told her so, himself. It didn't matter, he had said. He liked her for who she was. She still hadn't told him about Mr. Gifford, though. She'd work up to that story later. She didn't even want to think about it yet, let alone talk about it. Suddenly Dorisse remembered, Mike was leaving. He had to go back to San Francisco. She almost started crying again, but decided she would just enjoy the rest of the time they had together.

The following weeks whizzed by for both Mike and Dorisse and soon they sat having breakfast in the hotel coffee shop the morning he was to begin his drive back to San Francisco.

"So what are you gonna do here, Dorisse?" The two held hands across the table.

"I don't know. I found some reasonable rooms for rent in the paper. I'll probably go take a look at them. Then out to look for jobs, modeling maybe." She had enough money to get settled with and tie her over for a while.

"That's a good start for an actress." Mike looked at Dorisse's hand as he played with it. "You know, I hear there are great modeling jobs in San Francisco."

Dorisse smiled widely. "You know, I think I heard the same thing."

Mike took each of Dorisse's hands in his and squeezed them, "You know, Dorisse I have to say that you have really stolen my heart. And very quickly too. Right from under my nose."

"So it's my property now," Dorisse said, "and I wouldn't let it go for all the gold in California,"

"Well, I couldn't possibly go to San Francisco and leave my heart in L.A. It's supposed to be the other way around." He had thought about this for the last week and a half. "Would you like to come with me?"

"Mike?" Dorisse leaned across the table toward him and smiled. "I thought you'd never ask."

CHAPTER NINETEEN

Mike dialed direct long distance to San Francisco from the hotel as Dorisse packed in the other room. The phone rung several times and a voice answered right before Mike hung up.
"Hello?"
"Louis?" Mike talked into the receiver.
"Yea. Mike? Hey, what's happening buddy!? You back?"
"No. Leaving today."
"Great. So, you should be home later this evening, right?"
"Yea."
"Everything go as planned out there?"
"Sure did. Except one thing I hadn't expected. I met the most wonderful woman in the whole wide world."
"Is that right?" Louis laughed.
"Really, man. Her name is Dorisse and she's a walking angel. I think this is serious, Louis. She's coming back to San Francisco with me."
"Hey, this *is* serious."
"You'll have a chance to meet her later. After this thing blows over."
"Yea. The sooner the better."
"You said a mouth full, man. I'll give you a call tomorrow."
"Alright. Hey. Take care of that little lady, buddy."
"I won't let her out of my sight!"
Dorisse immediately called Ann and told her she was in Los Angeles and was on her way to San Francisco. She was delighted to find out that Ann was the mother of a beautiful baby girl now. She knew Ann had to be a fabulous mother. She was good at whatever she did. Ann told Dorisse on the phone that she had a lot more to tell her but that they would get caught up when she got there. Dorisse couldn't wait to see Ann. She had some things to tell her too. She missed her so much. She also couldn't wait for Ann to meet Mike. She knew she'd love him.
The drive to San Francisco was great, nothing like that horrid ride on the bus from Louisiana. Mike drove the shiny red Mercedes Benz two-seater up highway one, on the coast, with

the top down. Dorisse gazed at the small, chrome emblem that guided the sports car down the highway. The car rode so smooth and fast it was like riding on air to Dorisse. It seemed to glide over the bumps as if it was smoothing them out as it went along. The view sat still like a giant postcard as they drove past it. Dorisse stared at an endless, green ocean and layers of distant mountains that looked a giant oil painting. She rolled her car window down, let her head fall back on the headrest and the crisp ocean scent rushed into her nostrils and blew over her closed eyelids. The air was different in California to her. Everyone talked about the smog, but it seemed light and gentle to her. It seemed to touch her face ever so softly, then make its way through her hair easily like quiet fingertips. She licked her lips and tasted the salt from the ocean and smiled. She glanced over at Mike as he drove to make sure she hadn't drifted off into some fantastic dream, to awaken next to the old lady with the heavy coat that she'd ridden next to all the way from Louisiana. She hadn't. Mike's handsome profile looked straight ahead. He had a certain boyish appearance to Dorisse, especially when he was alone with his thoughts. A youthful handsomeness. It was easy to picture how he must have looked as a child. Probably a delightful, energetic boy who liked to climb trees and collect frogs and play little league baseball. Dorisse smiled at the thought of a darker-haired ten-year-old Mike that jumped and laughed, and wondered what a child of theirs would look like. She grinned at the side of his face as she transformed it to her image of how a son of theirs would look. He must have felt her looking because he glanced over at her.

    Dorisse's chin pointed back toward the sky as she rested her head on the headrest again. She looked at Mike downward, out the corners of her eyes, making her look incredibly sexy to him. If anyone could become a movie star, it was Dorisse, Mike thought as he took small glances at her. She possessed some natural sort of beauty, very untraditional, the kind Hollywood agents looked for. Mike knew pretty faces were a dime a dozen. He had seen plenty of them, out at nightclubs or prancing around the beach, but Dorisse's personality was as fresh as the ocean wind that blew through her hair. What made her even more beautiful then the dark sexiness of her eyes, was the warmth that came from them each time she looked at him. Not only the soft suppleness of her lips, but the simple innocence that came out each time she spoke, the sincerity. She was as genuine as a person could be, and as gorgeous as any woman had ever been made.

Mike thought about how frightened Dorisse had looked when she told him she was black. He wondered what it was like for her living in the south, since she actually looked white. What problems she may have had, what racism she had experienced. Well this was California and she never had to worry about those things again. Good old, California.

Mike tugged at his collar, which suddenly seemed uncomfortable. He knew that good old California had as many bigots as any other place. People just didn't talk about it as openly in California. It wasn't quite as acceptable. Oh, everyone claimed that they felt like Blacks deserved to be treated equally, but behind closed doors it was quite a different story. He had heard people make racist comments many times. Mike thought back to his years in Catholic school. The nuns wouldn't answer questions about sex to save their lives, but they never neglected to mention was that God had created all men in his own image, and that we all belonged to one race, the human race. As corny as it sounded, Mike really did believe it. He never remembered his parents saying it, but to them, people had just always been . . . people. Nothing more, nothing less. It was people's *actions* that made them scum, his dad had said once. He could hardly wait to take Dorisse to meet his parents. They might be a bit surprised to learn that Dorisse is Black, mostly because she simply didn't look it, but Mike knew that if *he* loved her, they would too. His parents, like all parents, Mike supposed, just wanted him to be happy. And Mike was happier than he could ever have imagined.

The hours passed quickly and Dorisse couldn't believe she was in San Francisco as they drove past the city limits sign. The tall skyscrapers fenced in by the golden bridges formed a breathtaking scene to her. Dorisse could never have imagined even visiting a city like this, let alone living in one. San Francisco. The city by the bay. Mike's home town. She could have guessed a person like Mike would be from a place as beautiful as San Francisco.

Mike lived in Marin county, directly across the Golden Gate Bridge from San Francisco. He pulled his car into the garage underneath a tall building. Dorisse couldn't believe her eyes. First, the garage door opened by itself when Mike pulled up to it. Then, they took an elevator from the garage straight up to a long carpeted, mirrored hallway, then entered his apartment through a side door. Mike led her by the hand through the dark apartment and flipped on the living room light. Dorisse and Mike stood in the middle of a room that couldn't compare to any living room Dorisse had ever seen in any magazine, dreamt about, or could even have imagined. One whole entire wall in the living room was covered with windows that framed the Golden Gate Bridge like a giant velvet picture. The midnight water sparkled like liquid sapphire and blended with the bay sky into one brilliant indigo masterpiece. Mike stood behind Dorisse and wrapped his arms around her shoulders. As beautiful as the view was, she closed her eyes and leaned her head back onto his chest. He kissed the side of her face and smelled her black hair. In spite of their long drive, it smelled sweet, like a child's. He turned her body around to face him and held her chin up to meet his.

"Do you mind if I kiss you?" he asked her in a quiet voice.

"Mind?" She answered softly, "I've been waiting for you to kiss me all day." They pressed their lips together, letting some moisture escape into the kiss, then suctioned them apart loudly.

"My little Creole doll," He smiled happily at Dorisse. "Do you speak French?"

"*Oui, monsieur.*" She answered and remembered she and Ann's pact to speak to each other to retain their language.

"Do you think you can teach me some?"

"*Oui, Oui!*" she answered. "Repeat after me . . . *Je'taime.*"

Mike repeated, "*Je'taime.*"

"*Je'taime toup.*" Dorisse said to him. He understood already, very well.

Dorisse felt right at home in the huge apartment and slept like a baby, but the next morning she woke to an empty bed. She almost thought she had been dreaming again but she was still in Mike's luxurious apartment, lost in his king-sized bed. She rolled over on her stomach into a stretch and saw a note on the nightstand with her name written on it.

Dorisse,

I had to leave early, some people have to work you know. I couldn't bear to wake you. You looked like a sleeping angel. I'll be home this afternoon around three. Help yourself to food in the kitchen, and I hope you don't get bored or change your mind and decide you don't like me anymore. Even if you do, at least wait until I get home. See you later. Je'taime.

Leaving Basile

Mike

This all had to be a dream, Dorisse thought. Mike was like Sidney Portier and Rock Hudson and Tony Curtis all rolled up into one. Was it possible to fall in love in so quickly? Dorisse would never have thought so... until now. She was so glad she had come to California. Dorisse turned back over and buried her face into Mike's pillow. She breathed in deeply and smiled at the fragrance Mike's soft, brown hair left on his pillowcase. She hugged the pillow as if it were him and drifted back off into a deep, blissful sleep.

The soft, mechanical ring of Mike's telephone awoke Dorisse. She didn't know if she should answer it or not, but it might be Mike. It rang again and again. Finally she picked it up.

"Hello," she answered hesitantly.

"Hello, sweetheart."

"Mike?"

"Who else phones you at my house and calls you sweetheart?"

"Nobody but you, sweetheart." She was so happy to hear his voice.

"Well that's a relief. I thought you had met someone new already while I was at work."

"No. Not a chance."

"So what do you want to do today? Don't tell me...the wax museum."

"No," she laughed. "Whatever *you* want to do."

"Well, I have some more business to tend to but I think I can pick you up this evening around sixish. We're going out for some *San Francisco* sightseeing this time."

"Sounds good to me," Dorisse said, sleep still in her voice. Mike kissed her over the phone and hung up.

Mike drove up the avenue and eased his foot down on the brake pedal as he approached the red light. He sighed deeply and smiled a bit to himself. He had hated to leave Dorisse this morning. It was so nice and warm lying next to her that he had to pry himself from bed. But he had to take care of this last bit of business and this whole deal would soon be over. Six months, it had been, since he had gone undercover to work on this case. Now, finally the bust was about to take place. Then, he could pick up Dorisse, they could go out on the town to celebrate and he'd tell her the whole story. He knew he couldn't tell her he was a police detective working in Los Angeles undercover. He couldn't talk about the case to anyone while he was working on it. Fortunately, Dorisse, in all her innocence, hadn't asked any questions.

The traffic light changed and Mike turned left onto Ocean Boulevard toward the boardwalk. The warm weather that day had driven crowds of San Franciscans out of their homes and onto the beach. This is good, Mike thought. The more public, the better. A public place was necessary. A neutral atmosphere. He'd make the drop, collect the money, and it would all be over.

The sound of laughter, screams, bells and whistles got louder as Mike drove closer to the boardwalk with the car window rolled down. He could see the giant white scaffolding of the roller coaster from the distance. The train of cars dipped and dove like a giant metal caterpillar over the roller coaster tracks. The huge neon letters PLAYLAND hovered above the amusement park framed in white lights that lit up the entrance way at night. Mike parked and grabbed the small leather suitcase from under the front seat and walked toward the park.

Although running these kinds of busts undercover could be extremely dangerous, Mike wasn't nervous in the least bit. He was happy and relieved. He would no longer have to be Mickey Rollins, drug smuggler. In no more than a few minutes he'd be Sergeant Mike Branigan, again, San Francisco Police Detective, Narcotics Division. Mikey Rollins would be an alias lost in the files of the SFPD.

The sweet smells of cotton candy and pink popcorn pervaded the air and traveled into Mike's nostrils as soon as he crossed the street with dozens of other people. Mike stood in line at the Playland gate.

"One adult," he told the lady at the ticket booth and walked through the turnstile with the handle of the leather bag held tightly in his right hand.

Mike immediately heard the familiar cackling laughter of the gigantic fat lady behind the glass wall. The large, mechanical puppet held her plastic belly and leaned backward and forward in uncontrollable fits of laughter. Mike smiled and remembered being afraid of her as a small boy. She exposed her tonsils and peered at him over her big, red nose as she rocked. He used to think she was laughing at him. But not this time, Mike thought. This time he would have the last laugh.

Mike switched the suitcase to his left hand and lightly

Leaving Basile

brushed his right hand over the forty-five automatic that was strapped against his side in it's holster. The gun was loaded and ready to shoot. Seven rounds in the clip, and one in the chamber. He hoped and prayed he didn't have to use it at a place like this. He always hoped and prayed he didn't have to use, no matter where he was. But he especially hoped he didn't have to use it at Playland. The fat lady wouldn't find that so funny, Mike thought.

Mike walked through the crowd of people. Young couples holding hands. Parents pushing strollers. Mothers leading their toddlers by the hand. Mike wondered for a moment if he looked out of place. How many people were carrying a leather suitcase? He looked around. None.

He forgot about his conspicuousness as he spotted the meeting place. The merry-go-round. Mike watched the painted horses move up and down as the base of the ride, slowly turning counterclockwise. The old-fashioned organ music churned along with the rotating ride as children hung onto the necks of colorful animated horses. Mike stopped in front of the ride's entry gate and held the suitcase in front of him with both hands. The transaction would be smooth and quick.

Mike guessed that the pick up man had seen him already. He was probably watching Mike at that very moment, standing off somewhere, making sure there were no cops around. Mike mentally laughed at the irony and thought about the surprise that was in store for him. While the pick up man was breaking his neck looking for cops, the goods were nestled tightly in Sergeant Branigan's hand. Good ole Mikey Rollins *wasn't* good ole Mikey Rollins after all.

Mike wondered if Jake himself would do the pick up. If this Jake was *really* Mr. Big like Mike had heard, then someone else would be the mule. One of his boys. The quantity of drugs Mike was carrying, six kilos, was too much for the big man not to be in direct charge of the operation. If he wasn't doing the pick up, he would be very near by with the amount of money that was involved. This exchange was on a high level. It was a big job. Well, *Big Jake*, sorry to botch up your plans, Mike thought, but all sick things must come to an end.

Mike waited calmly and patiently. He tried not to glance around too much. They knew who he was. There was no reason for him to try to find them. But something caught Mike's eye. A man reading a newspaper had pulled it down from in front of his face for a second and then lifted it again quickly. Mike peered around at the man, trying to look around the paper at the his face. Shit! Mike *thought* he had recognized the man! He was a cop! Cops were there! God damn cops! Mike looked around quickly and saw a tall suited man lighting a cigarette. Another one! Two . . . no three of them! What the hell were they doing!? They stood around looking even more obvious than uniformed cops! If *Mike* noticed them so easily, crooks could smell cops like these from miles away. There was no way the exchange was going to go through now. No way! Shit! There was no way the pick up guy would approach Mike with these cops hovering around like vultures waiting for the switch to take place. Mike walked away from his post. He couldn't approach the stupid cops and ask them what the hell they were doing. Then *his* cover would be blown. He had to leave. Then he had to find out what the entire goddamn department was doing at the site of an undercover bust.

Mike walked back to his car, threw the suitcase under the seat and drove off.

"Shit!" he said aloud and hit the steering wheel with his palms as he drove. He habitually glanced in his rear view mirror and sped along the boulevard, trying to figure out what the hell had happened. Something had gone very wrong. Did the contact get word that good ole Mikey was a cop and call to check up on him? If that had happened the department would deny any knowledge, then send some backup cops to protect Mike in case Jake's boys had something bad planned for him. That was a possibility. But, no. Their precinct's boys would never have stood out so obviously. These boys definitely were not used to undercover work, whoever they were. Mike looked for a telephone booth as he drove. Louis might have some idea what had happened. Mike and Louis had known each other ever since Mike had come to the narcotics division. Louis had taken Mike under his wing and trained him to be one of the best men on the force. It was Louis' expert training, Mike always felt, that had gotten Mike assigned to detective work right along side Louis, then promoted to sergeant. Mike pulled over to a telephone booth at the corner and dialed Louis' number at the precinct. No answer. He got back in the car. If Jake and his guys knew Mike was a cop, he was in trouble and they would be after him. If they didn't, the switch hadn't gone through and they'd be upset about that. Either way, something had to happen.

Leaving Basile

With no answer from Louis, Mike thought about what steps to take next. He wanted to find Jake before Jake found him. It would be better that way. He got back in the Mercedes and drove toward the tenderloin district. Mike would be happy to turn this car back in to the department, he thought. It was a beautiful car, but it reminded him of the slime he had been dealing with for the past few months. He knew Jake and his kind very well and he hated them. These people would do anything for money. They'd kill their own grandmother if she got in the way.

Mike pulled over on Sixth and Mission and walked up the block leaving the suitcase under the car seat of the locked Mercedes, its hard top securely latched in place. These streets smelled strongly of spoiled garbage or puke or both as Mike stepped over a sleeping mound of tattered, brown blankets on the sidewalk. Across the street, in front of the liquor store, Mike saw who he was looking for.

"Sam, my man." As Mike nudged the man leaning on the brick wall, he stumbled, loosing the wall as his crutch.

"Hey, man," he grumbled at the ground before struggling to look up at Mike. He squinted at the daylight and pulled his soiled, baggy pants up by the waist. Sam smelled as if the garbage Mike had passed a minute ago had come to life and named itself Sam.

"Sam, where can I find a guy by the name of Jake?"

"Jake?" Sam rubbed his forehead and pulled the knit cap he wore down over his eyebrows. "I don't . . ."

"Bullshit, man!" Mike grabbed Sam by his arm and some hardened matter cracked on Sam's sleeve and began to crumble. Mike let go. "You know him just like I know you."

Sam continued to look at the ground and shook his head.

Mike pulled a ten dollar bill out of his pocket.

Sam looked closely at the bill and scratched his rear end through his filthy trousers. The bill helped jog his memory. "Stubby's pool hall, man. Over on Third Street."

Mike held the bill at arms distance and stared at Sam incredulously.

"One of his boy's name is Chuck. I'm telling you, man." Sam weaved a bit then steadied himself as he eyed the bill. Mike held the bill out toward Sam and pulled it out of his reach again as he swiped for it.

"Oh, yea. How would I recognize him?" Mike stared at Sam

as he rubbed his nose loosely and squinted in thought.

"He's a big guy." Sam held his hand up to about six feet. "Yea, big." Mike continued to stare and held the bill out. "Oh, yea!" Sam pointed at Mike as if he just remembered something else. "He has a gold tooth." Sam tapped his own single front tooth with his forefinger. Mike dropped the bill on the ground and walked away as Sam scrambled for it before the wind picked it up and carried it into the gutter.

Dorisse walked out into the kitchen. She had decided to make some *mas-pa* for breakfast. Sugar, flour . . . Mike's kitchen wasn't stocked very well. She found some cornmeal, decided to make *cush-cush* and ate that instead. Dorisse wasn't used to having so many television stations available, so she watched TV all day long and dosed off in front of the set.

Dorisse woke up and stretched. She felt like a lazy cow. She'd go look for work tomorrow. She couldn't live off of Mike. He already had supported her for the last two weeks. She had plenty of money saved but he hadn't let her pay for a thing. She looked at the clock. Oh my God! It was almost four o'clock and she looked like hell. She'd take a shower and get prettied up before Mike got there.

Dorisse showered and put on a little make-up and looked through her clothes trying to decide what to wear. She wondered what they'd do that day. Maybe he'd take her dancing or maybe there *was* a wax museum in San Francisco. She went into the bathroom and fiddled with her hair. He had huge mirrors all over the bathroom that allowed you to see yourself from every angle. She had to do something with this hair of hers. She had always worn it pulled back off her face with a headband, but it was about time she did something more sophisticated with it. She was in San Francisco now. Women there dressed well and knew all the latest fashions. She had to buy a magazine to catch up. Dorisse stood in front of the mirror for so long, she didn't realize it was way past six and Mike wasn't back yet. Just then, there was a knock at the door. Well it's about time, she thought. She ran to the front door, not stopping to think that Mike wouldn't be knocking at his own door, and swung it open. It wasn't Mike. The last thing she saw was a huge fist aiming straight for her face, then blackness, as black as the bay sky.

CHAPTER TWENTY

Paul sat on the bar stool at Henry's bar as he always did when he and Ann had a fight. He rested his elbows on the bar and held on to his bottle of Coors with both hands, trying to decide if he should order another. Henry decided for him as he slid another his way. Henry had gotten used to seeing Paul hunched over his beer bottle with the same troubled expression on his face. Every few weeks or so Paul showed up, sat on the same bar stool toward the left end of the bar, and ordered one Coor's after another. He would usually end up drinking two, or sometimes three if he had more then usual to think about. Henry counted the bar seats from the left and remembered the number to see if Paul really sat in the same seat every time or if it was just that general area that he liked.

Henry's was located a few blocks down and around the corner from Paul and Ann's apartment. Paul passed by it on his way to and from school each day and had been meaning to stop in and look around for months. The first time Paul went in, he stopped in the middle of the dimly lit room and looked around, scoping out the place. The bar was empty that day except for a middle-aged man in a dark suit seated in a booth with a neatly dressed middle-aged woman, his wife maybe, maybe not, but they looked comfortable with each other. Co-workers perhaps, yes, Paul had decided they were coworkers out for a happy hour cocktail. He was hoping Henry's wasn't a pick up joint so that some woman would come ask him to buy her a drink as soon as he got comfortable, or worse some guy. He wanted a place to kick back and relax alone with his thoughts. Henry's was quiet and Paul liked that. Of course it *was* one o'clock in the afternoon on a Tuesday, but it was quiet at that time, nonetheless. The walls were decorated with an aluminum Coca-Cola advertisement from the twenties, some old movie posters, and a couple of stuffed animal heads bolted to wood . Paul wasn't sure if any of these things were authentic, but it gave him something to look at, something to wonder about while he nursed his beer.

Henry had watched Paul look around the first day he came in. He had chosen a seat at the bar, and introduced himself to Henry. He had told Henry his name and that he lived a few blocks away and then, Henry remembered, Paul had taken a big sigh before he ordered his Coor's in the bottle. Since that day he didn't say more than a few words to Henry when he came in. Usually just "hello" and "thanks", before he walked out the door a bit more relaxed than when he came in. He seemed a nice enough guy. Kept to himself, didn't start any trouble. He seemed to just want a little solitude in the afternoons to think things out. That seemed like a fair enough request, so, Henry gave it to him.

Things had not been easy lately, Paul thought to himself as he sat at Henry's one evening. And things were getting more and more difficult all the time. School, caring for Miette, and dealing with Ann. Ann complained constantly, and about everything. The upper division classes Paul was taking were no piece of cake and trying to study while Miette woke up crying every few hours was not making them any easier. How dare Ann get upset with him? He should be the one that was mad. Offering to do the right thing by marrying her and she couldn't even find her stupid husband to get a divorce. How many places could a hillbilly like that go? She obviously didn't realize all Paul had given up for her. Packing up and leaving his friends and family and moving across the country to be with her. He worked day and night to finish his education so he could make enough money to care for his family properly. Classes all day and studying all night while watching the baby. Miette did sleep through the night most of the time, and he didn't mind taking a break from his studies to sit and rock her back to sleep. She was as sweet as any child could be and he loved Miette more than anyone on earth. But it was not easy for him to be a full-time student and care for a baby at the same time and all Ann could do was bitch about it. *He* was able to pursue *his* education, she'd say. Did she think it was fun? Reading hundreds of pages of required reading, writing fifty-page essays, studying until all hours of the night for exams? It certainly was not the picnic Ann made it out to be. Ungrateful. That was what she was sometimes. An ungrateful little bitch.

He turned his first beer upside down and let the last of it bubble up into the tinted bottle and fall back down into his throat. He saw a blurred figure through his bottle sit on the stool next to him. Paul was in no mood for talking to anyone, so he turned his shoulder away unsociably from the stool being occupied. The last thing he wanted to do was listen to some fellow describe the Giant's game he had watched on the tube inning by inning, shouting into Paul's ear like some sport's announcer. Paul just wanted to sit and stew his thoughts in his beer, but instead of a gruffy sports fanatic's voice, a soft, female one asked him for a light. He picked up a book of matches from the ashtray that sat in front of him and turned toward a striking woman with chocolate brown skin, almond shaped eyes and black hair cut into short curls that taped off at her neck. She wore a grey blazer, black skirt, tinted stockings and high heels that strapped around her ankle. Paul struck the match and held it up to her long, thin cigarette. She puffed on it with full, frosty lips and nodded thanks. She inhaled, sat back on her stool, and talked small clouds of smoke into the air.

"Thank you . . . uh . . .," she said through the smoke.

"Paul," he answered.

She reached out a feminine hand toward him. "Winnie." She leaned over and pulled the clear ashtray toward her and thumped her cigarette against it, although no ashes had a chance to form on its end yet. Winnie faced forward after looking at Paul for an extended moment and puffed on her cigarette.

Not bad, she thought after eyeing Paul quickly. Interesting looking guy. Handsome. He looks like he may be mixed with Spanish, maybe, she thought. Nice bod too. Tall, broad shouldered, just the way I like 'em, she nodded to herself. Oh yes, definitely, Winnie thought. He definitely has potential.

"So what brings you to Henry's, Paul?" Winnie said, after deciding he'd be worth her time. She swung her bar stool around to face Paul and rested her right elbow on the bar and crossed her left arm over her chest. She sat back and held the cigarette far out in front of her with her right hand as if she were about to conduct an orchestra with it. Winnie held her small nose in the air and smiled down at Paul, stretching her darkly rimmed almond eyes up into thick slants.

"Nothing in particular."

"I've never seen you here before."

"Doesn't mean I haven't been here," Paul said caustically, his eyebrows held high. He was a bit perturbed by this woman starting a conversation with him when his body language clearly said, leave me alone, and questioning him like he had to give *her* a reason for being there.

"Oh," Winnie let out very quickly, as if saying, Okay, I get the message and took another hit of her cigarette. She stared at one of the movie posters. Marilyn Monroe and Richard Widmark in *Don't Bother to Knock*. Marilyn leaned back in the picture, jutting her breasts forward as they fought to get out of the tight, strapless dress she wore.

Paul looked at Winnie's three-quarter profile. Her black eyeliner whipped up at the corners of her eyes made her look exotic and sexy. Her face looked chiseled, sculptured, perfect. She was an exquisitely attractive woman. Poised and refined. Everything in place, spit-shined, so to speak. He felt a little bad about snapping at her and tried to dilute his original tone.

"I'm sort of new in this area," he said pleasantly. "I come into Henry's every now and then to . . ., "Paul thought about the reason he always came into Henry's, ". . . to have a few beers."

Winnie looked back at him and smiled, teeth perfect and straight. "Well, from your expression I'd say you were trying to . . . drown your sorrows?" She lifted an eyebrow inquisitively. Winnie had seen guys like Paul before. Woman problems no doubt, she thought. Another guy unable to make some woman do things his way, and he couldn't handle it, so he came here to drink to try to forget the fact that he was not always in charge. Winnie never had that problem. She was always in charge, she thought to herself. Always.

"Does it really show?" He didn't mind this Winnie being so presumptuous with him now. He liked her approach. Nonchalant, sure of herself, but not cocky. Confident. She smiled a very small, narrow smile. A smile that was almost . . . condescending. A smirk was what it was, an arrogant little smirk. Actually, Paul thought, she seemed a bit out of his class. More mature, more serious. Paul had never met a woman *he* thought was out of his class, but this one was, and he kind of liked it.

Winnie removed the grey jacket. The black skirt turned out to be a black dress. Paul eyed her as she readjusted herself on the edge of the stool. The dress seemed to hug each curve of her body the way an expensive sports car hugged each turn on the road. Her slightly slanted eyes were as dark and catlike as she seemed to be — sleek and mysterious.

"No, not really. I'm just very perceptive." She stared at him for a moment, then leaned across the bar to get Henry's attention. She didn't wave her arm or shout Henry's name, she just looked at his profile and he instinctively turned and walked toward her.

"Gin and tonic, please, Henry."

"Twist of lime?" he asked her as he grabbed the green bottle of gin from the back wall. She and Henry had obviously been previously acquainted.

"Definitely," she smiled at him and carried the smile back over to Paul's waiting face. "I'm a good listener, Paul." She shifted on her bar stool as if getting in a suitable position for listening and then sat still and leaned in toward Paul. Henry placed her cocktail in front of her and she nodded at him and looked back at Paul, awaiting the beginning of his long, and surely pathetic story.

Although Paul barely knew this woman, he felt comfortable talking to her. All the problems he had been having with Ann poured out like a hole had been cut into the bottom of his thoughts. He told Winnie about the nights he sat up until four or five in the morning studying. He told her how he spent his Saturdays and Sundays in the library while Ann was able to stroll around the park with Miette. He told her how Ann complained about how he was able to have time to himself and she was always either working or keeping Miette. He'd love to be spending time with his daughter, he told Winnie, rather than hunched over some text book at school, and he'd hardly call sitting in a classroom with a hundred other people, having time to himself.

Winnie sat and nodded occasionally as he spoke, taking small sips of her drink and looking attentively into his eyes. She would never have expected this handsome young man to have so many responsibilities. A college student, a father . . . and a good one it seemed. Paul continued to talk and told Winnie how he and Ann had met and about Edward and how they ended up in San Francisco. That part of the story was very interesting to Winnie, very interesting indeed, but Winnie didn't have much sympathy for any of them. You make your bed, you lie in it, she thought.

"Well," she finally said after Paul had stopped talking to hail another beer from Henry. "It seems as though you two need to sit down and have a nice long talk." She reached into her purse and pulled out another cigarette, but paused before lighting it.

"Don't you think?" She lifted an eyebrow and waited for him to answer.

Paul shook his head. "I can't talk to her. She just . . . she won't listen." He waved his hand resignedly.

Just as Winnie thought. He couldn't make this Ann agree with his way of doing things. Ann just didn't know how to handle men, Winnie thought. She didn't know how to put her own ideas in his head and make him think they were his own. Oh well, Ann was just a naive country girl and Winnie really wouldn't expect her to know any better.

Winnie shrugged and finally lit her cigarette. Paul watched her as the match spotlighted her face in the dim bar and her cheeks hollowed as they puffed on the cigarette. Her brown cheekbones sat unusually high and Paul watched her full lips as she puckered them around the thin filter. After three beers, Paul thought she looked like a panther perched on a rock, her black dress caressing the S of her perfect posture like a cat's own silky coat would. She looked up from the flame and smiled at him a little, the white edges of her teeth contrasting against her dark skin. She shook the match out and resumed her customary position, right hand displaying the cigarette, left one crossed over her chest.

Paul liked Winnie. She hadn't made any stupid comments about him and Ann. She just listened, let him get it all off his chest and nodded non-judgementally. Maybe that was why he didn't mind telling his story to someone he hardly knew, because she could be objective and she was right — she *was* a good listener.

"I've been babbling on about my problems . . . tell me something about yourself, Winnie."

"There's not much to tell. I'm a legal secretary. I was born and raised in San Francisco. I have two brothers, both of whom, along with my parents, still live here in the city."

"Are you married?" Paul asked her, never thinking for a minute that she might be. She didn't *look* married, or even attached. She almost seemed the type no one could pin down.

"Nope. Never been married, no children."

He wasn't surprised. He nodded confirmingly. "How old are you . . . if you don't mind me asking." Paul didn't think she'd mind.

"Thirty-three," she answered without hesitation.

She looked great, Paul thought. Her brown skin was

Leaving Basile

incredibly flawless. Not a line anywhere in sight and her long legs were as toned as a cheetah's.

"Thirty-three!? You look a *lot* younger than that!"

"Thank you, Paul." She said as if she had heard it a million times and took a hit off of her cigarette, unaffected by the complement. She finally snubbed the butt out and shook the ice cubes around in her glass.

"Can I buy you another?" Paul offered. He didn't want her to leave just yet. She had done such a good job of making him forget about Ann for a while.

"No, thank you." She smoothed back the edges of her hair very lightly and turned toward Paul. While he was spilling his guts to her about Ann, She was thinking about asking him to join her for a little excursion and decided that it would be a good idea. "I know a great little blues club in the east bay. The entertainment is good and the food is excellent. Would you like to go?" She thought Paul would make a handsome accessory for her arm.

Paul paid Henry for the drinks and the two headed over the Bay Bridge towards Oakland.

Paul sat across the kitchen table from Ann and watched as she spooned homemade baby food into Miette's tiny mouth. He shoveled the same food Ann had mashed up for Miette into his own mouth, in whole pieces though. It was some concoction Ann always cooked, chicken and okra with tomato sauce over rice. She said it didn't really have a name, but Paul kind of liked the taste of it. Miette slapped some of the food off the spoon as a reddish clump hit the table cloth with a splat. Ann fussed at Miette quietly in French as Paul got up for a second helping and thought about something his friend Winnie had said to him in the car on their way home from Oakland the night he had met her. She had asked Paul what nationality he was and he had told her he was a Negro. She had laughed that slight, smirk of a laugh and said that Black was a preferable term. Black, she said, was what Americans of African decent should be referred to as. Black, she said, was a name representative of a proud race of people, who worked their way from slavery to freedom and who still in this century and in the coming century would not be completely free of the chains of racial prejudice that they were still bound by. "Negro is a name the White man has given us," Winnie had said, "just a slight variation of the word they prefer to use — nigger." Paul thought about his background, growing up in the south. He wasn't used to people asking him what his nationality was. Mainly because to them, if you weren't White, it didn't much matter what you were. You just weren't White.

"Ann," he asked her as he returned to the table to eat meal number two. "Has anyone ever asked you what race you are?"

Ann looked off to the side in thought and shook her head, "No, not that I can remember. Why?" She was curious now.

Paul started to tell her that there was no reason, but then asked her, "Do I look Black to you?"

"Black?"

"Yea. That's what Negroes are called now. Negro is just a name the White man has given us. Black! That's what we are now. Black!" Paul felt incredibly noble, like he was reciting Shakespeare.

Ann looked at Paul like he had just said he was Abraham Lincoln or something. "What the hell's gotten into you?"

"Nothing's gotten into me. It's about time Ann, that we became more aware of our Afro-American heritage."

"I'm quite aware of *my* heritage."

"Not that Creole shit. I mean what we really are. Black people!" Paul began to feel noble again and Ann continued to stare at him like he'd lost his mind. "That's why we're failing as a people, because we need to stick together as a race instead of separating ourselves into subgroups that just make each one a weaker minority. We can't deny our race, Ann."

"I've certainly never denied my race, Paul. It was kind of hard to do when I couldn't go to the high school that was two blocks away from my house but instead had to walk for an hour to get to the Negro high school across town."

"*Black* high school!"

"Whatever!"

"Well you don't have to do that anymore, Ann. Times and places have changed and we need to take a stand and teach our daughter what the White man has done to us as a people."

"Our daughter will be quite aware of the history of . . . *black* people in this country, and she'll also be aware of her Creole heritage. It's very important that she know her true heritage."

"Oh, what? That white men from France raped the slave women that had been brought there to work for them. Well *that's* something to be proud of," Paul said sarcastically to Ann. He was standing now as Ann still sat in her chair facing Miette. "And I don't want you teaching her that ridiculous slave language

Leaving Basile

either. I won't have it!" Paul turned around and said to Ann.

"Slave language? What the hell do you think English is!?" Now Ann was getting a bit upset herself.

"English is the language of the country that we live in and will *be* living in. She will need to master English in order to survive and be successful here. That other language will be totally useless to her."

"What about preserving our culture?" Now Ann was standing, walking toward Paul with her hands on her narrow hips. "If our generation forgets our culture, and everyone follows your *stupid* theory, the culture of our people will disappear like it never existed. Miette and myself are the only Fruge´s that exist, Paul. There is no way on this earth I'll let the history of *our* family, however it was formed, be forgotten or lied about. You're getting all pushed out of shape because someone obviously didn't know if you were a Negr . . . a *black* person or not. Yes, you look a little different than the blacks they're used to seeing in the movies or on television or whatever, but its you Paul. *You're* the one with the problem. *You're* the one who never knew enough about your own heritage to explain it — not to others — but to yourself. No wonder you're confused." Ann rolled her eyes and walked back toward Miette.

"Confused? I'm not confused! You're the one who's confused if you think looking different will make things better. Worse maybe, not better."

"Did I say that?"

"You think that, don't you."

Ann rolled her eyes again and shook her head. "Sit down and eat your food!" She pointed to the plate of food he had fixed.

"I'm sick and tired of eating okra, and shit with tomato sauce, and weird fish dishes with no names," Paul yelled across the living room. "I'm going to get a hamburger!" Paul grabbed his jacket off the couch and walked out the front door.

A hamburger, Ann thought. An all American hamburger.

Winnie wasn't quite sure what prompted her to ask Paul over to her parents house for dinner a few weeks after they had met. A few weeks earlier, they had gone to *Ruthie's* in East Oakland and listened to a woman named C.J. Thompson belt out songs that could make the most demure souls stand up and shout back at her to "tell em about it, C.J." as some did that very night. C.J. weighed about three hundred pounds and wore a sequined dress that hung over her fatty shoulders like a Christmas table cloth. Paul gnawed on bar-b-qued ribs and washed them down with two more beers and Winnie ate chicken wings and ordered a gin and tonic afterward . . . with lime.

    Winnie's parents liked Paul, but she knew they would. That was one of the reasons why she invited him to their house the next time she ran into him at Henry's, the night he had argued with Ann. Winnie had stopped into Henry's for a drink that night, before she went to her parent's house for dinner, as she did two or three nights out of the week. Paul had stopped in for a beer, the first time since he had met Winnie there a few weeks before. She had called her parents and told them she was bringing a guest. They were delighted. They both worried that Winnie would end up unmarried and they'd have no grandchildren from their only daughter. Winnie's father didn't worry about it half as much as her mother did. She had suffered the empty nest syndrome since her youngest son had left home eight years ago and gotten his own apartment. Winnie's mother listened to he daughter's biological clock tick loudly as she dated dozens of men, but made no plans to settle down with any of them. Winnie had told her mother a little sternly once that she had no intentions of getting married anytime soon and she hadn't asked Winnie about it again since. But her mother knew, if Winnie was bringing this young man to their house for dinner there was a possibility that he might be the one. Winnie's father told her not to blow things out of proportion, but she fixed a dinner that was like a love potion. No man could have resisted.

    Paul sat comfortably in Mr. and Mrs. Johnson's den after the best dinner he had since he left Baton Rouge. Chicken fried in a Dutch oven to a gorgeous shade of brown, mashed potatoes with just enough lumps to let you know they were real, and vegetables that tasted like they had just been picked from the garden, drenched in butter. Mrs. Johnson served hot steaming rolls and his favorite, peach cobbler for dessert. He leaned back on their sofa a little to give his bulging stomach room to spread out. He was a little apprehensive about having dinner there at first. He thought he might be uncomfortable, maybe have to put on that Eddie Haskell routine in front of them, but Mr. and Mrs. Johnson were as easy to talk to as the Cleavers themselves. He felt like he had known them for years. It seemed strange that a woman as sophisticated as Winnie

Leaving Basile

would have two of the most down to earth parents that existed. Right off television. Mrs. Johnson wore an apron that she wiped her hands on often and took off before serving coffee in the den, and Paul saw where Winnie had inherited her perfect teeth from each time Mrs. Johnson smiled. Their small house was clean with too much furniture and dozens of tiny knick knacks lined up on every horizontal surface available. An old sepia photograph of a woman that looked a lot like Harriet Tubman to Paul, and a family portrait of Winnie and two men that had to have been her brother, probably taken in the past five years or so, sat perched on top of the console TV. Mr. Johnson smoked a pipe and had his own chair, an old recliner with an Afghan thrown over it that Mrs. Johnson had probably crocheted herself. Mr. Johnson leaned back and told corny jokes that the women seemed to have heard a million times. He told Paul a few, slapped him on the back and pointed at Paul as he laughed one of those hoarse laughs that ended in a wheeze, and amused himself with his own wit. Mrs. Johnson waved her hand at him and told him to quit it, but laughed along with him all the same. He called Paul son, and laughed over his pipe as he told Paul funny stories about Winnie when she was small. Winnie blushed and crossed her fingers that they wouldn't pull the old photo album out with pictures of her in the second grade with missing front teeth and black braids that stood straight out all by themselves like Pippi Longstockings.

"Well, honey," Mr. Johnson said to his wife, "I think I'll turn in. Why don't we let these youngsters talk amongst themselves for a while."

Mrs. Johnson would have loved to stay and pump Paul for information about his intentions, but she knew the best approach was to let nature take its course. It was hard, but she agreed that she too was tired and bid Paul and Winnie goodnight as the two elder Johnsons disappeared into the back of the house.

Paul stood up, a very gentlemanly gesture Mrs. Johnson thought, and thanked the two repeatedly for having him over and for the magnificent dinner. Mrs. Johnson told him that they loved having him and that he was welcome back anytime. Her approval of him was hardly hidden, as she grinned Winnie's smile at him and held her own hands under her bosom .

Paul and Winnie sat on the sofa side by side and Paul slid down on the tapestry sofa a bit more, resting his head on the off-white doily on the cushion back and crossed his ankles under the coffee table. Winnie sat sideways, facing him with her right elbow on the sofa back, her face resting in her hand, and her right leg folded under her bottom.

She smiled at Paul's relaxed physique. "Thanks for coming, Paul."

"Are you kidding? My pleasure! I haven't had a meal like that since my mother cooked for me." Paul thought about his mother briefly. He missed his family. "Don't tell my mother I said so. . .but maybe not even then!"

Winnie laughed softly. "They like you, you know. They like you a lot."

"I like them too. I just met them and this feels like home away from home," he looked around the small room. "They took me in like adoptive parents."

"Well, you heard them, you're welcome anytime."

Paul locked his fingers behind his head and closed his eyes. He hadn't felt this much at ease in a long time. He had forgotten all about Ann and midterms and the paper he had to turn in the following week, and quickly drifted off into a heavy, food induced sleep.

Winnie stared at his profile as his breaths became long and deep. What a handsome man, she thought. He had such a unique look about him. Soft black curls and a creamy smooth complexion with a little, black stubble growing over it. He had a masculine jaw, like Paul Newman's she thought, but lightly tanned to a beautiful shade. She covered Paul with another Afghan that sat on the end of the sofa and went and slept in her old bedroom.

Paul awoke more leisurely than he had in a long time, stretched and yawned before he realized he was still on Winnie's parent's sofa and it was six o'clock the next morning.

"Oh, my God!" he said softly but out loud. Paul looked around and grabbed a pencil and notepad from the mantle.

Winnie,

Thank's so much for inviting me over for dinner. Tell your mother she'll never get rid of me now, she's made a friend for life. . .and so have you. See you at Henry's!

Paul

Paul folded the Afghan and tiptoed out of the house and caught the bus home. Ann had been off the night before so he hadn't had to keep Miette. He hoped Ann would still be asleep.

Leaving Basile

Sometimes Miette woke her up quite early, he hoped this was not one of those days. How could he explain this to her?

Paul inserted the key into the door very slowly and turned it, very softly pushing the door open with his other hand, gritting his teeth at the small creaks the door made as it opened. He closed the door from the inside just as quiet and turned to head to the bathroom. He'd take a shower and dress and tell Ann he had gotten up early to go do some research at the library, which he actually really needed to do. The first step he took when he turned around froze as it landed on the living room carpet. There stood Ann in her house coat, arms folded, her slipper patting the floor and she wore an expression that spoke before she did. She looked straight into Paul's eyes without blinking. The kind of stare the teacher gave you in elementary school when you were talking during class and you were always the last one to see her. Then when you did notice, she always stared a little bit longer. Just long enough to make you *feel* the stare. Well Paul felt this one. It burned into him like a hot poker, making him wince and squirm in his shoes. Still, Ann didn't speak, didn't blink, didn't move, except for that slippered foot which patted the floor irritatingly like a dripping faucet. Paul thought he'd take this moment of silence as an opportunity to speak first. On the bus on his way home from Winnie's, Paul had thought about telling Ann he was studying all night at a classmates house, but remembered that was the same line she had given Edward night after night when she stayed in Paul's dorm room. Not a good story to use. Paul decided to tell the truth and use the "nothing happened" approach.

"Good morning," he smiled one of his wide, bright smiles at her and stretched his arms out toward her. She looked as still and gray as a statue in the park, her stare just as hard. "You know Ann, I . . .," he let out a nervous laugh, "I know you're probably wondering where I've been." He laughed again. "You know I was, well you see . . .," the more he thought about how the truth would sound the more he decided against using it. "You see I was up studying all night at . . ."

Ann cut him off, finally breaking her vow of silence. "If you ever walk through this door at six a.m., ever again, it'll be your last time walking through it at all . . . PERIOD!" she said loudly and Paul flinched.

This time Paul was actually scared. Maybe because he knew he didn't have any excuse. "Hey, I didn't do anything wrong," he shouted to her back as she walked into the bedroom, but Ann didn't turn around. She closed the bedroom door and got back into bed. Paul showered and got dressed quietly and left for the library. He thought it might be a good time to leave so Ann could calm down. He thought it might be a very good time.

Leaving Basile

CHAPTER TWENTY-ONE

Winnie laughed when she read the note Paul had left on her parent's sofa. "A friend for life", he had written. She didn't really have any friends. No real friends. The girls she had lunch with sometimes, the ones she grew up with, were gossipy and nosy. She had known them all her life and felt a bit of an obligation to keep in touch with them. And men well, she had never met one that wanted to be her *friend*. Actually, she had never met one who she wanted to be *friends* with. Especially ones who looked like Paul. Her eyelids lowered and her lips opened slightly as she thought about his black, sparkly eyes and the sexy way his lip curled up on one side when he smiled. Winnie had met handsome men before, enough to open an escort service. Some *extremely* handsome men, there were tons of them in San Francisco. She would go out with them three or four times, and ultimately lose interest. The ones she hated the most were the ones who latched themselves on to her like leeches, calling her every night, wanting to monopolize all of her free time. That drove her crazy. Then when she stopped returning their calls they'd call her with the same pathetic questions. What did they do wrong? When could they see each other again? What had happened to their relationship? Nothing had happened, Winnie thought. That was just it. Nothing. She just didn't like them. It was that simple. Couldn't they accept that? Were they going to force her to insult them even *more* by telling them they had practically bored her to her grave on the last three dates they had?

Most of them were lawyers she met at the firm she worked at. Lonely men in expensive suits, hair graying prematurely from the stress of their work. Men just wanting someone to spend time with, something pretty to look at across the dinner table, someone to tell their depressing problems to. Ex-wives taking them for all they were worth, mortgage payments, grown children of theirs who still wanted to be supported. Not for me, Winnie thought, not what I call a dream date. Oh, she had met a few she liked, handsome, funny guys who liked to have a good time, but none of *those* guys were ever serious. They usually got intimidated by her personality and took off after they slept with her once or twice, and the ones she loathed always wanted to marry her. Marry those creeps? The last thing she wanted was to be the obedient wife of some chauvinistic attorney. She could see herself in an apron like her mother's cooking him dinner every night, getting him his pipe and his slippers. She might as well carry then to him in her mouth like a well trained mutt. She hated the idea so much it made her cringe. So why did she feel like she could see Paul every day of the week and never get tired of him? Probably because she knew he was taken and she knew how much he cared for Ann and his daughter. A challenge. Something Winnie hadn't had in a long time, not a good one anyway. Once, she had gone out with a young handsome lawyer who was married to a nice wifely type who he had brought with him to San Francisco from Beatrice, Nebraska where they were both born and raised. There weren't girls like Winnie back in Beatrice, Winnie had suspected, and she had taken him aback with her city sexiness and charm. She didn't seduce him. He was just intrigued with her and she thought he would be fun for awhile but the two eventually became very close and Winnie really fell for him. She fell so hard that she asked him to leave his wife and he had told her, while they lay in her bed naked one morning at three a.m., that he knew he shouldn't see her anymore, that he couldn't see her anymore, and he didn't. It broke Winnie's heart. But she felt that it was the fact that he was married that made her fall for him so hard in the first place, and if that was the case, she was destined to have the same problem over and over again.

  Was it the same thing with Paul? All she knew was that she hadn't seen him in two months, even though she had stopped in at Henry's each evening after work. But Paul was never there on that barstool near the end where he always sat. She wanted to see him. She wanted to see him desperately. She couldn't remember wanting to see anyone so bad since the young, married lawyer. She had decided too, that when she did see him, she would have him for herself. Paul would be hers. Winnie always got what Winnie wanted.

  Paul didn't go back to Henry's for two months. In a way he was afraid he'd run into Winnie and he didn't want to do that. Then he'd have to tell her why he hadn't been to Henry's sooner, and he loathed telling her that Ann had threatened him

Leaving Basile

that morning when he came home and scared the wits out of him . . . and that he didn't want her to be that mad at him ever again.

What scared Paul even more was the fact that he had liked Winnie. He liked that confident, sophisticated air she carried around on the tip of her nose and the way she seemed to know she was attractive. She was so sure of herself, so in charge. He remembered liking that same confident air about Ann when he had first met her. He remembered how smart and ambitious she was. How direct and positive she had always been. She had changed, though, bitching about everything he did, whining about what he didn't do. She wasn't the Ann she used to be since she had come to San Francisco. She wasn't the same at all, Paul thought.

Paul couldn't believe it but his final exams were over. He hated summer courses because they were so condensed. They rushed you through an entire semester's worth of material in eight weeks. That meant class five days a week and a test practically every week. Also, it was even harder to sit inside a stuffy classroom when the weather outside was gorgeous. He had decided to walk home from the last Muni train where he usually transferred to a bus. He had sold his text books back and gotten back about half of what he paid for them. He whistled and pushed his hands down into his pockets, moving around the money from his books. He usually had a load of books with him that a mule couldn't have carried, but he rolled his book money around in his pockets with his free hands instead.

After Ann's blowup the morning he came home from Winnie's, she hadn't said another word about it and Paul knew it was better off forgotten, so he hadn't brought it up since and neither did she. He and Ann had both been in better moods lately because Paul had gotten a job on campus and this gave them extra money, plus he had more time to spend with Ann and Miette since it was summer. Paul looked over at Henry's bar as he crossed the street heading home and the thought of a nice cool Coors trailing down his throat seemed incredibly appealing. The thought of running into Winnie there also crossed his mind briefly, but he was in such a good mood that he figured it wouldn't be so bad seeing her-it wouldn't be bad at all.

He unconsciously sat in his usual seat, and Henry smiled at him.

"Long time, partner." he said to Paul.

"Yes sir, it has been. Fix me up Henry."

"Coming right up." This wasn't the tone Henry was used to hearing from Paul. He was happy, cheerful, even excited this time. He was glad to see his friend in a good mood for a change. He slid the Coors to him saloon style and Paul caught it as it passed in front of him on the shellacked bar. He nodded thanks to Henry and took a long, hearty swig. He looked around the bar and a few couples shared cocktails in booths but Paul had the bar all to himself. He felt great. His classes had gone well and he was expecting good grades. His job paid much better than the bookstore job back home and he would try to save enough money during the summer to buy a car. Boy, Paul hadn't felt this good since he had laughed after dinner with Winnie's parents that night.

As if she had read his mind and tracked him there, Winnie walked into Henry's and sat on the stool — her stool — next to him, smiling at him sweetly as he turned to face her slowly. Her black eyeliner was even more dramatic than usual as it swept her eyes up into the shape of a feline's. He smiled back immediately."Winnie!" Without stopping, he reached out and hugged her tightly. She wore a red knit dress that crisscrossed in the back and gold spheres dangled from chains on her earlobes. They swung back and forth as Paul pulled her body toward his, pressing his cheek against hers. She was a bit surprised at his enthusiastic show of affection but enjoyed it all the same.

"Paul! Oh my!" She showed all of her straight, even teeth to him in a happy smile. "I haven't . . . where've you been?" She still grinned at him broadly.

"Working hard, baby . . . in those books!" Paul said still happy. "But not any more. Today was my last final."

"Well, no wonder you're in such a good mood. We'll have to drink to that. Henry." Winnie called him over. "How about a drink, huh!" She smiled as happily as Paul did. Henry reached for the gin. "No. Not gin this time Henry. Let me have a beer. . .in honor of my friend here." Henry opened her a Coor's, but before he got the glass to her, she and Paul were clicking their bottles together in a toast. "Friends for life?"

"Friends for life!" Paul answered, and both he and Winnie took big bar room swigs out of their bottles, and laughed.

Paul and Winnie laughed and talked and polished away

eight beers between them before they knew it. Five for Paul and three for Winnie. Winnie wasn't quite used to the lethargic effect of chug-a-lugging beers and the way it made her speak her mind and do as she pleased.

After Paul payed the bill, Winnie picked up Paul's hand without warning and led him out onto the sidewalk. They laughed together and staggered out toward her car.

"Do you think you're in any condition to drive?" Paul asked, certainly in no condition himself.

"I only live a few blocks away," she said and blinked very slowly. "Come on," Winnie waved him toward her car in a loose, unrestrained movement, "I'll give you a ride home." They climbed in and she raced the small car down the street, darted around a few corners and parked in front of her own apartment as Paul looked around in confusion.

"Where are we?" His head swung around uncontrollably.

"At my house. I have to make a phone call. You wanna come up for a drink?" She leaned in close to Paul as she talked. "Come on," she coaxed him on. "One for the road?" She hit Paul on his thigh and her eyes stretched up even more catlike then usual as she squinted from the bright street light that reflected into her face through the windshield.

He got out of her car and followed her through the iron gate up to her apartment as easily as he walked into a new class on the first day of school. He stared at her hips as they swayed inside the red knit dress on her way up to the third floor. She took slow, even steps and seemed to contemplate each stair as she placed her foot quietly on each one and pulled herself up with her toned legs. Paul eyes studied the curves of her dress, and the crisscross on her bare back seemed to be trying to tell him something. Maybe the way a railroad crossing sign meant a train was approaching. Maybe the way the crossed bones under a skull meant poison. Maybe the way cartoonists drew X's for eyes when someone was knocked out cold. Maybe like the way an X over almost anything meant not to touch it, danger, warning, but there are those people who try to beat the train before it reaches the crossing, they feel lucky, they take a chance. Paul looked beyond the red crisscross up to the nape of Winnie's neck, at the earrings that swung like pendulums on a clock, as he counted the seconds that passed until they reached her front door. When she got to the top she turned to face him before she opened the door and the gold sphere on her left ear swung in circles over her shoulder like a hypnotist's watch. One last warning. He followed her in.

Winnie's apartment looked like her, dark and sultry. Two huge palms stood by the window spreading jungle like shadows onto the floor, over the tan-colored sofa. She had a large black-and-white zebra-print chaise chair between the two trees that Paul could tell was *her* chair as much as her father's recliner was his. He pictured her brown body stretched out on it like Cleopatra, queen of the Nile. A zebraskin rug lay on the floor in front of Winnie's chair, its flattened limbs spread out in each direction as if bowing to her. A giant picture hung on her wall, a woman's silhouette smoking a cigarette from a long holder with the shadow of a trail of black smoke floating from it into the air and off the frame. The outlined woman held her nose in the air and her lips apart as a cloud came out of her mouth like dark, visible words.

"Have a seat," Winnie stood with her back to the front door, "I'll be right back," she said and disappeared into the back.

Paul stepped slowly, cautiously into the room as if her were in the uncivilized jungles of Africa. He wouldn't have dreamt of sitting in her chair so he sat on the couch and looked over at Winnie's chair by the window. The street lights came into the window and spotlighted it like center stage. The two palms swayed a little from the small breeze that came in through the window and fanned the chair like two obedient male servants. Her stage was set and as Paul had expected, Winnie emerged from the back, walked over to her chair and extended her body along the length of it like no one but Cleo herself would have. She smiled that slight smile at him.

"Fix us some drinks. The bar's there." She pointed to a completely mirrored table in the corner that Paul had totally overlooked. Neither of them needed more to drink but he stood behind it and mixed Winnie a gin and tonic, then decided to fix himself one too to see what she liked so much about it. Maybe it would make him confident and arrogant and he'd smirk at her the way she did at him. He looked at her, she had kicked off her shoes and was staring out the window in her leonine position.

Paul thought about Ann for a second while he squeezed a plastic lime over the cocktails. He remembered how she had looked at him with eyes of stone that morning, the contempt on her face, the concreteness of the few words she had said to him. He carried the two glasses over to Winnie and sat on the edge of her chair near her waist. She took a small sip from hers and placed it under the palm.

"I like your apartment." Paul said, staring at Winnie now.

"Do you?" She smiled and squinted a little.

"Yea. It's so . . . so," Paul looked around, searching for one complementary word to describe it. "It's so exotic." He looked back her.

"Yes. It is exotic, isn't it?" Winnie looked around the room too. "Do you like . . . exotic, Paul?"

"Yea," He smiled and nodded softly. "I like exotic." The two laughed a little and Paul took two swallows from his drink.

"What else do you like . . . *Paul*?" She emphasized his name. "What do you really, really like." She spoke slowly and sensuously and looked him right in the eye.

"I like *you*, " Paul said automatically, like he had rehearsed those lines from a script. They fit in so well that he couldn't pass up the chance to use them "I like you a lot." He leaned over her reclined body and kissed her full, moist lips, taking them between his and running his tongue over each one within his mouth, then slowly withdrawing, leaving them wet and glistening against the outside lights.

Winnie looked up at his face, his eyes dark and glossy from the beers and swallows of gin. Winnie took the glass from his hand which he still held on to, and placed it under the palm next to hers. Then she softly pushed Paul out of her way and stood up. Winnie reached up, slipped the red dress off her shoulders, slid it down off her arms and over her hips, and dropped it to the floor. She stepped out of it and kicked it out of her way, and there she posed, her brown body harnessed in a bright red, lacy bra, red string panties, and a red contraption that held up her stockings and let her soft thighs show through between the red straps. The red almost blinded Paul, like a flashing red stop light against the city night, telling him to stop. Warning him to stop. But to Paul, Winnie may as well have had on all green, because everything he saw definitely said go, and Paul could have bet that Winnie's father never used his chair the way he and Winnie used her's that night!

It was easy after that, for Paul and Winnie to meet at least once a week. Paul used to take Miette to the babysitter's sometimes when he had especially big tests to study for. Now, he took Miette to the sitter's at least once a week. Ann didn't get home from work until eight thirty in the morning, and by that time he had picked Miette up and gone home. Then, he left for school as soon as Ann walked in.

It was as if Winnie had hypnotized him, Paul thought. He couldn't stop seeing her if he tried, there was no way. She became unbelievable beyond the iron gates of her building, within her jungle apartment. She was like a wild animal that had been tamed, but you could never knew when she might regress, the danger was always there. It seemed she could lap up a bowl of milk or become carnivorous all in one night.

Leaving Basile

CHAPTER TWENTY TWO

Ann gathered some of Miette's things in a bag to take with her to the sitter's. She brushed Miette's hair into two short pony tails and curled each around her finger and dressed her in a small corduroy jumper. Miette was a spirited, active child, who had become quite spoiled. She was the spitting image of her father. Her black eyes dominated her small face. She did have her mother's personality. She was strong, stubborn and determined. Once she had made up her mind to do something, she found a way to do it.

After struggling the jumper onto Miette's moving body, Ann finally got her off to the sitter's. Back home, Ann sat on the sofa holding a cup of hot coffee and put her feet on the coffee table. She had taken Miette to the sitter's because she needed to run some errands and it would be nice to have a small break from the baby, have some time to herself for a change. It had been a busy night at the coffee shop and she couldn't wait to take a long hot shower, run her errands then fall into her bed and rest until she picked up Miette at three o'clock. She finished sipping her coffee. She would have no problem sleeping, even with the coffee in her system. She only drank that cup to keep her awake long enough to run out and take care of her business. Ann got up and rubbed her face up and down hard and yawned. She stretched and started heading for the bathroom but a knock at the door interrupted her plan for the shower. She looked through the peephole and an immaculately dressed woman stood tugging on the tops of her gloves. She must be selling cosmetics or something, Ann thought, and opened the door.

"Ann?" The woman addressed her by name.

"Yes?" Ann looked at her, puzzled.

"My name is Winnie. Winnie Johnson. May I come in and speak with you?" She smiled slightly at Ann. For some strange intuitive reason, Ann knew exactly what she was going to say.

Winnie walked into the apartment and looked around. Some of Miette's toys and dolls were lying on the table. It looked to Winnie as if a family lived there-a happy family.

"May I sit?" she asked Ann respectfully. Ann nodded, still suspicious. Winnie lowered herself down onto the sofa at an angle, loosening her gloves by pulling on each finger. Ann sat down across from her, taking in every single one of Winnie's very distinct moves. She stuffed her gloves into her handbag and lifted her perfectly made-up face so she'd have to look down at Ann to talk. She lifted her eyebrow before she began her sentence.

"I don't think you're aware of the facts I'm about to state-and they are facts-but Paul and I have had a continuous affair over the past several months." She looked at Ann without a bit of emotion in her darkly lined eyes.

Ann's eyes squinted in disbelief and her mouth slowly dropped open. Paul would never...this couldn't be true. Ann's back seemed to droop. He wouldn't do this to her. He just couldn't

Ann got her composure. She straightened her posture and tried to look as confident as Winnie did. "You're lying."

"Oh?" Winnie let out a little laugh that made Ann want to kill her. "I think not," Winnie said, pouring on the cynicism. She lifted her chin even higher and took a deep breath. "I just want you to know, Paul is in love with me. And the only reason he stays with you is because of his daughter."

Ann began to breathe hard. Her lips got tight.

"Oh, and also to help pay his way through school."

That was it. Ann stood up. "Now you listen to me, you cheap dime store bitch." Ann put her hands on her narrow hips. "It would be in your best interest to get out of my reach as fast as you can because my only worry at this moment is that I won't be able to dispose of the body. But if you stay a minute longer, I don't think even *that* will stop me from killing you."

Winnie stood up and took her gloves from her purse. "You may be used to wrestling those alligators in the bayou, but I'd rather be a little more ladylike about it." She moved toward the door. "I just thought you'd want to know where your boyfriend is late at night when you and your daughter are all alone." She opened Ann's front door and gave her one last scowling look. "Ciao." She lifted her eyebrow and left Ann standing in her living room trembling with anger.

Ann collapsed onto the couch and cried from frustration and anger. That stupid son-of-a-bitch. How could he? Ann cried into the sofa long and hard. Maybe, she thought, maybe Winnie just wanted him and knew she could never have him. Maybe she was just jealous of Ann. Yes. She was just jealous. Who Winnie? She and her fancy, city looks? Her exotic, perfectly tailored beauty? Winnie who walked into Ann's house and took over as if it was a public forum? Winnie? Jealous of Ann? Ann cried more.

That evening, Ann decided not to say anything to Paul about her visitor. Not just yet. She didn't know why at first but she soon realized it would be too easy for him to deny. When it came time for Paul to come home, she cleaned her face of her afternoon tears and gave him a homecoming smile when he arrived. Ann decided she'd find out the truth for herself.

Paul had asked Ann if she could drop Miette off at the sitters on her way to work because he needed to go out to the library for a while around ten. This was it. Ann was ready. She dropped Miette off at the sitter's early and called a taxi to wait for her outside of her apartment at ten o'clock that night when Paul was leaving for the so-called library. She'd make it to work on time at eleven all right. Her plan wouldn't take longer than an hour. Paul left, walking, and turned into Henry's. Ann followed in her taxi asking the driver to park across the street from the bar. To the library. Yea, right, Ann thought. She wore a scarf tied under her chin and a pair of dark glasses. She pulled the shades down briefly so she could see Paul's figure through the bar window more clearly. She could barely see his back seated at the bar, but he did seem to be talking to someone. Was it Ann's imagination? Was it the bartender he was talking to? Maybe Paul had just stopped in for a beer on his way to the library. Ann couldn't tell. She'd wait. It was cold and musty in the cab and the driver sat reading the daily newspaper, unconcerned about anything but the fare he was making. Suddenly she saw Paul's figure rise from the bar stool. He emerged from the bar and walked around to the passenger seat of a small sports car that was parked in front. Ann's heart began to beat faster as a woman walked out behind him. It was her. All wrapped up in a long, fur collared coat. Although the fur stood up around the woman's face, Ann recognized her the minute she put one high-heeled pump outside the bar door. Winnie climbed into the driver's seat of the sports car, let Paul in and the two zoomed off down the hill.

"Follow them," Ann said quickly. "Follow that sports car! Hurry!" She sat on the edge of the back seat speaking frantically in the driver's ear. He took off after them. "But not too close," Ann added. She stayed on the edge of her seat, dark glasses pushed up to her face, and hid partially behind the driver, peeking around him. The driver was glad to have a little excitement on his rounds tonight. He kind of hoped something would come of it. At least it'd keep him awake. They drove a few blocks, turned a few corners and finally the sports car parked at the curb.

"Park over there." Ann pointed to a spot behind them, a few doors down. The cabbie pulled over. Ann sat and watched Paul and Winnie as they walked into the building. She even saw a light come on a few moments later on the third floor. Ann sat and watched from the taxi. She saw Paul's figure in the window, but Ann waited. She wanted to wait. Twenty minutes later the lights went off slowly. Ann still waited. Then ten minutes later she asked the driver to wait, walked over to the building and looked at the buzzers. Johnson, it read. Three-ten. Ann looked at the iron gate that opened only when buzzed open from the inside. How would she get in? She walked over to the gate and touched it. It swung open. Now Ann's heart really began to beat. She was in. She walked toward the staircase and took each step slowly and quietly. She reached three-ten far too quickly, although it seemed the longest walk in her life. She looked at the numbers on the door. Her heart was beating so loudly she was sure they could hear it through the door. She listened for any voices but heard none. Nothing. Her trembling hand reached for the knob. She slowly turned it clockwise and pushed it inward at the end of the turn. Oh my God, she thought, the door is open. What the hell was she doing? This was breaking and entering. She could go to jail. All the thoughts that ran through Ann's mind didn't stop her hand from opening that door. What if it was the wrong apartment? What if some nervous old lady with a shot gun lived there and blew Ann's brains out thinking she was a burglar? The room was pitch black. A tiny light emerged from the back of the apartment. Ann had come this far. There was absolutely nothing that could make her turn back now. She had to know. She had to see.

She crept toward the small, faint light. Her heart seemed to stop beating at this point. It was waiting, as she was. She heard very slight sounds, now that she had gotten closer. She looked through the narrow opening in the door. She wasn't quite sure at first, but then realized she was looking into a mirror on the bedroom wall. The reflection came into focus all at once. She would know Paul's bare, tanned back from a mile away, and there were Winnie's pedicured feet wrapped around it, latched onto each other like a padlock, pinning Paul down against her naked body. Ann covered her mouth to stifle her scream. Sheer terror covered her face and tears were forcing their way through her frowned eyes. But no facial expression Ann could ever muster up could express the horror Ann felt when she peered into the mirror and saw Winnie's cat eyes staring directly at her through the mirror from around Paul's shoulder. She gripped Paul's waist while he buried his face in her pillow, stroking away, oblivious to what was actually happening at that moment. Winnie's eyes burned into Ann as it seemed Satan's would. They even seemed to smile. Mission accomplished, they said. Ann backed away from the bedroom door without even touching it, her hand still over her mouth. Now It seemed as if she were in a horror movie. As if she had been watching it from the safety of her living room and all of a sudden found herself catapulted into the scene, living it instead of watching it. She backed into the hall until she felt the wall behind her, then turned and ran out leaving the heavy iron gate wide open. She jumped into the cab and rode home. She wanted to scream, she wanted to cry. But she couldn't. Instead she changed into her uniform and got to the coffee shop just after eleven. "Ann, can I talk to you?" her boss asked while she placed a fresh pot of coffee on the warmer.

"Sure." She was only a couple of minutes late. Maybe he sensed something was wrong and was going to tell her to take the night off. That would be a blessing. She was moving around the coffee shop like a zombie. Her nerves were in knots. She could certainly use the evening off for a change.

"Ann. I'm really sorry, but business has been slow lately. Especially at night, so we're going to have to let you go. We really only need one waitress at night and, well, you're the low man on the totem pole...I'm sorry, Ann. You're a good worker. I wish there was something I could do."

"Don't worry about it," Ann said. "I kind of needed the night off anyway."

CHAPTER TWENTY-THREE

The room spun in several directions above Dorisse's head and her temples throbbed after each turn. She blinked and squinted, trying to make the room stop, but it only slowed down a bit and her temples continued to ache. Her eyes hadn't made out any distinct figures in the room, only dark shapes and a pale background.

A large hand shook her by the shoulder, wobbling her body like a marionette. Her neck and face hurt with each movement. She felt terrible. What had happened? Where was she? She thought hard through her pounding temples. She was . . . at Mike's house and . . . the door, she'd opened the front door. Oh God, where was she? The large hand palmed her entire shoulder and shook harder. The dark shapes began to sharpen into furniture and the background into pale, green walls. A wide, muscular arm attached to the giant hand that shook her so violently came into view. Her eyeballs hurt as she moved them upward to look at him, so she moved her neck up instead, and even that was painful. She followed the arm up to a tall, broad-shouldered man who wore an expression like granite. His herculean frame was clothed in a giant dark suit that blocked Dorisse's view of the room as he stepped in front of her. She tried to form her lips to speak, only to find them numb and painful. The man removed his hand and peered down at Dorisse.

He spoke in a deep, husky, animal-like voice, "Once again, honey, where is he?" His expression remained hard and his words were as stiff as his thin, wide lips. Gold sparkled from inside his mouth.

"I . . . I," she put her hand up to her forehead in confusion.

"Where is your boyfriend, huh? Where's Mike?" He got louder and grabbed her upper arm, jerking her face toward him. Dorisse's mouth hung open and tried to say something.

"He has a package he's supposed to deliver to us," the man said a little deeper. He leaned down toward Dorisse and held her arm tightly. The gold tooth blinded her like the sun reflecting

Leaving Basile

off of a mirror.

"He . . . he's at work," Dorisse said with much effort.

The broad-shouldered man stood up straight and then broke out into a deep, wicked laughter. The edges of his jaw expanded like a cobra's. His teeth looked like they could chew through steel, like a pit bull's. The gold tooth sparkled and flickered mockingly as he laughed.

"At work?" His laugh tapered off, but an evil grin still plastered his face. "If he were at work *you* wouldn't be here." He bent over again, now face to face with Dorisse, "Where can we find him? We just want our package. We ain't gonna hurt him. But if you don't tell us where we can find him so we can get our package," he began to clench his teeth as he spoke, "then *you* will get hurt," He looked straight into Dorisse's eyes with his beady ones, "real, real bad." He stared at her, switching his monstrous gaze from one of her eyes to the other. Then without any type of forewarning, he stood up straight, swung back his large hand and slapped her across her face with the back of it. She fell from the chair she was seated in and lay sprawled on the thinly carpeted floor. She kept her eyes tightly shut. It felt like he had hit her with a brick instead of his open hand. Her head seemed to spin completely around on her neck.

"Maybe that'll help you think a little," she heard his grating voice say.

"Should I tie her up?" For the first time Dorisse realized there had been someone else in the room, another man.

"No. I don't think she's stupid enough to try to go anywhere. We'll leave her alone to think . . . for now."

"Ok. I'll park outside."Dorisse heard the door shut but she didn't move. She lay on the carpet and began to cry. She buried her face in the fold of her arm and cried hard as saliva and tears formed two puddles in the crease of her arm. Package? What were they talking about? What did they want from Mike? What was he mixed up in? Did Mike work with these men? Where? He had never really told Dorisse what kind of work he did. She had never thought to ask. Business, he had always said. He had business to take care of.

The thin, worn carpet had a damp, rotten odor that made Dorisse feel nauseated, but she didn't have the energy to pull herself up from it. She opened her eye a crack. Dorisse wiped her nose with the back of her hand and a streak of dark blood spread across it. She sniffed in and the salty taste drained into her throat. She closed her eyes again, covered her bloody nose with her hand and cried harder. Dorisse's body ached terribly. They must have thrown her into the car while she was unconscious and driven her to this horrible place. They had actually thrown her into the trunk of the car and she'd bumped around inside like a piece of luggage as they drove to a seedy motel where the manager never asked questions. She lifted her aching head and looked around. It was dark outside and the ugly room seemed even scarier with the dark shadows that stretched across the walls. A fresh drop of blood fell from her nostril and landed on her right hand. She laboriously pulled herself from the floor, aching with every movement, and looked around for the bathroom. The small room she stood in had nothing in it except for a bed and one nightstand with an old tattered lamp on it. The bed was nothing more than a mattress and box spring stacked on the floor and its shabby spread made it look less inviting than the bare mattress would have. The old carpet's intertwining pattern was worn off in spots near the bed and the front door, and reappeared as huge winding cracks in the corroded green walls. A fading picture of a child and dog, both with huge, sad eyes hung over the bed and stared down at Dorisse. She'd be sad too if she had to hang on these walls, she thought. She crept toward the window and peeked out of it at an angle. A long, brown, older model Mercedez Benz sat in the parking lot facing her room with a man in its driver's seat. The license plates first three letters ironically read B-A-D. Yea, Dorisse thought, they were bad alright. The plates must've been a warning to other drivers. Don't blow your horn at these guys. Just pull over and let them pass. The man in the driver's seat was motionless except for the slow rise and fall of his shoulders as he breathed. She moved her eyes around the parking lot. The building enclosed the parking area leaving a narrow driveway to the street outside. From her corner motel room she had no view of the street. Only of the rest of the motel, which was painted a sickly shade of orange, the color of a piece of rotten fruit. She had no idea where she was. She listened for a moment but only heard the sound of distant car horns and a faint, whistling wind. She looked back at the man, decided he was asleep, and drew back into the dismal room.

  Dorisse walked toward a partially opened door that she suspected to be the bathroom. She felt along the wall for a light switch and clicked it on. A dim, yellow bulb that hung loose on

Leaving Basile

a wire from the ceiling barely lit up the small room. A group of startled cockroaches scattered throughout the small room and disappeared between cracks in the bile-green walls. Dorisse walked toward the mirror over the sink and almost screamed at the hideous sight she saw. A swollen, black and blue mess where her face used to be. Bluish-purple crescents shadowed her edematous eyes and crusted blood encircled her nostrils. Her lips were swollen to twice their normal size. She pulled away and gasped in shock through pillowed lips at her reflection. Through the brown blood Dorisse could see that her nose was crooked. She started to cry again and slowly reached to turn the water on. The porcelain sink was stained black and brown and one last cockroach made his way across the peeling faucet. Dorisse jerked her hand away at his surprise appearance and waited for his leisurely exit. The cold water stung as she patted it onto her battered face, and she looked back into the mirror. The yellow bulb swung back and forth and she could see the reflection of the sad eyed child looking at her from the other room. Tears spilled out of her eyes and made their way through the water on her face. She could feel a familiar tickling in her nose and a drop of blood splashed into the sink. She pinched her nose, held her head back and headed toward the bed. A dust cloud emerged from the musty spread as Dorisse laid down and coughed through her tears. She stared at a moldy water stain on the ceiling as she squeezed her nose and swallowed the blood that drained into her throat. The broad-shouldered man would be back, she thought. She knew it, and she had nothing to tell him. She didn't know where Mike was. The man would end up killing her. She could tell. His eyes were hard and ruthless. She could see he had no remorse for his actions. He could kill her with his bare hands, she thought. He could crack her head open like a coconut and leave the jagged pieces on the motel room floor for the housekeeper to come sweep up the next day like a broken vase. Dorisse would be stupid to lie there and wait for him to return. She had to leave before he came back. She had to get away.

    Ann stood in the middle of her dark living room and stared into the blackness of the apartment. Paul. That stupid son-of-a-bitch. Ann really wished he were dead. If someone had walked into that door right then and told her Paul was dead, she would have hoped it was a slow painful death, and that he had suffered endlessly. Ann felt a hatred she'd thought she was incapable of feeling toward another human being. A vicious, heartless anger. She stood in the middle of the room and her anger built up slowly the more she thought about it. She pictured Winnie's legs wrapped tightly around his back. She remembered Winnie's evil gaze in the mirror. Ann's face tightened and she breathed heavily. Her hazel eyes squinted in the dark. She didn't know if she wanted to cry from hurt or scream from anger. The two emotions tugged at her throat until she felt that she was going to explode.

    She picked up a wooden chair and flung it across the room. It crashed into the wall and snapped in two like a wooden pencil. She picked up the seat and banged it against the floor, cursing and screaming with each strike until the chair was kindling for the fireplace. She then turned toward the kitchen table and swept her arms across it. A full glass of water smashed against the wall. Bottles and dishes flew everywhere. She then lifted the table by its edge and flipped it onto its side. She flung the chairs out of her way one by one and headed toward the bedroom. She opened the closet and yanked each one of Paul's garments out of the closet and onto the floor. She kicked through the tangled clothes and hangers and snatched the spread off of their bed, then the blankets then the sheets and wrestled them all to the floor. She tried to shove the bed but couldn't. Ann then built up an enormous amount of strength and leaned against the bed with all her might. She screamed and moved the bed from one end of the room to the other and there she broke into tears. Ann lay on the floor next to the bed where she and Paul slept, amongst piles of clothes and blankets, and cried an endless ocean of tears. She grasped the mattress between her fists as she wailed and tried to cry the pain away. It didn't go away though. It stuck in her throat the way it did when she had wanted to see Paul so badly in Baton Rouge, when she deceived her husband night after night for him, when she rode on a bus, pregnant and alone, two thousand miles to this giant city by the bay to get away from him. She had never known this kind of pain until she met Paul.

    He's not going to win this fight, Ann thought. I won't let him. Now I have nothing else to lose. Ann picked up the phone, called a taxi and headed back to Winnie's apartment.

    "Who is he? A John Doe?"

    "No. He has I.D." The emergency room intern opened the wallet for the medical social worker to see. "Edward Broussard.

Leaving Basile

No local phone numbers, though. There's a number in Port Allen, Louisiana. A couple of addresses in somewhere called Basile, Louisiana. No phone numbers there."

"Okay. I'll call the number in Port Allen."

"You'd better get started. This guy isn't doing very well."

"He looks awful! What's wrong with him?"

"Upper G.I. hemorrhage."

"Jesus! His belly looks like he's eight month pregnant!"

"Ascites," the intern answered. "Fluid in his abdomen. We'll have to run a few diagnostic studies on him. In the mean time, try to get some family on him, would you?"

"Consider it done." The medical social worker took Edward's wallet back to his office and called the number in Port Allen, Edward and Ann's old apartment. Disconnected. The only other thing he had to go on was a general delivery address in Basile, Louisiana. A Mrs. Erma Thibideaux. No phone number though. He got directory assistance for Basile. "Do you have a listing for a Mrs. Erma Thibideaux?"

"In Basile?" The heavy southern accent asked him unbelievingly.

"Yes."

"Ain't too many telephones in Basile, sir. Not no residences no how."

"How about the post office? Do *they* have a telephone?"

"Just a minute." The operator answered.

"Jesus! Where am I calling? Hooterville?" The social worker said aloud to himself.

"Here's your number, sir."

"Thank you." He wrote the number down and called it. "Yes, hello. Do you happen to know how I can reach a Mrs. Erma Thibideaux. She's a . . ."

"Hold on." The voice cut him off and yelled to someone in the background. "Hey, John. Go run and get Erma Thibideaux. Tell her she got a phone call here. Hold on," the voice said into the receiver again. He held on to the phone for at least ten minutes before he heard fumbling and soon a voice spoke into the receiver.

"Yea. Who's dis?"

"Mrs. Erma Thibideaux?"

"Yea?"

"Do you know Mr. Edward Broussard?"

"Yea. I know him."

155

"He's here in San Francisco in the hospital and we're trying to notify his family, if possible. Are you, or do you know where we can reach his immediate family, Mrs. Thibideaux?"

"In de hospital? Whas wrong wit him?" Mrs. Thibideaux put her hand over her heart. It was beating fast. "He hurt? Someting happen to him out de?"

"Yes. The doctor's aren't quite sure what yet. They're running some tests on him right now. Are you related to him?"

"No, I ain't, but I can get in touch wit his wife. She der in San Francisco."

"Could you do that for us please and give her this telephone number?"

"Yea. She der . . . in San Francisco. I give it to her"

"Wonderful. Thank you so much, Ma'am."

I had to call half way across the country to get to a relative right here in the city, he thought. Oh, well. At least he has someone close by. By the time someone would've come over from Bumfuck, Louisiana, he'd probably have kicked. Poor guy. He thought about Edward's appearance and shook his head. Hope he makes it.

CHAPTER TWENTY-FOUR

The first thing Mike had to do was get rid of the red Mercedez. It would draw attention on Third Street like a naked woman in a prison courtyard. Mike drove back toward his house. He would exchange the Mercedez for his own Chevy Impala. The Impala wasn't that great to look at, but it had functioned as a faithful means of transportation for Mike for many years. Its smoke-grey body was long and heavy with a wide, light blue stripe stretched out along each side. It looked like a dark rain cloud in a stormy sky. The grill stretched across the front like a big chrome smile. It was the kind of car that easily blended into the background. He could park that old thing *inside* the pool hall and no one would notice.

Mike drove the Mercedez into his garage and parked it next to the Impala. He took the elevator from the garage up to the tenth floor and entered the apartment from the hallway through the side door into the kitchen. He would have to explain to Dorisse that he had a bit more work to finish and he'd be back in a few hours. He hated to disappoint her but this was the kind of job that couldn't go unfinished. Once it was over, Mike thought, he and Dorisse would have a long talk about what it would be like having a police detective for a boyfriend.

"Ha," Mike laughed sarcastically. "Never a dull moment."

"Dorisse." Mike stood in the hall and yelled back toward the bedroom. "Dorisse." He peeked into the kitchen. It was unusually quiet in the apartment. Even more quiet then when no one was there, it seemed to him. Mike sensed something was wrong,. He pulled his forty-five out and turned toward the living room. Mike stopped abruptly when he saw the remains of the front door. It hung open from one hinge. A splatter of blood was strewn across its white surface and pieces of splintered wood hung from its frame like loose teeth. Mike walked slowly toward the dreadful sight. "Oh God, they've been here," Mike said. He turned and walked, then ran toward his bedroom. He burst through the bedroom door, picked up the telephone and dialed Louis' number at work.

"Sorry. Not here," an unsympathetic voice said.

"Please have him call Mike Branigan . . . right away!" Mike slammed the phone down and opened his closet door. He pulled a shoebox out from the middle of two others and placed it on his bed. His covers were still disheveled from Dorisse's late awakening. Mike removed a short, silver-toned gun from the shoebox. He pulled back on the slide of the thirty-two caliber automatic to chamber a round and shoved the gun into his belt against his back. Mike replaced the empty shoebox in the closet and walked over to his dresser. He pulled the bottom dresser drawer completely out of the cabinet and reached down onto the floor inside. He took out a beige leather ankle holster and his five-shot, Smith and Wesson revolver. The "Chief's Special", they called it. It was also Mike's special. His back up weapon. It wasn't a gun used for long distance shots, but for a gun small enough to wear on your ankle, it had the power of a thirty-two. At closer range, it could blow a nice sized hole in someone. He snapped it into its ankle holster, pulled his pants leg down and headed for the garage. If Dorisse was hurt—Mike's heart ached at the probable thought, he would never forgive himself, and whoever was responsible . . . was a dead man.

Stubby's was a hole in the wall, as were most of the establishments on Third street. Only three people were inside, two guys shooting a game of pool and a woman with lavender crushed velvet shorts and spike-heeled shoes who sat on a bar stool chewing gum and smoking a Kool's Filter King cigarette. Mike sat three stools away from her. He crossed his leg and felt the "special" clinging to his ankle inside its holster. Two twenty dollar bills sat on the edge of the pool table as one of the men carefully aimed his cue at the white ball. No words were spoken between them men as they played. The woman chewed her gum and smoked and never even looked Mike's way. Every other chew made a popping sound like a cap gun that irritated Mike intensely. He turned his back to the pool game and leaned over the bar until he heard the cues being replaced in the rack. Mike looked to one side and saw one of the men pick up the bills, fold them in half and push them into his front pants pocket. He headed toward the front door. The other headed toward the bar. Mike looked at each man. They were both pretty big, over six feet tall. He decided to stick with the one who had lost his money. He approached the bar, sat next to the woman and pulled a cigarette pack from the breast pocket of the black leather jacket he wore. He placed the cigarette between his lips, balled up the empty pack and smashed it on the counter. Mike didn't want to stare inside the guy's mouth, looking for the gold tooth Sam had told him about, so he thought he'd listen for a minute to see if the guy handed out any information on his own. The man sighed a few times and smoked his cigarette in silence. The woman slid from her stool and disappeared into the ladies room at the far corner of the room.

"Tough luck, huh?" Mike nodded toward the man.

"What?" The man looked at Mike.

"I said, tough luck. The game." Mike tilted his head toward the pool table."

"Yea, right." No reflection in his mouth from the light.

"Say, uh. . .maybe I can help you out," Mike said. This caught the man's attention. "and maybe you can help *me* out, too." Mike pulled forty dollars from his pocket and put it on the counter. The man continued to look at Mike, but said nothing. Mike continued. "I'm looking for a man named Jake." Mike paused. No reaction from the man. "You know him?"

"Who wants to know?" The man sat up straight now.

"Mikey. I have a package for him. We were supposed to meet today but, uh. . .we didn't."

The man eyed Mike from head to toe then put his cigarette out. He pocketed the forty and stood up. "Follow me." Mike left his car parked on the street and climbed in the car with the man from Stubby's.

"So, uh . . . Chuck, " Mike paused to see if his guess was correct, "Where's Jake," Mike said as they rode together.

"If you want me to take you to him keep your mouth shut and I will." Poor old Chuck was too stupid to ask Mike if he had the package with him. He didn't even ask Mike how he had known his name, but Mike kept a vigilant eye on Chuck nonetheless. It didn't take that much intelligence to kill.

They pulled into the parking lot of the motel and Mike saw the brown Mercedes parked in the lot. Chuck got out and walked over to the car. He leaned over, tapped on the car window and seemed to startle the man behind the wheel awake. They talked for a minute, the man got out and walked up to the motel office.

"It'll be a minute," Chuck said into Mike's window. "Can you step out of the car and take off your jacket?"

Mike looked up at Chuck's wide face. "What for?"

"Cause, Jake don't like guns, that's why."

"What makes you think . . ."

"Just take off your jacket, would you. Make life a little easier for the both of us, huh?"

Mike stepped out of the car slowly and stood between the car and the open door. Chuck slipped his large hands in the sides of Mike's jacket, easily removed the forty-five and the thirty-two and shoved them into his own belt. He and Mike looked each other in the eyes for a few seconds but said nothing and Mike got back into the car. Chuck walked around the car, retrieved his seat behind the wheel and rested his hands behind his head. Mike watched the other guy return from the office and get back into the brown Mercedes. He looked back at Chuck, who had closed his eyes and his mouth was slowly falling open. These guys must get some of their best sleep behind the wheels of cars, Mike thought, and stared around the parking lot at the peach-colored building for at least twenty minutes until another car drove up. The man got out and walked over to their car. He glanced at Chuck's snoozing face but was staring at Mike. Mike could tell, even through the dark glasses the man wore, Mike could tell.

He reached into to Chuck's open window and slapped Chuck in the back of the head. Chuck jumped he same way the other guy had when Chuck woke him up.

"Hey . . . hey Jake." Chuck sat up straight. "This here's Mikey. Says he has business with you."

Jake stood at least six-three, Mike thought, and as Sam had said, he was a *big* guy. The dark suit he wore made him look solid, like a steel vault. Jake stared into the car for several minutes. Finally, he said, "Follow me," in a deep, monotone voice.

Even if the small window in the bathroom hadn't been on the first floor Dorisse would have jumped anyway. She could hear the deep, heavy pounding of her heart as she perched herself on the ledge. Everything seemed pronounced and exaggerated. It couldn't have been more than about eight feet from the window sill to the cement ground below, but it seemed like she was bailing out of an airplane without a parachute. The skydive placed her on the balls of her feet and her knees bent on impact. She fell forward but caught herself with her fingertips. A projectile splatter of blood from her nose sprayed the ground in front of her. It couldn't have been more painful if

Leaving Basile

she *had* jumped from an airplane. It seemed as though her entire skeleton had crumbled on impact and the broken pieces lay in the lower half of her body, poking her tissue with its splintered edges. And now, in addition to the rest of her body, the soles of her feet stung like they had been slapped with wooden paddles...hard. But she had to get away.

Dorisse tiptoed from the back alleyway onto a quiet city street and began walking. The crisp chill in the night air bit into the deep bruises in her face and her feet still stung with each tiptoe of a step as she struggled to carry herself up the deserted street, but her mind wasn't centered on her physical suffering. She listened intensely, trying to take in every sound that was made within miles. Her ears hung on every thump that might be a footstep, and every car that approached the street she walked on. Her sore legs barely supported her body but she had to get away, to escape. A gripping spasm accompanied each step, shooting from her neck down into the sidewalk. Her face began to feel completely numb. It seemed as though another face had been placed on top of hers and her own was buried somewhere beneath this swollen, bloody mask she wore. An occasional drop of fresh, thick blood fell from her right nostril, timed to land on her right foot as it stepped forward.

Although she had walked for hours, she had gotten nowhere, as if the sidewalk moved against her steps. Maybe it moved back two steps for every step she took so she was only half as far as she should have been, and each step was too loud, far too loud. It seemed they might drown out the sound of an approaching car that would complete the job that had been started.

The inside of her head spun around in its battered shell. She staggered on her already unsteady feet and reached out for some imaginary crutch. As she steadied herself in mid space she began to sob, quietly talking to herself.

"Please," she pleaded, "Please help me. Please, please, please . . .," she continued to cry, rocking back and forth, her pleas turning into silent lip gestures.

Dorisse's sobs were abruptly halted by the sound of a car's motor. An old car, coughing and wheezing as it drove along, followed by and a scraping metal sound which got louder as the car came closer. She turned into a dark alley to escape the street lights that glared upon her. She coughed a thick, mucousy cough, tears diluting the blood from her nose. Her dark pupils had instantly dilated like a cat's, trying to adjust to the alley's black spaces ahead, but failed to judge distance. She ran into a stucco wall, her knees finally gave way, and she fell. The cold concrete caught her as small pebbles and broken pieces of green glass embedded themselves into her back. She lay on the painful alley bed, unable to move, but felt a presence. Now she knew it was too late. She hadn't gotten away after all. Dorisse tried to pry open her puffy eyelids to see the face she knew awaited her, but she couldn't. She parted her swollen lips to scream but only a wet gurgle came through as old blood drained down through her nose into the back of her throat. She fought to breathe.

As Dorisse's young body lay silently in the night, the florescent full moon slowly moved into the alley, casting a blue highlight along her dark hair. Am I dead? Is this what it feels like to be dead, she thought? She could think. She could even see now. She tried to move her hands but they lay like anvils on the ground beside her. She couldn't budge. She tried to pull herself from the floor of the alley but no part of her body cooperated with her attempts. Out of the corner of her eye she could see the movement of a brown spider making a path across the alley heading for her left cheek but she was helpless, and surrendered to be his walkway to the other side. The hairy tentacle tickling her face was unbearable. Dorisse turned her eyes to try to stare the spider away and she saw it. The dark suit.

"Oh, no," she cried. The streets were abandoned except for the shadow that stood over her. When the large hand landed on her shoulder she knew she hadn't gotten away. It shook her like a puppet as it had done before. It was too late to try to run now. She couldn't any more. The gargantuan hands reached for her thin neck and then wrapped themselves around it and began to squeeze, overlapping each other more and more as they squeezed harder and harder. Dorisse felt her face began to turn hot from her neck up. All bloodflow to and from her brain slowly ceased, turning her fair complexion into a deep shade of eggplant to blend with the midnight sky and camaflauge her swollen body against the night.

Ann got out of the taxi and asked it to wait. "This won't take long," she said in a hard, serious voice. She walked through the iron gate that swung open the way it had an hour earlier. Winnie had planned this whole thing, she thought. That's why the gate

Leaving Basile

was opened and the door was unlocked. That devious little bitch. Ann walked quicker and leaped the steps two at a time. She hesitated only for a brief moment before she knocked on Winnie's front door. She heard high heeled footsteps heading for the door and Winnie's face graced the doorway.

"Hello Ann," she smiled slightly.

Ann pushed her aside. Paul sat in the living room in his underwear with his bare feet stretched out on Winnie's couch. At Ann's entrance he jumped to attention as she walked straight over to him. He formed his mouth to say Ann's name as she balled up her skinny fist and poured all her anger into a championship right cross, bouncing Paul back on the sofa. Ann then turned and headed back toward the front door where Winnie still stood holding it open, eyes widened from Ann's attack.

Ann looked up at Winnie's perfect face as she backed away. "*That's* what I learned from wrestling alligators. Would you like a personal demonstration?"

Winnie huddled further away behind the door. Ann looked over at Paul cradling his bloody mouth on the sofa and Winnie wincing behind the door, and shook her head. "You two deserve each other," she said looking at them contemptuously, and walked back to her waiting cab.

Jake and Chuck walked behind Mike as the watchdog from the brown Mercedes opened the motel door with a key he had removed from his pocket. The four men entered the dark, empty room. Jake nodded toward the bathroom and the watchdog opened it entered, and returned to the main room with a nervous, frightened look on his face.

"Where is she!?" Jake shouted at him.

Mike lurched toward Jake, but Chuck already had a pistol barrel resting in the small of Mike's back. Jake and the other man had both reached inside their jackets but stopped when Mike put both hands slowly in the air.

"You moron," Jake said to the watchdog How stupid can . . ." A small knock on the motel room door interrupted him. Jake peeked through the curtains and opened the door just enough to let the person in . It was Louis. He walked in and pulled a revolver from inside his jacket.

"Louis! Thank God you're . . . " Mike began to let his hands fall to his sides.

"Get those hands back up, buddy." Louis pointed the

revolver at Mike. Mike stared at Louis in disbelief. Not Louis. God dammit, not Louis, Mike thought as he stared at his friend. His friend.

Louis looked at Mike. His expression was cold and flat. "Sorry, Mike." Louis said dryly. Chuck buried his gun a little deeper into the flesh in Mike's back and he slowly raised his hands again but stared at Louis with unblinking eyes. Louis returned his revolver to its holster and sat in a chair in the corner.

Jake turned back toward the watchdog. Jake's face had turned into furrows of frowns and grimaces, and for the first time Mike saw the gold tooth sparkle in his mouth like a cobra's venom.

"You stupid idiot!" Jake said, the gold tooth gritted against the one below it. "How did you let that bitch get away!?"

The watchdog shrugged. "She must've gone through the window, Jake." He backed away a bit. "Hh . . . how could I have known. She . . . she didn't make a sound, Jake. I swear it! I . . . I swear it, Jake." The watchdog must've known it was coming, and sure enough Jake kicked him between the legs . . . hard. The watchdog fell to his knees and cupped his crotch with both hands. He fell another level from his knees onto his side and lay motionless, whimpering and moaning on the floor. Jake swung his large leg back and kicked him again in the side. Mike felt Chuck's hand drift down a bit toward his own crotch, feeling some of the watchdog's pain. With Jake's back now to Mike and Chuck sympathizing with his buddy, Mike thought quickly. He ducked and grabbed Chuck's hand so that his gun flew up into the air and landed on the other side of the bed. Mike, still bent over, grabbed for his "special" from the ankle holster. He felt his hand on its handle and pulled it out of its holster. Mike was quick . . . but Jake was quicker. He leaned over Mike's back and hit him on the back of the head right above his neck. Jake's balled up fist felt like a steel mallet to Mike. Mike fell to the floor and made one last attempt at reaching for the special, then lost consciousness.

"Get up! Both of you!" Jake yelled at his two henchmen. Louis sat in a chair in the corner, laughing and shook his head at the whole scene. Jake peeked out the front door. "Hurry up, stupid. Carry this guy out and put him in the trunk!" Chuck grabbed Mike's shoulders and the watchdog limped to pick up Mike by the ankles.

Leaving Basile

    Jake stared at Mike's limp body as they carried him out the door, blood dripping from the back of his head. Jake had killed three people in the past with his bare hands. He had gotten a pretty good thump on this guy, too. He'd felt Mike's skull give way a little on impact. He'd even hurt his hand this time. He rubbed it on its side. No. By the time they got Mike where they were taking him, he'd have bled to death through his cranial artery, Jake thought, or at least enough to put his brain out of commission. Jake smiled and nodded with satisfaction. "This guy's a cop fellows. Take him to the cop graveyard." Jake and Louis began to laugh in unison.

    As Chuck and the watchdog drove through the city, Mike slowly opened his eyes inside the trunk. His head ached and the motion from inside the dark, cramped trunk was making him sick. The two drove to the city's dump and unloaded Mike on top of a pile of rubbish. They covered him with smelly, rotten garbage as Mike held his eyes tightly shut. Then they drove off.

    Mike lay still until he heard the car's motor trail off in the distance. He could see absolutely nothing in the darkness he was in, but the reek of garbage was overwhelming. Where could he be? The blackness of his surroundings was solid and the odor...it was indescribable. Mike's equilibrium swayed as he sat up slowly. He still couldn't see a thing and his brain seemed to swell with each deep pulsation. He positioned himself on all fours and began to crawl. He pawed his way through pieces of paper and wet, squishy things. He banged his knees into hard, sturdy items and clanged into what may have been a tin can or two. Mike finally found himself in a clear area and pulled himself to his feet. He walked out a ways, his hands waving through the darkness, but still, no light. The foul stench was lessened as Mike walked. He stopped for a moment and listened for familiar sounds. Excruciating pain throbbed from the back of his head and radiated throughout his entire skull. A train's whistle and some barking dogs echoed from some ways away. He felt a slight breeze which carried the fetid odor back within his reach. A breeze. He walked again with his hands out in front of him and reached out and touched something. It was a fence. A chain-link fence. He was outdoors, but... Mike put his hands over his eyes. He blinked heavily and looked up toward the sky, then down, then out around him. He touched the fence again. Jesus! Mike frowned and gasped from fear.

    He couldn't see.

* * *

The hands moved Dorisse back and forth and a voice spoke out, "Hey, wake up." But it wasn't the broad shouldered man's grimy voice, or his watchdog, it was a woman's voice. Dorisse opened her eyes to face the wide, pleasant face of a young woman.

"Hey!" Dorisse's terrified expression scared the woman. "Its okay! You're alright, honey. You were just having a bad dream."

Dorisse slowly began to focus on the source of the voice and stared at the woman's face for a moment. The cold cement was now a soft, warm mattress and the full moon had become a bright, spherical lamp at her bedside. Dorisse looked at the woman again and tried desperately to orient herself.

"Oh, God." Dorisse finally became aware of her surroundings. The bed she was in was warm and clean and dry and she finally realized that she wasn't on the alley floor. She *had* been having a nightmare. She relaxed into her pillow and breathed a sigh into the air.

"Here, have some cold water." The woman held a glass up to Dorisse's lips and she eagerly puckered them around the edge of the glass. But instead of the cool, quenching drink she expected, a throbbing pain radiated through her mouth. She reached up and touched her lips and was horrified to feel two large flaps of swollen flesh that were numb to her touch. Her throat felt raw. She turned her head toward a mirror that was across the room and stared at the same hideous, purple and blue mess that she had seen in the motel room mirror. She leaned away and gasped in shock through pillowed lips. She grabbed the woman, burying her face in her chest. It wasn't a dream.

"Don't worry, honey. It'll be all right." Dorisse began to cry in the woman's arms.

"Where am I?"

"You're in the hospital, honey. Don't worry. They're taking good care of you. Before you know it, you'll be good as new. Look at me, I got a broken arm. But they fixed it for me. Don't cry, sweetie." The woman softly patted the frightened young girl on her back for comfort. "Do you want me to get your nurse?"

"No, thank you." Dorisse sniffled. "I'll be alright. How'd I get here?"

"I don't know. What happened to you? Do you remember?"

"Yes, I . . .," Dorisse frowned and put her hand up to her head.

"You don't have to talk about if you don't want to. It looks like it was pretty bad."

"Yes." Dorisse tried to remember what happened to her after she fell in the alley. The woman put the glass of water on Dorisse's night stand and got back into her own bed next to Dorisse's.

"Mine was bad, too. I broke my arm." She pointed to the white plaster cast on her left arm hardened at a right angle. She looked over at Dorisse, who sat up in her bed looking like she had just acquired an acute case of amnesia. "Are you sure you're alright, honey?" This one may have had a few screws knocked loose, she thought.

"Yea. I . . . I think so." Dorisse was still trying desperately to remember the rest of what had happened to her. It was coming back slowly, bit by bit as the woman talked.

"I broke up with my boyfriend at first because, well . . . he drank a lot. He had stopped drinking, though, he said, and we got back together. I believed him too. I think maybe he did, but the first time he got drunk, this is what happened." She pointed to her cast again. "My friend Ann tried to warn me, but I didn't listen. I should've listened to her, you know, but some things, you have to learn for yourself, you know?"

"Yea." Dorisse looked up into the woman's red hair not hearing a word of her story. "Ann was only looking out for my best interest. I miss her, too. But, she has a family of her own, you know. The sweetest little girl you'd ever want to see, and a boyfriend to die for. Yes, I'll have to call her sometime. Ann Fruge´ is probably one of the best friends I've ever had."

"Did you say Ann Fruge'? Oh my God!" Dorisse started to cry.

"Do you know Ann?"

"We grew up together . . . in Basile." Dorisse's face hurt when she frowned.

"Are you Dorisse? Sweetie, I've heard an awful lot about you." Liz reached into her nightstand and took out a box of chocolates to munch on as she told Dorisse about how she and Ann had met.

There was a small knock outside of the girls closed hospital door and two tall, suited men entered Liz and Dorisse's hospital room and walked over to Dorisse's bed. Liz got out of bed, walked over to Dorisse's bed, sat down next to her and looked up at the men.

"Miss Guillory?" A tall, dark-skinned Black man addressed Dorisse. Her heart started beating frantically. Oh God, it was them! The men from the motel had found her and sent their gorillas to the hospital to get her.

"Who are you? What do you want?" She looked back and forth between the two men and huddled close to Liz.

The dark man reached inside his jacket and Dorisse's eyes grew in anticipatory fear. He pulled a wallet from his breast pocket and flipped it open toward Dorisse. A metallic glare flashed in her face as he announced his title to her. "Lieutenant Henderson. San Francisco Police Department. I'm with the narcotics division. This is Officer Williams. May we speak with you privately please?"

"I'd like for my friend to stay." Dorisse squeezed Liz's hand.

The officers looked at each other and nodded slightly. Lieutenant Henderson pulled up a chair to Dorisse's bed and Officer Williams handed him a picture. He held the picture in front of Dorisse.

"Miss Guillory, do you know this man?"

Dorisse looked at the picture and tears immediately filled her eyes. It was Mike. She nodded softly through her frowned face and closed her eyes to his handsome photograph. Liz handed her a tissue.

"Miss Guillory, this man is a police detective and we believe he's in trouble. He disappeared while working on an undercover assignment. You told the emergency room physician you were abducted from your home and the address you gave them was that of Detective Branigan."

Abducted? Dorisse remembered being knocked out at Mike's front door and waking up in the motel. Mike? A police detective? Dorisse put her hand to her mouth. Now she was really confused, but she remembered everything before that very clearly. "Yes," she answered Lieutenant Henderson. "We had just come back from Los Angeles the day before." The two policemen looked at each other knowingly again.

"So he made the connection," the Officer said to Lieutenant Henderson.

"Can you tell us exactly what happened, Miss Guillory?" Dorisse told them the whole story and described the two men to them. She told them as much as she could remember about the

Leaving Basile

motel and the surrounding location as the officer took notes.

"Is their anything else you can tell us about the men, Miss Guillory. Had you ever seen any of them before? Did you know them?"

"Of course not!"

"Did they call each other by name?" Dorisse shook her head back and forth and stared off into space, her forehead frowning like a child on the verge of tears.

"Bad." Dorisse said the single word like part of a baby's limited vocabulary. Officer Williams looked at Dorisse ruefully. Poor girl, he thought. They must really have traumatized her. She was in a childlike state.

"Bad." Dorisse repeated the word, but this time looked as though she had just remembered something she had been trying to think of all day.

"We know. They were bad, bad men," Officer Williams said consoling her.

"No," Dorisse said, her attention now back with them. Bad. B-A-D. The license plate. The letters were B-A-D." Dorisse looked back and forth between the two policemen. "Bad."

Officer Williams whipped out his notepad again and began writing. "What about the numbers? Do you remember them?"

Dorisse thought back to the brown car in the parking lot and remembered staring at the man behind the wheel through a round, chrome emblem. "No, but it was a Mercedes Benz." Officer Williams started writing again. "A big, brown one."

"That's wonderful, Miss Guillory. This will help us tremendously," Officer Henderson said. "Miss Guillory we'd like to move you to a private room, under protective custody."

Dorisse tightened her grip on Liz's hand. "No! I feel safer in the room with my friend." She looked at Liz and the two girls smiled at each other.

Well, then do you mind if we place a guard outside the door? There's no doubt these guys are looking for you. You can identify them, and the hospital wouldn't be a bad place for them to start."

"Sure." She nodded at them.

"Okay, Miss. Thank you for the information."

"Lieutenant?" Dorisse said. "Do you think Mike is alright?" Tears started building up again as she thought about the picture they had just shown her.

"We certainly hope so Miss." He looked at her tearful face

and walked back over to her. "Would you like to keep this?" Dorisse looked down and he held out the picture of Mike. She nodded and took the photo. She tried to smile at the suited policeman but just managed to squeeze out several more tears.

"Thank you very much, Miss Guillory, I'm sure we'll be back in touch. The guard will be outside. Miss," Lieutenant Henderson nodded at Liz and the two officers left.

Dorisse ran her thumb across Mike's face as she held his picture in her lap. She spoke to Liz without looking up. "Liz, Mike showed me something I wasn't even sure existed in this world. I guess I must've known in my heart that it did exist, or else I would have never left Basile. But I used to tell myself, when I was little, that there was a place where people celebrated the differences in each other. Where being different didn't mean being strange or weird. It meant being unique. Where people could feel proud about who they were. Mike showed me how to feel proud about who Dorisse is. He loves all the unusual things that make me, me. Not in spite of them. He didn't want me to keep quiet and try to blend in, he wanted to know more. Where did you come from? What are people there like? What makes them that way? What was it like in Basile? Knowing about other people makes him like that. Ignorance about other people is what causes prejudice. Now I know," she finally looked up at Liz and smiled a bit," now I know that if more people like Mike exist, then there's hope."

*   *   *

The intern and his attending surgeon pulled their bloody gowns off and stuffed them into the receptacle. Their gowns were covered with Edward's blood.

Leaving the operating room, the intern pulled his blue mask down from over his face. "How effective will this treatment be for him Dr. Patrick?" he asked the surgeon in charge.

"Well, an upper G.I. bleed from the esophagus is extremely serious because the bleeding can be very profuse. He could have bled to death out there on the street. Many of them do, since its caused by drinking and often they don't even realize they're bleeding. About a third of the individuals who experience this type of hemorrhage die from it. Fortunately, he came in before he exsanguinated."

"So we got to him in time with this procedure?"

"The sclerotherapy we just did stops the bleeding fine, but it has, say, a seventy percent chance of reoccurring. One of the vessels could reopen and start bleeding again. All we can do is monitor him well, keep him on diuretics for his ascites and check with the pathologist for the report on that liver specimen we sent. It's almost certain he's got a micro nodular cirrhosis."

"At his age?"

"Yes doctor. . .at his young age."

The young intern began writing orders for Edward in the recovery room and shook his head again as he reread Edward's date of birth on the chart. The patient was younger than him, he thought! He looked down at Edward. He looked ten years older. The intern looked over at the PAR nurse as she hooked Edward up to dozens of monitors and said, "*That's* what alcohol can do, Meg." They both looked down at Edward, at each other, and then continued with their work.

CHAPTER TWENTY-FIVE

"Ann?"

"Yes?" Ann spoke into the telephone receiver. "Hello? I can barely hear you?"

"I know. I think we got a bad connection."

"Mrs. Thibideaux!?" Ann smiled broadly. She hadn't talked to her in months.

"Yea."

"Mrs. Thibideaux, how's everything? What's going on out there?"

"Listen Ann," she interrupted, "I know where Edward is."

"What?" Ann's happy expression changed abruptly "Where!?"

"He in San Francisco City Hospital."

"What!? San Franc . . . In the hospital!? What. . .what happened?"

"He sick Ann. Real sick. You gotta go. You gotta go real soon. Da doctas found ma address on him and call me down de road. You gatta go, Ann. You gatta go na."

Ann hung up the phone. Oh my God. Edward. She couldn't believe it. After all this time, and he's in the hospital. This was just too much happening all at once. She ran and grabbed her purse and headed for the front door when the phone rang again.

"Ann?"

"Liz!"

"Ann, how are you?"

"I'm fine, Liz, but I was just walking out of the door. I just found out Edward is here in San Francisco at City Hospital. Can I call you back later."

"*I'm* at City Hospital."

"City Hospital? What're *you* doing there"

"I'm fine. But guess what? Another friend of yours is here- Dorisse."

"What? Dorisse? At City Hospital?" A million thoughts shot through Ann's mind at once. Edward, Dorisse and Liz all at City Hospital?

"Oh, Ann. I can't wait to see you. Dorisse is with her doctor right now. She can't wait to see you either." Liz smiled into the telephone receiver.

"What happened to Dorisse?"

"Its a long story. I'd better let her tell you. We're in room two-seventeen."

Ann put her hand on her forehead. "I'm on my way."

CHAPTER TWENTY-SIX

Dorisse stared at the white ceiling of the examining room as she lay on her back waiting for the doctor to arrive. A white cotton sheet was draped over her body and Mike's picture was tucked neatly into the pocket of her hospital gown. She placed her hand over her pocket absently, and traced the edges of the picture with her fingers. Dorisse pulled the sheet up under her chin and closed her eyes. Mike's face drifted into the darkness of her mind and his voice spoke in the silence. She could see his lips smile as he talked. They had spent so much time talking, learning about each other. Just in the short length of time they had spent together, Dorisse felt she knew him so well. She had spent so much time thinking about the two of them. He had grown to be a part of her. But there were so many more things she wanted to know. She wanted to know what a man so wonderful wanted in his life. What kinds of things made him happy? What kinds of things were important to him? What were the things he thought about everyday? She knew they must be magnificent things. Grand, brilliant, noble things. She wanted to ask him about his family, his work, his dreams, his feelings. But more than ever now, Dorisse wanted to ask Mike if he loved her.

"Dorisse? I'm Doctor Bernard." A young, Black man in a short white jacket was standing at her bedside. "Do you remember me? I came to see you in your room." He swung around a pair of wire rim glasses as he talked.

Dorisse nodded. She only remembered him once he mentioned that he had seen her. He had come into her room and examined her nose, looked inside her mouth and ordered a series x-rays of her face to be taken. Dorisse remembered the monstrous machine pointing at her face and then Dr. Bernard coming back to her room several hours later and holding the smoke color pictures of her skull up to the light over her bed. The pictures scared her. The teeth grinned a deathly white on their grey background. This was just a picture of how her face would look after she was dead, she thought. A death-ray. Dr. Bernard held up the x-ray and pointed to a small line on the bridge of her nose with a pencil. Her nose was broken, he had said.

"Well, I told you then, Dorisse," he put the glasses on and pushed them up with his forefinger, "that when the swelling went down, I'd fix it for you. Remember?" He pointed at Dorisse's crooked nose. "So that's what we'll do today. It'll be *as good as new*" He smiled and looked at her as if waiting for her to give the go ahead. Dorisse hadn't even thought about Doctor Bernard since then. When he had walked out of her room it was as if he had never come in. His visit disappeared into the place she had put all the other things that had happened to her since she was abducted from Mike's house. She could recall them if she wanted to, but they were all in her mind's dungeon. Where she sent all the unpleasant stuff. She looked up at Doctor Bernard. He had a pleasant, youthful face. Too youthful for a doctor, she thought. The other ones she had seen all looked about a hundred years old. But this one didn't look much older than a teenager. His glasses made him look a little older, though. Wiser, anyway. Dorisse nodded and tried to smile back at him. He patted her shoulder and walked out of the room.

Dorisse hadn't looked at her face in the mirror since that first day. She hadn't even thought about it. It was in her dungeon, but it slowly crept out as she waited for Doctor Bernard to return. The black and purple blotches that colored her face like abstract splashes of paint. Her lips, two balloons of flesh. The way her nose had made a sharp turn at it's midpoint so she could see it's tip without the mirror. She had also sent her career plans into her dungeon. She hadn't seen many models in those magazines with black eyes or crooked noses. But Doctor Bernard had said, she'd be as good as new . Those were his words.

Dorisse sat up just as Doctor Bernard and a nurse came into the room. The nurse began drawing up some medication in a syringe as Doctor Bernard washed his hands.

"Doctor? Will my nose be the same as it was before, I mean, before it was broken?"

Dr. Bernard removed her x-rays from a large manilla folder and placed them on a board on the wall and flipped a switch that lit them up from behind. He pointed to the small line he had shown her before.

"This is where your nose was broken. This is-if there is such a thing-the best place for a nose to be broken . . . on the suture line. In other words, the place where the bones are naturally fused together. So it will be easier to fit them back together. If it were broken here," he pointed below the line where Dorisse's fracture was, "the break would be irregular and would probably break into several pieces. We call that a comminuted fracture and those are more difficult to fix because there are more pieces to the puzzle, so to speak. Yours only has two pieces that just need to be snapped back into place." Dorisse flinched when he said 'snapped'. She looked away from the death-ray. It still frightened her.

"Doctor?

"Yes?"

"Do you have a mirror I can look in? Now, I mean. . .before you fix it." Doctor Bernard looked at Dorisse and his nurse turned to look at her too.

"Sure," he said after a moment and smiled. He reached into a drawer, pulled out a hand held mirror and handed it to Dorisse. He stood at her side as she stared blankly at her reflection. Her lips were back to their normal size and the bruises had gone from purple to pale shades of green and yellow. The swelling *had* gone down, but her nose was still as crooked as Lombard Street. She handed the mirror back to Doctor Bernard and leaned back on her elbows. "Doctor . . . start snapping."

Doctor Bernard winked at Dorisse and this was the first time she felt his smile was real. Not that smile he gave to all his patients because he had to be nice, but to her because she had given him the go ahead. Like he wouldn't have been happy unless she did. He helped her lay flat and the nurse wheeled a metal tray over to the head of the bed.

"We're going to give you some sedation," Doctor Bernard said to Dorisse, "and when you wake up, it'll all be over." He turned to the nurse.

The nurse began to inject the medication into the port in the line that was already taped into Dorisse's vein. The last thing Dorisse heard was Doctor Bernard's youthful voice, "See you when you wake up."

Leaving Basile

CHAPTER TWENTY-SEVEN

Ann held her purse in one hand and gripped the vertical, steel pole tightly with the other as she stood on the crowded bus heading for San Francisco City Hospital. She stood behind the driver, sandwiched between two old women and stared out the front window reading each street sign as the bus passed it. Her thin arm stretched in and away from the pole as the bus went over small hills and bumps. One of the old women had one of those pull carts with wheels filled with groceries that she had inadvertently parked on Ann's right foot. Ann pulled her foot from under it as she bent over to the busdriver's side.

"Excuse me. How much further before we get to City Hospital?" She spoke into his ear.

"Uh . . . ," the driver rubbed his chin in thought. A patch on the right shoulder of his uniform read, Safe Driver 15 years. "I'll say . . . around another two miles." He nodded, agreeing with his own estimate.

Ann stood up straight again. Okay he's a safe driver, but was he a quick one? Ann patted her foot impatiently at each red light. After about two seconds Ann figured the light was stuck and would have run it if she were driving, but Mr. *Safe Driver* here would probably sit there until doomsday before running it.

Mrs. Thibideaux hadn't told Ann what was wrong with Edward, but there was an urgency in her voice that Ann had never heard before. The man Ann had spoken to from the motel, she remembered, had said Edward was drunk and hadn't payed his bill. Maybe Edward had staggered out into the street and gotten hit by a car? No. Mrs. Thibideaux said he was real sick. She hadn't said he was hurt. What could it be, Ann thought? Well, he was hospitalized so it must be something serious. Maybe he had a disease of some sort. But Edward was young. Maybe he had some sort of cancer or rare blood disease. Maybe he was dying? Ann's anxiety continued to build. What if he had tried to kill himself? What if he tried to commit suicide because of what she had done to him? What if she was too late and he had succeeded? She covered her eyes with her free hand. Her other one was white from squeezing the metal pole so hard.

"City Hospital," the driver yelled out leaning back and the bus doors opened. "This is it ma'am." He said to Ann over his shoulder. She looked up, startled.

"Oh. Thank you." Ann released her grip on the pole and wiggled her fingers to start the circulation again. "Thank you very much." She stepped off the bus and walked up the walkway into the hospital.

Ann slowly turned into the intensive care unit, where the front desk had directed her. The brightly lit hallway was lined with wheeled carts and small tables on one side, and glass doors on the other. Each door was slid open. A single bed parked at an angle inhabited each room, and a single patient inhabited each bed. The monitors beeped and buzzed from each room in an unsynchronized pattern. Red, green and white lights flashed numbers and patterns from the dimness of the rooms as the patients lay in silence, some with a nurse at their side, some alone. Ann approached the nurses station. The young woman who sat behind the desk had just hung up the telephone.

"I'd like to see Mr. Edward Broussard, please. Ann said, in little more than a whisper.

"Are you related to him, Miss?"

"I'm his wife," Ann said. A quiver waved through her words.

"He's in room number nine." The young lady pointed to Ann's right.

Ann looked up at the numbers above the glassed in rooms as she walked. Seven, eight . . . Ann approached room number nine not knowing what to expect. Would she recognize him? What would he have to say to her? He hates me, Ann thought. I'm the reason he's here. Ann clutched her purse to her chest and slowly entered the room. A nurse stood at his bedside with her back to Ann. She turned around as Ann stopped at the doorway and smiled at Ann. She then hung a bag of clear fluid on a pole next to another bag of yellowish fluid. A bag of dark, red blood hung from another pole and carried the blood from the bag into Edward's veins. Ann stared at the nurse's back as she manipulated the bag onto the hook and walked out of the room. Ann's eyes followed her until she disappeared around the corner of the glass door. She would rather have looked at anything else at that moment besides Edward. But she knew

Leaving Basile

she couldn't avoid it now. He was lying there in the bed in front of her.

Ann clutched her bag as tightly as she had the pole on the bus and looked at the foot of his bed in the dim room. The red light from the monitor silhouetted his still profile onto the wall next to his bed. Ann turned and looked below the shadow into Edward's sleeping face. She stood as immobile as he was. Even more so, because Edward's chest moved up and down as he breathed in his sleep. Ann stood holding her breath. Sheer terror had rendered her motionless for several seconds . Finally, her hand moved to her mouth and a gasp came through as her own lungs forced her to breathe. Ann's thin fingers began to tremble against her mouth as she walked closer to the head of Edward's bed. A narrow tube that extended from the bag of fluid disappeared underneath Edward's blanket at his side. Several wires emerged from under the blanket and led to the machine that visualized his heart beat with peaks and valleys. A monotonous beep accompanied each peak. A tube came out of Edward's nose that drained green bile into a jar on the wall. Ann stood over him and cupped her hand over the other one. Oh, Edward, she mouthed but only "ward," came out. Tears had already begun to drain down into her throat.

"What . . . " Ann stared at him in disbelief as tears spilled over her hands. What has happened, Ann thought. She shut her eyes tightly, then opened them again. Why do you look this way? Ann stood fixed in the space next to Edward's bed and stared down at his face. The young, freckled face Ann had remembered so well had become old and haggard. His hair was matted and gnarled into thick red knots. His closed eyes were sunken down into their sockets and if Ann hadn't seen him breathing she would have pronounced him dead herself.

The nurse who had hung the bag entered Edward's room. "Mrs. Broussard?" The voice jarred Ann although it was soft and quiet. Ann's head turned sharply. She placed both of her hands on Ann's shoulders. "He's probably sleeping pretty heavily right now. He's had some medication."

"What happened?" Ann managed to articulate through her hands which were still cupped over her mouth.

"He's had quite a bit of internal bleeding, Mrs. Broussard. He's lost a lot of blood."

"Blood? How?" Ann looked into the young Asian nurse's dark eyes.

"If you'd like to talk to his doctor, he will be here in the unit in about an hour." She placed her arm around Ann's shoulder and patted it lightly. We have some coffee in the lounge if you'd like to wait?"

Ann looked over her shoulder at Edward. "He'll be fine," the young nurse reassured Ann. Ann stared at him for a few moments and the two walked out of his room together. "I'll show you where the lounge is." Ann followed the nurse then suddenly remembered, Dorisse was in the hospital too — and Liz.

"Thank you, but I have to visit another friend. I'll come back in an hour."

Mike's nine by eleven foot hospital room might as well have been a runway at SFO, the fifty yard line on the field at Candlestick Park stadium, the Sahara Desert, the Pacific Ocean, the whole fucking universe, as far as Mike was concerned. Because his private room, along with his entire world was now a vast, infinite chamber. Solitary confinement with the world as his jail. The grand ballroom of prison cells, if you will. Can you direct me to the world? I seem to have gotten lost. Mike smiled cynically at his mental joke. Well, at least I still have my sense of humor, he said to himself.

Mike had spent most of the morning talking to himself, since he had refused any visitors. Not his parents, not any goddamn reporters, and certainly not any of his fellow detectives. Why? So they could stand over him and tell him how sorry they were, then do something as simple as walk out of the hospital, get back into their cars and drive away. Something Mike would never do again. He could see them staring down at him, wondering if he could sense their pity, if he knew how they were grimacing at him. Maybe they would even wave their hands in front of him a few times to see if he was really blind. A couple of his friends from the department are here, they had told him. Friends? Oh, like Louis you mean? Maybe it was Louis himself. Maybe he had come to tell Mike that yes, he planned on framing him, but he never agreed to blinding him. That was all Jake's idea. Louis was only in it for the money. Still friends, right? Mike imagined Louis standing over his bed holding his hand out as a gesture of friendship. Mike shoved the standing tray that hovered over his lap and it tumbled over onto its side.

"Sergeant Branigan?" The nurse barged into his room.

"Get out," Mike said quietly through gritted teeth, then shouted it. "GET OUT!" He heard the door shut quickly. His fists were gripping holes in the bedspread and he began to shake vehemently. Mike covered his eyes with his hands and grimaced in frustration. The darkness made him angry. It was like a practical joke that had gone too far and everyone was in on it but him. Okay, joke's over. Turn the lights on. Who's idea was this. Louis'? He always did have a warped sense of humor. That crazy Louis. Where is that wacky guy? Where is that Louis. . .so I can blow his fucking brains out. Mike took a few swings through the air with his fist, then grabbed his ankle through the covers. Where's my revolver?

"Where's my revolver!?" Mike yelled from inside his room. "Where's my fucking revolver?" he screamed again and again as the nurse outside his room called his doctor for a psychiatric consult.

Ann got off the elevator on the second floor and marched to room two-seventeen. She paused at the door before pushing it open. Was Dorisse in some awful condition like Edward? What had happened to everyone? Ann knocked softly on the door before opening it. She walked in but the room was empty. Before she had a chance to turn and walk out, Liz came in from the bathroom fully dressed.

"Ann!" Liz squealed. Her pink face lit up like a Christmas bulb. She threw some small, plastic bottles onto the bed and opened her arms wide toward Ann. Ann ran into her them, welcoming the comfort of Liz's fleshy arms. They squeezed each other long and hard. Ann began to cry as she buried her face in Liz's shoulder.

"Now, there, honey," Liz led Ann to the bed. "You sit right here and just stop that crying." She handed Ann a tissue.

Ann sniffled and wiped her eyes. "I saw Edward, Liz." Ann lowered her head onto the tissue. "He's not good, Liz. He's not good at all." Ann began to cry harder.

"What's the matter with him?" Liz sat close to Ann on the bed.

Ann shook her head back and forth as she held the tissue to her nose. "I don't know. I have to go back in an hour to talk to his doctor. He doesn't look good, Liz." Ann looked up at Liz, her eyes red and swollen. Liz hugged her tight and rocked her back and forth.

"We'll find out, honey. Don't you worry, you hear?" She pulled Ann away from her and looked into her face. "We'll just find out." Liz rocked Ann until her sobbing subsided, then she smoothed Ann's wavy hair from her face and smiled at her again.

"Guess what, Ann. My doctor says I can go home today."

"What happened to you? And where's Dorisse?" Ann turned and looked around the room again, thinking maybe in her preoccupation with Edward she might have totally overlooked her.

"She had to go have her nose fixed."

"Her nose!?" Ann could never have believed so many things could have happened all at once. It was like every person she had ever known had gone through some earth-shattering crisis all at the same time. Everyone's life was falling apart and every aspect of Ann's life had been affected. She suddenly began to worry about Miette. She wanted to see her, she wanted to hold her. She wanted to feel to her baby soft skin desperately.

"Yea, her nose. But don't worry. She's alright. Well, she's still a little upset, I think."

"Upset about what, Liz?"

Liz told Ann the whole story Dorisse had told her. She also told Ann about the cops that had come to talk to Dorisse, and how Mike was missing and how Dorisse didn't even know he was a cop. She also told Ann that she had left Sam for good this time.

"Oh, Jesus." Ann said and turned her head.

Just then, the orderly came wheeling Dorisse back to her bed. Dorisse saw Liz stand up.

"Where're you going, Liz? You weren't gonna leave without. . ." Dorisse looked up and saw Ann's tenuous figure standing in her hospital room the same as she had last seen her standing in her small apartment in Port Allen. The same Ann. Ann leaned over and hugged Dorisse in her chair and Dorisse rose and got into bed. Although the sedation had worn off, she was still tired and slipped underneath her blankets.

"Dorisse, I can't believe it's you! Liz told me about what happened. I'm so sorry to hear about Mike." Dorisse reached out to hug Ann again as Lieutenant Henderson walked in the room wearing a grave expression. He walked over to Dorisse and looked down at her silently.

"Lieutenant?" Dorisse knew he had some news about Mike and she knew it wasn't good. She wished he wasn't looking at her like that. His brow was furrowed and he pressed and

Leaving Basile

released his lips as if trying to find the right words.

"Lieutenant!?" Dorisse said louder.

He looked at both Ann and Liz.

"They can stay. Whatever it is, Lieutenant, please tell me! Dorisse was ready to grab the Lieutenant and shake it out of him.

"Dorisse, we caught the guys who kidnaped you. They're in police custody right now."

"Where's Mike!?" The Lieutenant got that look again. Where *is* he!?" Dorisse shouted.

"He's here . . . in the hospital."

Ann could not believe it. Was there anyone who *wasn't* in San Francisco City Hospital?

"Is he all right? Tell me, please!" Dorisse shouted.

"Dorisse," the Lieutenant hesitated again. "Mike is in with the neurologists now. He was hit on the head and. . .," The Lieutenant took a deep breath in, then let it come out with his exhalation, "he was blinded."

Liz gasped and Ann covered her mouth in horror.

"Oh my God! Oh, God no," Dorisse's head dropped and she grabbed her hair at the sides with both hands. She gritted her teeth silently, then screamed tears at Lieutenant Henderson.

"I want to see him! I want to see Mike!" She scrambled underneath her blankets.

"He's with the doctors right now, Dorisse." Lieutenant Henderson held her softly back on the bed. Ann and Liz helped to calm her.

"I want to see him right now!" Dorisse cried and swung her arms and legs wildly. Ann and Liz tried to quiet her by gently holding her on the bed.

"Can I tell you what happened, Dorisse?" Lieutenant said softly.

Dorisse stopped swinging, but still cried hysterically in Ann and Liz's arms.

Lieutenant Henderson sat on the end of Dorisse's bed as Ann and Liz stood by. He took a breath and began to talk.

"Mike had been working undercover as a drug smuggler, bringing a large quantity of heroin from Los Angeles to San Francisco. Mike's assignment was to pick up the shipment and deliver it to a guy named Jake Madison, one of the biggest dealers in the city. Well, another detective named Louis had come to me and told me that Mike had confided in him that he planned on giving Jake the drugs and keeping the money they gave him for it and telling the department that they took off with both. So Louis asked if he could work on the case with Mike, then he could help catch Mike in the act. Well, actually Jake and *Louis* had planned on making the switch, taking off with the heroin, and giving *Mike* a suitcase full of dummy money. So, then when Mike came back to me and said they had given him dummy money, it would look like Mike was guilty, just like Louis had said."

Dorisse had stopped crying and was listening closely. Ann and Liz were both looking at Lieutenant Henderson intently as he spoke. He looked up at both the girls, then continued.

"Well, what Louis didn't know was that *he* had been under investigation by internal affairs for months. So I suspected all along what was happening. Anyway, I sent some guys to the trade-off spot to back Mike up in case things got ugly. There was no one there on his side. It turns out that two of *these* guys were on Louis' payroll and they purposefully made their presence known so the trade-off would *not* go through. In other words, they knew that if Mike saw cops there, he'd cancel the trade-off, so the pick-up guy wouldn't get caught by the other straight cops I had sent buying drugs from an undercover cop. All of this would have still been fine, but now Mike still had the drugs and they weren't able to frame him like they had planned. Now, the pick-up man knew absolutely nothing about any of this. He was just hired to make the exchange. So when he saw Mike take off before the exchange took place he didn't know what was going on, but he wasn't going back to Jake without the goods. So, he got some of his boys, found out where Mike lived, which isn't really Mike's apartment, it was just a set up for him, and went to wait for him. Then, when they found *you* there, well . . .," the lieutenant held his hands out, palms up, "they had themselves a hostage."

"Me," Dorisse said sadly.

"Yes, you. Anyway, once Mike caught up with Jake and Louis, they got into a scuffle and Mike got a pretty bad hit on the head . . . and . . . well," the Lieutenant looked down at his hands which he had folded together and twiddled his thumbs in front of him.

"Lieutenant?" Officer Williams stuck his head into the room.

"Yes," the Lieutenant was glad he had come at that time. It was difficult for him to talk about Mike's blindness. Especially to

Leaving Basile

Dorisse. It was like being the one to tell an officer's widow that she was a widow.

"May I speak with you in the hallway, please?"

The lieutenant excused himself, and stepped out into the hall with Officer Williams.

Ann and Liz looked at each other, then at Dorisse whose head rested in both hands, her face covered completely. Ann rubbed Dorisse's back in circles comfortingly and Liz rested her hand on Dorisse's knee as they sat quietly on the hospital bed.

"Liz, where are you going now?" Ann whispered. "I mean, do you have a place to stay?" She continued to rub Dorisse's back.

"Probably back to the motel where you and I met." Liz smiled sadly.

"You can come back and room with me if you want?"

"I couldn't impose on you and Paul."

Ann laughed a private laugh. "Well, that's *another* long story, Liz." Ann shook her head. "Don't worry. No imposition. Paul's made . . . other living arrangements."

Liz looked at Ann confused but decided she'd ask later in light of all that was happening. "Do you mind if I move my things in now?" Liz looked at her watch. "Now would be a good time."

Ann gave Liz the keys from her purse and Liz planted a full kiss on Ann's cheek. Liz lifted Dorisse's head gently from its cradle.

"Don't worry, Dorisse. Everything'll work out for the best. Okay? Everything'll work out for everyone." She looked over at Ann then back at Dorisse. Dorisse nodded, but she already felt like that possibility was hopeless.

Liz left the two girls and passed Lieutenant Henderson coming back into the room.

"Dorisse?" the lieutenant said to her. She lifted her head wearily. "You can see Mike now if you'd like." Dorisse's eyes widened zealously and she began climbing over Ann to get out of bed. Dorisse stopped and grabbed Ann's hand. "Ann, please come with me," and squeezed her hand tightly. Ann nodded and the three walked out to the elevator.

Lieutenant Henderson entered Mike's room first. "Mike?" The lieutenant had spoken to Mike's doctors and was aware of his mental state. He approached slowly and cautiously as if Mike was a suicidal friend on a ledge. "There's someone here who wants to see you."

Dorisse entered next and Ann followed closely behind. Dorisse walked slowly around the lieutenant and the tears flowed almost immediately as she saw Mike sitting up in bed, his back on the headboard with his hands folded neatly on top of the covers. He stared into space, his eyes drifting loosely around the room. Dorisse fought back the tears.

"Who is it?" Mike asked, squinting for sounds. "Who's there?"

Dorisse dashed toward him and knelt down at his bedside, grabbing his hands in hers. She held them tightly against her face and tried to swallow the tears before she spoke, but she didn't have to speak.

"Oh, Jesus, Dorisse." Mike recognized her smell, the feel of her skin. He released his hand from hers and touched her face then lifted her up to his chest. Dorisse followed and finally let her pent up tears spill over onto the front of his hospital gown.

"Dorisse!" Mike rubbed the back of her hair with one hand and squeezed her waist with the other. "Are you . . . ," Mike forgot about his own tears and fought back tears that had formed in his eyes for Dorisse. "Are you alright, baby?"

Dorisse nodded her head in his hand.

Mike suddenly felt incredibly selfish. He had forgotten about Dorisse. He was so lost in his own self pity and anger that he had forgotten the blood on the apartment door. He had forgotten how Jake must have tortured her in that horrid motel room. . .and that she had escaped. He rubbed the back of her neck, incredibly proud of her at that moment. She must have gone through so much, and here she was crying on his behalf. Ann and Lieutenant Henderson stood near the door. Ann had started crying silently and the lieutenant had put his arm around her shoulder comfortingly. He finally dropped his head toward the ground in order to keep from crying himself too.

Mike never wanted to let Dorisse go. He never wanted to let her out of his. . .his reach. Mike smoothed back her hair and kissed the top of her head. He pulled her back away from him and cupped her face in his hands. He used both of his thumbs and traced her lips with them. They felt soft and sweet. He used his forefinger and ran it along the bridge of her small nose. Although he did it gently, Dorisse flinched a little from the pain. It was still sore. Then he ran his thumbs over her closed eyelids. He felt her feathered lashes brush along his thumbs like gentle fans, as the tears she cried dampened her satin skin. Mike blinked through some tears that had begun to form in his own eyes and some reddened edges of light crept into the periphery of his now blackened view of life. Mike closed his eyes. Something was different inside his closed eyelids. The pitch darkness had become a maroon screen and obscure, murky shapes passed across it like dark ghosts. Mike blinked again and the lieutenant noticed his surprised expression.

"Mike? What's the matter?" Mike opened and closed and widened and narrowed his eyes, still holding Dorisse's face in his hands. He moved his hands to her hair and lifted a piece of it between his thumb and forefinger, then let it fall gently back into place. He could see a coarse, blurred movement of his hands and her dark hair as it wisped down onto the side of her face.

"I . . . I see that! I can see that!" Mike lifted her hair again and again and the lieutenant ran out of the room to get his doctor. Mike frowned and grimaced, trying desperately to sharpen the images that hovered in his cloudy field of vision.

Lieutenant Henderson met the neurologist by the elevator and the two walked briskly toward Mike's room.

"I told Mike there was a chance he could regain his sight," the doctor said, "but he was too depressed and bleak to hear me."

"Well, *something* is happening," the lieutenant told him, "He says he can see something."

"Mike was hit on the head over the occipital lobe of his brain." the doctor placed his hand on the base of his skull above his neck, "Here, where the part of the brain that controls vision lies. There was a great deal of swelling and those nerves cells were compressed-causing his blindness. I told Mike that the damage might be permanent, but that there was a chance that his vision could return if once the swelling went down the nerve cells returned to normal."

"Just like that?" The neurologist made it sound far too simple for Lieutenant Henderson.

"Sure. Just like that. I talked to Mike about all of this, lieutenant, but he wasn't hearing me. His psychological trauma was too extensive for him to get past it. " The lieutenant found it amazing that something like this could happen. That a person could actually be blinded and then be told that there was a *possibility* it could return, but maybe not. Lieutenant Henderson thought he would've gone crazy too. But if Mike really was regaining his vision- Jesus, the lieutenant prayed the rest of the way to Mike's room-it would be like waking up and finding the worse nightmare you'd ever had was just a bad dream.

Mike brought his hands up and placed them over his tightly shut eyes. He pulled them down along his face and left them covering his nose and mouth. The maroon background had turned a pale, grayish color with his eyes open. A brightness radiated from above, blended into the gray and darkened toward the floor. Mike lifted his head and slowly, very slowly, the room began to take shape right before his eyes. It was nebulous at first, like looking through a frosted bathroom window. Then the vague outline of Dorisse's face began to turn into individual features. He could see a shimmer of light off of her shiny black hair. Her pink lips fell open gradually and her dark, frightened eyes stared directly into Mike's pale blue ones. He stared at a face he thought he'd never see again.

"Your face . . . ," Mike looked amorously at each one of the features on her ivory face one at a time, "Your face is the most beautiful sight I've ever seen in my entire life. I love you, Dorisse." For Dorisse, Mike couldn't have said anything that would've made her happier.

Ann and Dorisse held hands tightly as they entered Edward's room. Dorisse had to pry herself away from Mike's side, but the doctor's wanted to run some more tests on him, now that his sight had returned. And when Ann told her that Edward was in the same hospital, there was no way she could let Ann go see him alone. They had just spoken to his doctor in the hall and he had explained to them that Edward's illness was a result of his alcohol consumption. Ann still dismissed the idea that Edward was an alcoholic. She denied it every chance she got-when he used to come home smelling like alcohol, when the motel clerk had called him a drunken so-and-so over the telephone, and even now, hearing his doctor tell her this, she just couldn't picture Edward drinking himself to the condition he was in now. He lay in the same position Ann had left him in before. The tube had been removed from his nose and he was no longer being transfused with blood. Only clear fluids ran into his arm. The lights in his room were on and Ann got a chance to see Edward more clearly than she had before. His once ruddy skin was a sickly shade of grey. White sprinkled the red hair that covered his head. Greyish stubble peppered his face. Ann and Dorisse stared at him in disbelief.

Leaving Basile

"Edward?" Ann spoke so softly you could barely hear her. "Edward?" She spoke a bit louder and touched his pale hand gently.

Edward's sunken eyes slowly began to open. He looked up and Ann's slender face came into focus as she stood by his bedside with Dorisse in the background. They pulled chairs close to his bed and sat down. He stared at the two girls he had grown up with. Both sat in silence as Edward licked his dry lips and began to speak.

"Ann," he spoke slow and quiet and the girls listened carefully. "I want you to know," he stopped and took a deep breath, then continued, "dat it ain't because of you dat I'm here. I know dat's what you thinkin." He coughed weakly.

Ann did not respond.

"I'm here because of my drinkin'. And do you know why I drank, Ann?"

She did not respond.

"Cause I was afraid to live life. I was afraid of things I didn't know about. Anything. Everything. I drank so I didn't have to deal wit new things. Things I might not be able to understan. Things dat might be too much for me to handle. Dere's so much mo to life den jus gettin up in de mo'nin. Dis worl is bigga den jus Basile. You said yo'sef, Ann, dat dere's so many places to see, so many places to go. Well, I was afraid of dose places, Ann. I didn't want nuttin cep to stay in a place where everything stay de same. I'm loss in a city like San Francisco. Dey don have no use for a simple man like me. I couldn't even get a job. De people here is different. Somebody like me jus get push into de backgroun. I would never be happy here, and dat's what it's all about, Ann —doin what make us happy. Dere's only one way to live. Whatever it is dat's out dere dat you want, you got ta go get it." Edward swallowed and breathed deeply through his nose. "Ann. . .I have a life insu'ance policy."

"Edward . . . " Ann said.

"Don stop me, Ann. I have a life insu'ance policy made out to you in case anything should happen."

"Edward, don't talk that way."

"Death is a part of life, Ann. *Death* is one thing I can't hide from."

"Oh, Edward," Ann stood up. She couldn't bear to listen. She turned and walked toward the wall with one on her hip and the other hand over her mouth to muffle her sobs.

Dorisse spoke for the first time since she had been in the room. "Edward?" She pulled her chair up to his side and leaned in toward him. "I was afraid too, Edward. I was afraid of things I didn't understand. I was afraid of tradition. Afraid of living the life my parents lived. But tradition keeps a part of our past alive. Did you know that? If we don't speak our language, it will disappear. If we don't teach our children about our music and the way we lived when we grew up, then it will all be lost. It's important, Edward, don't you see? We can remember the good things about our home. Basile will always be our home, no matter what, no matter where we go." Dorisse realized she was squeezing Edward's arm as she spoke, so she loosened her grip and rubbed the area she had been squeezing. "But all that doesn't matter anymore. All that matters now is that the three of us are here together again. You, and me and Ann. Just like always. We can do all the things we used to have so much fun doing. We can go to the movie show and I can sing and you can play your accordian. San Francisco is a wonderful city. We can do it here. We can still be together. We can." Dorisse paused, leaned back in her chair and smiled at Edward. "I met a wonderful man, Edward. His name is Mike and I want you to meet him. He's . . ." Dorisse stopped talking and stared at Edward. "Edward?" He had suddenly turned a ghostly shade of white right before her eyes as though all the blood had drained out of his face. He pulled himself forward to a sitting position.

"I don feel too good," Edward said weakly.

Ann turned to look at him, and Dorisse stood up quickly. "I'll get your nurse."

As Dorisse turned to run out of the room, Edward leaned forward and several liters of bright red blood ejected from his throat forcefully like water from a fire hose. A tidal wave of blood surged forward in thick waves, saturating his bed and half the wall beside him. Large sanguineous blotches splashed onto the glass door and began running downward in long red ribbons. Tiny red droplets sprayed the front of Ann's body like the splatter of a mud puddle from a passing car. Ann gasped, threw her hands up in shock and before she had a chance to recover, Edward's doctor, his nurse and two other people rushed into his room. One of them was pushing the red cart that had been parked in the hallway and Edward's nurse ushered Ann and Dorisse out into the hall. The two girls stood huddled together outside the room and stared through the blood stained glass doors of Edward's intensive care room. They watched as his nurse threw his drenched sheets into the corner and ripped his gown off, exposing a round swollen belly and thin, pale extremities. He looked like a starving child. His doctor removed a syringe filled with medication from a drawer in the red cart and quickly injected it into the I.V. port.

"Hand me the Minnesota!" he shouted. Edward's doctor inserted a curved, sturdy tube down into Edward's throat as another man hung bags of blood on the pole and opened them, immediately turning the tubing dark red. The other woman hung large bags of clear fluid on another pole and connected its tubing to a Y-port on his I.V. The urgent speed with which the team moved frightened Ann most of all. None of them stopped for an instant. They all moved independently and efficiently as the monitor beeped furiously in the background.

"He's in V-fib," Edward's doctor suddenly said aloud. The peaks and valleys had turned into wild scribbles of light on the screen and Ann watched in horror as the doctor swung his fist up behind his head and brought it down onto Edward's chest with all his might. She and Dorisse hugged each other tight and Ann covered her mouth, trying to silence the small screams she let out. Ann's muscles had contracted into tight, trembling bunches. The doctor looked over at the monitor then removed the two beige paddles from the red cart. The nurse squeezed clear gel on their metal surface and the doctor rubbed the two paddles together, placed them on Edward's bare chest and stared at the monitor again. A few seconds later he shouted, "Clear," and Edward's frail body was jolted a foot off of his bed as a sickening *thud* accompanied the jolt. The doctor yelled "clear" two more times and Ann screamed each time she saw them try to shock life back into Edward's body. Finally, the doctor stopped and everyone slowly and reluctantly backed away from Edward's lifeless body.

CHAPTER TWENTY-EIGHT
Basile, Louisiana

Ann and Dorisse sat in the dried leaves in the graveyard behind Edward's house where he was now buried. The spring weather in Basile was just as they had left it. Light and warm, the smell of soil and fertilizer heavy in the air.

"Ann?" Dorisse broke a crisp leaf into tiny pieces. "Do you wish we never would've left Basile?" She looked up at Ann's slim face.

Ann contemplated her question for several long, silent minutes. Ann remembered sitting on the very same tombstone she was on, wishing more than anything in the world that she could leave Basile. Waiting and planning for the day when her dream would become a reality. Thinking day after day of all the wonderful things she could do, of all the opportunities that awaited her outside of Basile, of all the glorious places she could visit-and of school-and of going to school. Ann still hadn't thrown the black, tasseled hat into the air, or squeezed the rolled up diploma with her name printed fancily on it in her palm. She never even finished her first year. Of course now, with the money Edward had left her, she could continue her education, but Edward had paid for it with his life. She wished Paul could've paid for her education with *his* life instead, but Paul's life couldn't have paid for a lead pencil, Ann thought, and Edward was worth his weight in gold. Her brow wrinkled. Oh, Edward, Ann spoke to him silently. How did all this happen? How could such misery have come from my ambitions? I only wanted to learn. I only wanted to read and write and do things no one else from Basile had done. Things some people didn't want them to do. Ann remembered Papa telling her that there were White people who didn't want them to learn to read. Who wouldn't sell them books in the store. People who didn't want them to learn. People who didn't want them to excel. And there would always be people like that. People who wanted them to stay in places like Basile and continue to plant seeds in the spring and pick cotton in the fall. Well, Ann didn't want to do that. She wanted

Leaving Basile

to be able to choose to do whatever she wanted-and to do it! And that was exactly what she would do. No matter what obstacles stood in front of her. No matter what problems arose. Keep going. Papa. . .and Edward would want her to. And when she did, they'd be the two proudest people in heaven.

"No, Dorisse. I don't wish that. I'm glad we left. And do you know what? We're going back. Don't ever let anyone or anything stop you from pursuing your dreams. Mike is waiting for you, Dorisse, and well, someone is waiting for me too. I have a date next week."

Dorisse looked at Ann, amused at her pleasant change in tone. "A date?"

"Yes," Ann smiled mischievously, "with Lieutenant Henderson."

"What?" Dorisse smiled broadly. The two girl stood up, brushed off their dresses and walked slowly through the leaves out of the graveyard behind Edward's house.

"Don't you think he looks a little like Sidney Poitier?" Ann put her arm around Dorisse's shoulder.

Dorisse clicked her tongue, widened her eyes and looked at Ann smiling. "You know I was thinking the exact same thing." Dorisse placed her arm around Ann's thin waist as they passed through the gate and headed up the gravel road through Basile.

The End